Unforgettable

Trevor Meldal-Johnsen

PIATKUS

Copyright © 1986 by Trevor Meldal-Johnsen

First published in Great Britain in 1986 by
Judy Piatkus (Publishers) Ltd of
5 Windmill Street, London W1P 1HS

British Library Cataloguing in Publication Data

Meldal-Johnsen, Trevor
    Unforgettable.
    I. Title
    813'.54[F]   PR3563.E435

ISBN 0 86188 557 0

Phototypeset in 11/12pt Linotron Times by
Phoenix Photosetting, Chatham
Printed and bound in Great Britain by
Mackays of Chatham Ltd

Chapter One

Samantha Barry was displeased. She swivelled her chair and stared bleakly out of the office window at the smog-shrouded buildings of downtown Los Angeles.

Her personal assistant, Maddy Shapiro, waited in the opposite chair, notebook in hand, pen poised to strike. When the silence lengthened, she spoke.

'What should I tell him? With Mark still in Hong Kong. I'd better handle it.'

Sam turned her chair back to face Maddy. 'Tell him that if he doesn't deliver by the nineteenth, I'll cancel the entire order today.'

Maddy raised an eyebrow. 'A little extreme, don't you think? There's no one else who could supply the fabric by then. Not now.'

Sam smiled, erasing the frown on her forehead. 'You and I know that, but he doesn't. If he picks up on it, just drop a hint about Hong Kong contacts. He knows our buyer is over there. That should scare the pants off him.'

Maddy made a note in her pad and rose from the chair. 'I'll give it a shot.' She glanced cautiously at her boss. 'Don't worry, Sam, we'll get it all handled.'

'I know. It's the same every season. I should be used to it by now.'

'Yeah, but if you were it wouldn't be any fun.'

'Well, some fun I can live without. Let me know as soon as you've talked to him.'

'Will do.'

Sam looked fondly after Maddy as she left the room. Once a dear college friend, she was now her strong right hand. She depended upon her, trusted her and paid her a small fortune. They had both come a long way since their days as art students at UCLA.

Sam Barry, Fashion Designer. Her name was a household word now. Not only was her new line of clothing eagerly anticipated each season in both America and Europe, but now there were Sam Barry table settings, linen designs, make-up accessories, shampoos and even furniture. She had built her initial success as a dress designer into an impressive fortune, licensing her name to manufacturers in a number of fields.

Clothing was still her first love, however. And her most lucrative area. And it took most of her time. The upcoming Spring show was giving her the usual headaches. The designs were done – in many ways, that was the easy part – but now there was the purchase of fabric, the manufacture of the clothes themselves, and the thousands of tiny details that went along with it. A constant battle against time and Murphy's Law. You could rely upon a hundred things to go wrong, and you never knew what they would be until they happened. A textile supplier falling two weeks behind the contracted delivery date was only one of many disasters to be overcome.

There was a knock at the door and Maddy came in without waiting for an invitation. She carried a bouquet of long-stemmed red roses in her arms and a broad grin on her face.

'Another one from your secret admirer,' she said.

2

She put them on Sam's desk and flipped open the card. There was nothing on it except an initial, a slashing '*T*.' in black ink.

Sam frowned. 'Give them to the girls in the office,' she said.

'But they're beautiful!' Maddy insisted.

'I don't know any *T*. and I don't like getting gifts from people I don't know.'

'It's probably just some shy guy, or someone working up to something,' Maddy said.

Sam looked down at the flowers again and felt a twinge of revulsion. It was totally irrational, she knew, nothing she could explain to Maddy, but this was the third batch of flowers from the anonymous donor and each time she felt more uncomfortable.

At thirty, Sam was a beautiful young woman, slim and tall, her heart-shaped face framed by lush dark hair. She had striking green eyes and a wide, determined mouth. There was nothing vapid about her beauty, as with many of the models she hired; strength and character marked her face. Although she was involved in no serious relationships, she was accustomed to attention from men. The problem was time. Her career demanded her full attention. The other problem was that most of the men she met, particularly in this business were either not interested in women or didn't interest her. It was unfair to generalise, she knew, but it seemed at times as if everyone she had contact with was either homosexual or married. This didn't stop many of the married men from approaching her, but she shot them down mercilessly. She despised cheats, in business and in personal relationships. Much of her business success was due to her reputation for honest dealings. She expected it from others as well.

She impatiently pushed the flowers across the desk.

3

'Take them away, Maddy. I don't have time for this.'

Maddy sighed. 'God, I'd kill for a guy who'd give me flowers like these. All I get are questions – like, "Wanna get laid?"'

Maddy had a pretty face and a bright wit, but where Sam was slim, she was rounded. Her weight was her Nemesis, constant in its presence due to her love of chocolates, pastries and sugar in all forms. It was more consideration than fact, however. She had an attractive figure, rarely more than seven or eight pounds overweight, and she was always able to lose it – for a while.

'Well, you take the flowers, Maddy,' Sam said.

Maddy grimaced. 'It's not the same.'

'Did you get Colton?'

'I have a call in. I'll let you know as soon as we've spoken.'

'We've got to get that fabric on time.'

'We will, don't worry,' Maddy said. She reached for the roses. 'Are you sure you don't want them?'

'They'll look lovely on your desk,' Sam said.

Maddy took the flowers, leaving the card on the desk. After she left the room, Sam picked the card up and looked again at the bold signature – *T*. The identity of the donor was a complete mystery. No old boyfriends with that initial, no current acquaintances, at least none who would be sending her flowers.

Well, she thought, three days of flowers in a row would presumably lead to something. Sooner or later the mystery would solve itself. She tossed the card into the top drawer of her desk and reached for the telephone. There was work to be done.

Samantha Barry displayed artistic aptitude at a young age. An only child, she delighted her parents with imaginative drawings from the moment she could hold a crayon. Her father, manager of a San Francisco clothing store, and her mother, who worked on and off as a legal secretary, had continued to encourage her. Instead of giving her dolls as presents, they gave her expensive sets of pastels, Windsor–Newton oil-paints, sable paint-brushes, sophisticated pens, easles and light tables. While she loved the Impressionists and painted excellent landscapes herself, by the time she was twelve she found herself leaning towards design.

At thirteen, she drew her first full line of dresses and gowns. They were little more than a young girl's fantasy. However, unlike most children who allowed their fanta-sies to evaporate in the winds of time, Sam made her's into realities. Intending to surprise her mother with the gift of one of her creations, she taught herself pattern-making and sewing and made a gorgeous white gown, working alone in her room in the evenings and weekends. It was a smashing success. Her father, although involved in the retailing of men's clothing, saw the possibilities and encouraged her even more. Unfor-tunately, hormones began their persuasive whispers and, due to a crush on a teenage poet in her school, Sam suddenly decided that poetry was her forte. For two years she wrote truly dreadful and depressing verse. When the love affair reached its foregone conclusion, after being suitably broken-hearted for the appropriate length of time, Sam returned to her love of art – much to the relief of her parents and, surprisingly, herself.

An alert and diligent student, she had no trouble entering UCLA, with the intention of majoring in Art History. She wanted to teach, she thought. The idea of actually making money from her art simply didn't occur to her.

And then, during her third year of college, life

5

changed. Her parents, driving down Highway 1 to visit her for a weekend, tried to avoid colliding with the drunken driver of a pick-up truck on the narrow, winding road. They landed at the bottom of a cliff, a few miles south of Big Sur, battered by Pacific waves, their lives shattered on the rocks.

Sam was devastated. All her life, her parents had been there for her to lean on. They validated her, supported her and gave her all the resources at their disposal, often denying themselves comforts for her progress. They were not wealthy people and, by the time the estate was sorted out, it amounted to a couple of thousand dollars. For the first time in her life, Sam was alone. And for the first time, she realised that in order to survive, she would have to produce something other than meandering drawings for her own satisfaction.

She had no idea what she was going to do. The urge to teach had dissipated. Her teachers couldn't paint worth a damn, she discovered, and neither could most of her fellow students. Somehow, the thought of teaching disinterested children about the history of art seemed a pale substitute for the act of creation. But 'everyone knew' that artists seldom made a living, and making a living had suddenly become of prime importance to Sam – alone, she thought, in a hostile world.

It was Maddy who guided her. A sharp-tongued, quick-witted Jewish girl, she heaped derision on the faculty and students. 'Despicable vultures of academia,' she called them at her kindest. They were great friends, the beautiful and talented Sam, the target of dozens of male overtures, and the comparatively plain but witty Maddy. They shared an apartment off-campus, one room in a house inhabited by students and retirees, both generations in a state of continuous war. Somehow, although every student who ever lived there was sooner

6

or later evicted, casualties of battle, Sam and Maddy never were. Perhaps it was because both had the ability to cross the dividing lines between generations and gain allies in the oldster's camp. Be that as it was, the two were great friends. Pettiness never marred their relationships. They did not compete and there was no envy or jealousy. They supported each other wholeheartedly. Sam consoled Maddy about her atrocious love life, and Maddy consoled Sam during the difficult time after the death of her parents.

During that morbid and fearful period, Sam kept her sanity by returning to her first love, drawing. She started a series of dress designs. The sense of fantasy that accompanied them balanced the harsh and omnipotent realities of the present. One afternoon, Maddy returned unexpectedly early from class to find Sam drawing. She picked her way through the papers strewn on the floor and asked Sam what she was doing.

'It's just a hobby of mine, designing clothes,' Sam said.

Maddy dropped to one knee and began to look at the drawings. 'This is beautiful,' she said, holding one up. 'Daring, original, fabulous!'

'They're just my little fantasies,' Sam said.

Maddy laughed. 'Jesus, Sam. You've been kvetching about money for weeks now and here you are sitting on a goldmine.'

'What are you talking about?' Sam asked.

Maddy swept her hand around the floor. 'These. These are worth money in the bank.'

'These drawings?'

'They aren't just drawings. They're original designs, Sam. Do you have any idea how much money there is in high fashion, kid? Fortunes! Millions, billions! We're talking Rolls Royces in Beverly Hills here.'

7

Sam laughed at her enthusiasm. 'You're dreaming. Who'd pay money for these?'

'Aaaar,' Maddy groaned. 'Stupid, stupid. People will pay money for it, I guarantee you.'

'Come on, you're dreaming,' Sam said, and returned to her drawing.

But Maddy didn't give up. Finally, at her friend's urging, Sam spent summer vacation trudging, portfolio in hand, through downtown Los Angeles' garment district to see who would pay money for her drawings. There was an endless stream of proposals, but they weren't the kind she was looking for. Finally, after two weeks, close to giving up, she met Moses Cohen, an elderly man with a small but thriving garment business.

Cohen looked at her drawings respectfully, but shook his head. Her stomach sank at the thought of yet another rejection.

'Your drawings are good, very good,' he said. 'These clothes are beautiful, but they're not the kind of thing I deal in. Too innovative. What I do is copy. I send my designers to the shows in Paris and New York and they copy the new fashions. We stick with the big names.'

'But that's stealing,' she blurted out.

Moses Cohen looked at her through drooping eyelids. He was old enough to have seen it all, but something about this beautiful and talented, not to mention naive, young girl touched him. 'It is not stealing,' he said. 'Everybody does it. It is how the business runs. It is reality.'

'But if you can get original designs, why not do it?' she asked.

'Because it is a risk. You go with what works, the sure thing. Well, there are no sure things in fashion, but some are surer than others.'

Sam began to rise. 'Well, thanks for seeing me, anyway,' she said.

8

Moses waved his hand. 'Sit, sit,' he said. 'I said the designs aren't for us. But you have talent and talent isn't to be wasted. I didn't say I wouldn't offer you a job. Would you like to learn this business?'

Sam not only liked to learn the business, but by the time the next semester rolled around, she dropped out of school. The money wasn't great, but she learned about fabric and sewing and pricing and marketing and negotiations and business, revelling in the new data, willingly putting in twelve-hour days and winning the heart of old Moses with her diligence and enthusiasm.

After two years, Moses took the risk he said he'd never take and put out a Fall line of Sam Barry Designs. Luck, circumstance, timing, call it what you will, it appears and disappears with unpredictable precision. That Fall it appeared for Sam. Perhaps it was a combination of her obvious beauty and the flagrant boldness of her designs, but whatever it was, the trade media was the first to pick up on it, soon to be followed by the glossy fashion magazines.

Moses was happy for her and sad for himself. 'Within a year you will be on your own. You have nothing but success ahead of you,' he said. Sam denied it, of course. 'I'm happy working here,' she said. 'It's the most exciting time of my life.' Moses just shook his head.

Moses was wrong. It took eighteen months. Moses didn't like being wrong, however. He prodded Sam into action by offering to bankroll her first line of Spring fashions. He charged her a hefty interest rate on the loan, but it was more out of pride than necessity, she suspected. Moses hated to come out second best on a business deal. Within two years she paid back every penny, and when the old man died a year later, she grieved as much as she had for her parents.

After her second successful year, Maddy came to

9

work for her. In the intervening time, her irresponsible friend had dropped out of school, worked in an art gallery, as a waitress, as a secretary and, briefly, enjoyed a career as a television game show entrant, winning a car, a set of atrocious yellow furniture and a few thousand dollars. They kept in touch, though, and when Sam saw the business cut into her valuable design time she approached Maddy with the offer.

'I know squat about clothes,' Maddy protested.

'You got me started in this,' Sam reminded her. 'And besides, you're bright enough to learn anything. I need someone I can trust. And I'll pay you a lot of money.'

It was true. Maddy was bright, and she learned remarkably quickly. Within a year she knew as much about the business side of things as Sam. And although she retained the title of personal assistant to Sam, she was much more than that. She guarded Sam like a mother hen, cutting off all diversion, particularly when Sam was in the middle of a heavy design schedule. 'Be an artist,' she would say. 'Let me take care of the grimy details.' Unfortunately, Sam was a perfectionist in everything, including the details of her business. She had to know everything that was happening at every moment. But they soon devised a workable system whereby, although Maddy would take care of many of the problems, she reported them all to Sam for final decisions. They were a team rather than employer and employee, and together they saw Sam Barry, Inc., grow in a handful of years from a small one-woman shop into a multi-faceted business with revenues in the millions of dollars.

It was, indeed, a long way from the one room apartment in Westwood.

Maddy was elated. 'He caved in,' she said, coming into Sam's office.

10

'Colton?'

'Said he'd have the fabric to us on time, even if he had to put two shifts on. Admitted we were his best customers.'

'Good job,' Sam said.

Maddy's voice grew dry. 'He said no matter how unreasonable our demands, he would do anything to see we were satisfied.'

Sam couldn't help but laugh. 'Sly old fox. I don't suppose he mentioned that he was the one who agreed to the delivery date weeks ago.'

'Of course not.'

'Well, that's great, anyway,' Sam said. 'One less problem to worry about. Keep on top of him though. Get progress reports every few days.'

'Right. By the way, I heard from Dallas. They want to meet with you. I think they're finally ready to talk a deal. I'm going to set it up, if that's okay.'

Huffakers, a national department store chain, headquartered in Dallas, had approached Sam a few months earlier with the proposal that she design a line of dresses for young girls. The idea had intrigued her, particularly as there was a void in the market. Jeans for girls in the six to twelve age bracket were plentiful, and so were dresses, of course. But the dresses looked suitable only for weddings, there was nothing practical and commonsense for everyday wear for the millions of children who still liked to wear dresses on occasion. It was the type of challenge she enjoyed. Marketing would be a key factor, but Huffakers had a reputation as an aggressive and efficient up-and-comer and a few questions in the right places revealed they had plans for major expansion.

Sam and Maddy had met with executives from the company twice already, exchanging a few ideas in a

11

tentative feeling-out process. Big money moves cautiously, however, and it was only now, six months after the original contact, that Huffakers was ready to get down to specifics. If the deal went through, and if the designs truly filled a need, and if the marketing was spot-on, and if a few more ifs were fulfilled, the deal had a potential of millions of dollars. A lot of ifs. Sam had learned not to get too excited until they were all disposed of.

Still, news of progress was encouraging, and she couldn't suppress a surge of excitement.

'Go ahead,' she said calmly to Maddy. 'It'll be good to get it rolling.'

The telephone on her desk rang. She picked it up.

'It's a man who says he's T.,' her secretary said, her voice thrilled. The whole office knew about the flowers and T.'s identity was a topic of speculation among the secretaries.

Sam rolled her eyes. 'It's T. on the line,' she said to Maddy.

'Take it, take it,' Maddy urged, leaning forward, wishing she could hear.

Sam grinned at her and flicked on the speakerphone. 'Put it through, Anne,' she said.

'Hello,' she said.

'Hello, Samantha.' The voice was deep and smooth.

'Who is this?' Sam asked irritably. She hated to be called Samantha.

'Did you get my flowers?'

'Yes, thank you. But who are you?'

'For the time being, I simply prefer to be known as T.,' the man said. His voice was well-modulated, his accent educated. A trace of East Coast in it, she thought. Maybe New England. And something else she couldn't quite put her finger on.

12

Maddy put her hand over her mouth to hide a giggle.

'I'm afraid I'm too busy to play these games,' she said.

The man's voice sharpened and grew faster, as if to prevent her from hanging up. 'This is not a game, I assure you. I am merely attempting to prove my devotion to you.'

'I don't even know you. What are you talking about?'

'You know me. Indeed you do,' he said.

'Then why are you hiding behind this anonymity?' she asked.

'I want us to meet, but not until you are ready,' he said.

'Sorry, but I'm not interested,' she said flatly. 'I've no idea who you are and I don't have time for games.'

'You know me,' he said again.

'Have we met somewhere recently?' she asked. 'Are you someone I knew at college or in high school? Where?'

'Before,' he said.

'Before high school?'

'Just before.'

Sam grimaced at Maddy and shook her head. Maddy shrugged, still smiling.

'Well, like I said, I don't have time for games,' Sam said, finality in her voice. 'I must go now.'

'Wait!' the man said. There was a pause. 'We knew each other before. You must believe that, Samantha.'

'What?' she questioned. Maddy began to giggle again.

'It's true,' the voice said. 'I'm going to prove it to you.'

'Look,' Sam said calmly. 'I don't think you'd better bother me again. I'm really not interested in playing a part in your fantasies.'

The man's voice changed subtly. 'Don't be afraid,' he said. 'I promise I won't hurt you. Not this time. It's going to be different.'

Sam felt goosebumps rise on her arms. She had no

13

idea why. All she knew was that she didn't want to talk further to the voice at the other end of the line.

'Look,' she said. 'This is enough. I don't want you to send me flowers again, I don't want you to call me. I want nothing to do with you. Do you understand?'

'Samantha, you don't understand. You –'

She hung up, cutting him off.

'Wow!' Maddy said. 'I've heard some lines, but that's the weirdest yet. Kinda interesting. Why'd you hang up?'

Sam looked moodily down at the phone. 'It's spooky,' she said.

'Hey, he was just coming on,' Maddy said.

Sam shook her head. 'No. I didn't like it. It's weird.'

The next day, a letter came in the morning mail. Inside was a card and a faded newspaper clipping. It was a photograph, cut into a square inch so that only the head of a woman showed. There was no caption visible, nothing to show what the subject was. Inside the card was a short message.

Who is this? was all it said. Below was the familiar *T*.

'That's it,' Sam said vehemently. 'This is getting too strange for me. I want you to call the police, Maddy.'

Maddy was incredulous at her reaction. 'What on earth are you so uptight about? It's just some guy on a trip.'

Sam was standing at her window, her back to Maddy. She folded her arms, clasping them with her hands.

'Something about it scares me,' she said faintly.

'Come on,' Maddy said, walking over to her. 'It's nothing. The guy's just coming on to you. If you ignore it, he'll fade away.'

Sam shook her head. 'This is different. I can't explain

14

it, but I feel it. God, I feel it! I want the police brought in. Say he's harassing me.'

'You're overreacting.'

'Maybe,' Sam said,

'There's no point in calling the police. We don't know who the person is and he hasn't done anything against the law. He hasn't even been harassing you, strictly speaking.'

Sam turned to her. 'Humour me, Maddy. There's something about this person that's not right, something dangerous. I swear it.'

Maddy looked at her for a long moment, then shrugged. 'All right, Sam. I understand your concern. But there's really nothing we can do about it other than for you to be careful. You know how it is with the police. They only come in after a crime has been committed. So far, there's no crime, right?'

Sam sighed. 'Right. Yes, you're right. It's just . . . I don't know. A feeling . . .'

'Well,' Maddy said with finality. 'Just be extra careful. I'll bet you anything the whole thing fades away.'

'Okay, Maddy. I guess I'm just being silly. Let's forget it.'

Maddy took a last concerned look at Sam and went back to her office. She hadn't seen Sam this spooked before. Not Sam – tough, determined, able to hold her own in the knock 'em down and drag 'em world of business, overcoming some of the sharpest and most ruthless minds in industry. This was a different Sam – afraid, uncertain, even paranoid. She didn't understand it.

Sam didn't understand it either. She sat back at her desk and looked at the papers she was supposed to read. None of them made sense to her now. The voice on the telephone overshadowed them.

15

Was she paranoid, she wondered? Had the strain of work begun to affect her? There was nothing she could put her finger on. Probably, to anyone else, the caller would sound perfectly natural, a little off the wall, perhaps, but not dangerously so.

No matter what anyone said or how foolish they thought her, she knew without doubt, that beneath the calm, assured manner of the caller's voice was a layer of menace, a can of worms bubbling to get out.

Chapter Two

On Saturday, while talking to her gardener, Sam noticed she had a new neighbour. A moving van, engine groaning under the load, pulled into the driveway of the house next door. After putting it on the market for four months, the owners finally pulled out of the house, leaving it vacant for another three. The new owner probably picked it up for a song.

Sam lived in the foothills of Studio City in a blazingly white two storey Spanish house. Of all the cities that now choked the once verdant San Fernando Valley, she liked Studio City best. In some ways, it retained the spirit of a small town. Five cents could still get you thirty minutes on a parking meter, and many shopkeepers continued to greet you by name.

She moved there from West Hollywood two years earlier. The house was large for one person, but she had a live-in maid and used about one-third of the house for her design work. This was her creative space. She thought of the downtown office as her 'paperwork office'. At times the house seemed as frantic as the office. During busy periods, the workspace usually had a couple of dressmakers cutting and sewing, the buyer, surrounded by bolts of fabric and samples, and Maddy,

17

trying to get a word in and hold what she called 'instant meetings'.

In fact, Sam loved the house, and tried to work there as often as possible. It sat on almost an acre of rolling green lawns, separated by flower beds and trees. The prolific trees bore apricots, oranges and loquats and enough avocados to keep the office staff in guacomole all year. Solid and graceful, the house had giant curved windows, stucco walls, hardwood floors and dark wood banisters, mantles and shelves throughout. An open-air patio in the back, led to a swimming pool, hot tub and sauna. A greenhouse languished behind the pool; so far she had done nothing with it. The maid's quarters consisted of a studio apartment above the garage to the side of the house. All in all, Sam felt she had everything she needed there. She often thought how nice it would be never to have to leave.

She watched the red and white moving truck park next door and for the first time noticed a white Mercedes parked in the driveway as well. After a moment she heard the truck's back doors open, the machinery of the ramp as it descended, and the curses of one of the movers. She turned back to her gardener.

'Is it all right if I pick some of the roses, Felix?' she asked.

'Only those over there,' he said, pointing at a bed of red and yellow roses.

Although he came only three days a week, Felix ran the garden like a martinet. As far as he was concerned, he owned it. An elderly Mexican-American, he did all the maintenance, but his true strength lay in his ability to make things grow. When she saw him she often thought of Shakespeare's quote about gardeners being of 'Adam's profession.' Felix was probably an illegal; she paid him in cash, at his request, and never saw any identi-

18

fication from him. She didn't care – he was worth every penny. The fruits of his knowledge made even his tyrannical rule of her garden worth putting up with.

Sam went to the patch he had indicated and began to cut red roses low on the stem. When she had a dozen, she gathered them up and walked back to the house.

A BMW screeched through the front gate and pulled up behind her Jaguar with only inches to spare. It was Maddy.

'Hi, kid!' Maddy shouted, jumping out like an energetic ball.

One of the reasons they got on so well together was that neither was a clockwatcher. When necessary, they worked on nights, weekends and holidays. Sam never had to tell Maddy to work. In fact, last year she had found herself insisting that Maddy take some vacation time. After a week of a planned two weeks in Baja, Maddy appeared back at the office, saying she was dying of boredom.

'What's up?' Sam asked.

'Just a short meeting,' Maddy said. 'Want to go over a couple of things with you.'

'Let me get these roses in a vase and then I'm all yours,' Sam said.

After clipping the stems and placing them in a tall crystal vase, she carried it into the living room.

It was an elegant yet casually furnished room with large overstuffed sectionals and cabinets and tables of dark teak. A couple of vaguely Impressionistic paintings hung on the walls, and abstract bronze sculptures and ornately carved Japanese netsukes sat together on the mantle and a display table, giving the room an eclectic effect.

They sat on a couch and Maddy mysteriously produced a sheaf of papers and a pen.

'These are the new orders for your signature,' she said, handing some pages over.

Sam glanced at them and signed.

'This is the contract with Solomon,' Maddy said.

After Sam read it over and gave it back, Maddy said. 'And I set up the meeting for you with Huffakers. In Dallas on Wednesday. They're expecting both of us.'

'I can't go now,' Sam said. 'There's too much to do.'

'Trust me, you'll be able to fit it in. I went over your calendar carefully. We can leave in the morning and be back in the afternoon, no problem.'

'Maddy, you drive me too hard,' Sam said. For a second Maddy looked worried and Sam quickly added, 'I don't know what I'd do without you.'

Maddy shrugged. 'You'd hire someone else.'

Sam was shocked. 'You don't think that do you? You know how invaluable you are. I couldn't find anyone to do what you do half as well, let alone trust completely.'

'I know, I know. But it does me good to remember every now and then that without your creativity this little empire wouldn't even exist.'

'You're having man problems again?' Sam said. The seemingly non-sequitur remark was based on her knowledge that whenever Maddy turned slightly maudlin a man was involved.

'I just got dumped again,' Maddy admitted. 'What hurts is that the guy wears gold chains around his neck, polyester trousers and has the IQ of a frog. I mean, if I was dumped by someone worthwhile it wouldn't be so bad. But where does this leave me?'

'Probably a lot better off,' Sam said drily. 'Want a beer?'

'I'd have something stronger, but it's still morning,' Maddy said.

Sam went to the kitchen and returned with two bottles

20

of beer. When they went out, both usually drank white wine, particularly during business lunches and dinners. But ever since they had known each other, they enjoyed beer from the bottle, and it was what they usually drank together.

Sam handed Maddy a bottle and clinked hers against it. 'Cheers!'

'Cheers,' Maddy replied. She took a swig. 'What is it about men and me? Do I walk around with a sign saying "Kick Me"?'

'Maybe you're just too available.'

'A girl's got to have some fun. If I lived like you, I'd be too horny to think straight.'

'You should try celibacy. It might surprise you,' Sam said.

'It's been enforced on me before. I don't like it. It's about time you got laid, anyway. You've been getting cranky lately.'

'I haven't,' Sam protested. 'And if I have, it's the show, not my sex life.'

'Huh!' Maddy said disbelievingly.

The front doorbell rang.

'I didn't hear a car, it must be Felix,' Sam said. She went to the door, beer in hand.

A tall, well-built man in his mid-thirties stood on the porch. He looked at the bottle in her hand with a glint of amusement in his green eyes.

'Hello. Are you the lady of the house?' he asked.

'Yes,' she said. 'May I help you?'

Dark, curly hair topped a lean face that just missed being handsome. It was the nose, she realised. It was aquiline in shape and a shade too large, subtracting from the overall good looks.

He held out his hand. 'I'm Nemo Riley. I just moved in next door.'

21

'Sam Barry,' she said.

He shook her hand firmly, with none of the limp condescension some men used.

'The designer?' he asked, raising a dark eyebrow.

'None other,' said Maddy, appearing at Sam's elbow. Curiosity widened her eyes.

'This is Maddy Shapiro. She works with me,' Sam said.

'You're a corporate lawyer, right?' Maddy said.

'You've heard of me?' Nemo asked.

'Couldn't forget a name like Nemo Riley,' she said. 'Besides, the aerospace case you handled last year was all over the financial pages. And *Los Angeles Magazine* listed you as one of our most eligible bachelors a few months ago. Now I can see why.'

Nemo smiled. His face, slightly cynical before, filled with warmth, 'I'm flattered.'

'What can I do for you, Mr Riley?' Sam said, suddenly feeling strangely irritated by the stranger.

'Please call me Nemo,' he said. 'We're going to be neighbours.'

She looked coolly at him, not acknowledging the invitation. He scratched his head. 'I'm not here for the proverbial cup of sugar, but I'm afraid I didn't do any shopping and I do need some milk. I was going to make some coffee for the movers.'

'Well, at least that's a twist,' Maddy said. 'Come on into the kitchen.'

Sam shot her a dirty look, but said nothing.

'Of course,' Nemo added, 'now that I see those beers in your hands, they look ten times better than coffee. Could you lend me three bottles? I'll repay you with a six-pack after I go to the store.'

'Interest isn't necessary, Mr Riley,' Sam said.

'Nemo,' he reminded her, 'and it isn't interest, just a

22

gesture to acknowledge your generosity.'

'I'll get your beers,' she said, nullifying Maddy's invitation to the kitchen by walking off.

When she returned with three cold beers in her hands, Maddy was chatting to Riley like an old friend.

'Here you are,' she said, interrupting them.

'You're very kind. Thank you,' he said, taking the beer from her. 'Moving furniture is thirsty work.'

He looked at them uncertainly for a second and then said, 'Well, back to work. See you later.'

'Goodbye,' Sam said.

'Don't get a hernia,' Maddy joked.

When they got back to the living room, Sam said sharply, 'God, Maddy, no wonder men take advantage of you. You're like a puppy with its tongue hanging out.'

'God, but isn't he a hunk!' Maddy said, unabashed. 'He has the sexiest mouth.'

'I didn't notice,' Sam said.

'And he lives right next door.'

'You're incorrigible.'

'See what I mean about you being cranky?'

Sam stifled a nasty retort and shook her head instead. 'You're right.' She slumped on the couch. 'I don't know what's going on with me. Yes, I do. It's that guy.'

'Your secret admirer? You're still worrying about that?'

'T.,' Sam mused. 'I guess I am. Every time I see a man, particularly a stranger, I wonder . . .'

'He hasn't called you since that last time two days ago. Like I said, if you ignore it, he'll just disappear. Anyway, it probably wasn't anything to worry about.'

'I suppose you're right,' Sam said. She tipped her bottle back and drained it.

'Of course I am. Now let's talk about the guy next door. I'm already fantasising.'

Sam giggled. 'He is attractive. I have to admit it.'

'Attractive?' Maddy said derisively. 'We're talking hunk here. Attractive? Jesus, and he doesn't even wear gold chains!'

'You're over being dumped already?'

'All it takes is the sight of a handsome man to remind me that the ocean pullulates with life,' Maddy said philosophically.

'You mean that there's more than one fish in the sea,' Sam said.

'Exactly.' Maddy smiled with all the satisfaction of a satiated cat.

Maddy left shortly before lunch, refusing the invitation to stay because of her new diet. 'It's the only one that works for me – not eating,' she said.

Sam gave her housekeeper the rest of the day off and spent the afternoon working on drawings to show the Huffakers people in Texas. She was working on the theory that young girls liked elegance just as much as older girls, and was trying to incorporate elements from her other work into the children's clothing. The obvious drawback was that girls under twelve didn't have the attributes of a woman. But that was no reason they should be forced to wear prissy clothes that dripped with lace and other trivia. Even though young, they had a right to clothes of good fabric that hung well with some elegance.

It was the type of challenge she loved. When the phone rang at five, she looked at her watch in surprise. As usual, she had hardly noticed the time pass.

'Hello,' she said.

'Hello, Lela,' a man's voice said.

'I'm sorry, you have the wrong number,' she answered

and began to lower the receiver.

She jerked it back up to her ear with enough force to sprain a muscle. The voice – it was *him*!

'What do you want?' she said, inexplicably breathless.

'I wanted to talk to you. This is me.'

'How did you get my home number?' she asked, regaining her composure, her voice growing harsh.

'Lela, love can move mountains. You know that,' he said patiently.

'My name is not Lela. Why are you calling me that? What are you talking about?'

'Your name *is* Lela. I want you to think about that, to reflect on that. You must remember me. Remember Lela. Lela. Remember Lela.'

'What the hell –' she began, but then she heard the click as he put down his receiver. The line was dead.

She held the phone until the dial-tone came on. When she put it down, she realised she was shaking.

'Oh, God!' she said finally.

What did he want of her?

He had her home phone number. Did he have her address?

Why was she frightened? The fear rose like uncontrollable bile from her stomach.

He had not threatened her. He said nothing overtly violent. He was just weird. Why was she reacting with such intensity? She'd had horribly obscene phone calls before and handled them with unruffled aplomb, feeling either pity for the callers, or anger at the invasion of her privacy. Never fear.

She didn't understand it. The thoughts flooding her mind weren't helping either.

She held her hands out in front of her. They were still shaking. She felt her heart thump against the walls of her chest. There was sweat on her palms. It was ridiculous.

The front doorbell rang.

She started as if something had struck her and looked wildly towards the front of the house.

She was alone.

The bell rang again.

She took a deep breath to calm herself, realising that she was near hysteria. He had just called. It couldn't be him. Could it?

On trembling legs, she walked through the house to the front door. She stopped a foot away from it and called.

'Who's there?'

She heard a man's voice but couldn't make out the answer.

'Who?' she called again.

'Nemo Riley.'

Nemo who? The man next door! The realisation hit her in a wave of relief. It was her new neighbour.

She opened her door quickly. He stood with a six-pack of beer in one hand and a bottle of wine in the other and smiled at her.

'Yes?' she said, her voice still shakey.

His face grew concerned. 'Are you all right?' he asked. 'You look pale.'

She leaned against the door jamb and closed her eyes. 'I'm fine,' she heard herself say.

He transferred the wine to the hand holding the beer, came forward and took her arm in a firm grip. 'What's happened? Is there anything I can do to help?'

She opened her eyes and looked up at him. 'No, really. I'm all right.'

'Nonsense,' he said. 'You need to sit down.'

Still holding her arm, he stepped into the house and led her to the living room. She sat unresistingly on the sofa.

'Now, tell me what happened,' he said, and sat beside her.

'It was nothing, just a phone call. A man.'

'An obscene call?' he asked, his eyes narrowing.

She shook her head. 'Not really.'

'Tell me about it,' he insisted.

She found herself blurting it out then. She told him about the flowers, the calls, the last one to her home.

When she mentioned the name the caller had given her, he rolled it around his mouth as if trying to taste it. 'Lela,' he said. 'Lela. I must admit you look more like a Lela than a Sam.'

'It's such a bizarre thing to do,' she said, repressing a shiver.

Nemo shrugged. 'Maybe it's an attempt at intimacy, to give you a pet name, a secret name, you know.'

'I don't know why I'm so upset about it,' she concluded. She rubbed her temples. 'I guess that upsets me more than anything, this feeling of being so powerless before my emotions and not understanding why.'

'Has he done anything else? Threatened to harm you in any way?'

'No,' she said, looking at him in embarrassment. 'Do you think I'm snapping? Am I just being paranoid? There's something about this guy that really makes me feel scared.'

'I believe in intuition,' he said carefully. 'Something about this is threatening to you. A little voice is warning you, even though the reason may not be apparent. I don't think you should ignore it.'

'Really?' she asked, surprised.

He nodded. 'Sometimes the things we *know* are not backed up by anything rational. We still know them. I wouldn't belittle what you're feeling.'

She leaned back and put her hand on her chest. 'I'm so

relieved to hear you say that. Maddy thinks I'm crazy. I was beginning to think so myself.'

'Whenever I get into trouble it's because I didn't listen to the little voice that knows,' he said with a smile. 'I couldn't suggest that you don't listen to yours, right?'

He gestured at the table on which he had put his beer. 'I've returned your beer, and I brought you a neighbourly bottle of wine from my cellar. You don't only drink beer, do you?'

'No, I also drink wine,' she said.

'Well, I was kind of hoping that the wine was something we could share,' he said. 'There's no better way to get to know a neighbour.'

'Yes, of course,' she said.

'If you lead the way to the kitchen I'll put the beer in your fridge and open the wine,' he suggested.

She got up. Her hands had stopped shaking and her legs felt stronger.

He put the beer in the fridge, took the corkscrew she handed him and opened the wine. He held the bottle for a moment and then said, 'We're going to need glasses.'

'Oh, I'm sorry.' She still felt discombobulated.

She removed two wine glasses from the cupboard and handed them to him.

'Have you had dinner yet?' he asked. 'Do you have any plans?'

'No. My housekeeper has the day off. I was just going to have a snack.'

'How about I cook dinner for you – here?' he suggested. 'I don't have all my kitchen stuff unpacked yet, otherwise I'd invite you over.'

She realised then that she didn't want to be alone. Not yet. She couldn't dismiss the fact that the man had her phone number. Nemo's suggestion hinted at security.

'That would be great,' she said. 'It's an even better

28

way to get to know a neighbour. But I'll cook.'

'Trust me,' he said. 'I'm a marvellous cook. I'll cook you a meal to remember.'

'Well . . .'

'Chauvinism, hey?' he said, kidding her.

'You cook,' she said.

Nemo prepared the food with dazzling skill, deboning chicken thighs and slicing the meat into bite-size pieces. While rice cooked, he chopped vegetables into neat piles on the cutting board. After parboiling a couple of the hardier vegetables, he threw peanut oil into her wok and began to fry the chicken. Throughout the performance he chatted effortlessly. When it was close to done, he threw in the vegetables and spices, whipped up a sauce, took off the rice, and placed it all on the table with perfect timing.

'It's delicious,' she said, taking the first bite.

'Just a little something I whipped up in a few minutes.'

'So how many lawyers on your staff now?' she asked, picking up where the conversation had left off.

'About twelve,' he said. 'My partner and I are trying to keep the size manageable. Once you have a big success and it's picked up by the media, client's come like bees to honey. I've found in the last year that I can be more selective and I like that.'

'I suppose the same thing happened to me. One big success and then the doors open,' she said. 'The secret is to maintain the momentum. I'm always afraid I'm going to lose it, which is why I diversified so much. I think you work twice as hard when you're successful.'

Nemo laughed. 'You bet. I always thought that one day I'd get rich and lounge around on the Riviera or something. Well, I'm starting to get rich, but I'm putting in double time.'

'But you enjoy it, don't you?'

29

'Of course. In spite of the bullshit I have to put up with every now and then. I love it, just like you probably love your work.'

'Guilty,' she conceded. 'I'm very lucky.'

'I don't believe in luck,' he said. 'Not that kind, anyway. We create what we want. You did it, not luck.'

'You mean Fate doesn't play a part?'

'Maybe it does,' he said, 'but only up to a point. It might present opportunities to us. At least, that could be argued, I guess. But we have to grasp them. That takes talent and ability and sometimes even courage.'

Sam was more relaxed than she had felt for a long time with a man. Nemo's casual, undemanding manner had made her feel safe. It was comforting. She knew she could say anything and not upset him. And although he apparently found her attractive, there was no artifice or sexual undercurrent to deal with.

At ten o'clock, two bottles of wine later, he looked at his watch. 'I'd better run. It's been a long day and I've got more unpacking to do tomorrow. The place is still a shambles.'

She felt an unexpected surge of panic at the thought of being alone. He must have seen it, because he said, 'You're okay now, aren't you?'

Was she? She hadn't thought about her caller for hours. Now it all came back and with it that fearful feeling in her stomach. What if he called again? What if . . .

'I'm fine,' she lied. 'I had a wonderful evening.'

'So did I,' he said. 'You're the nicest neighbour I've ever had. And the most beautiful.'

They were sitting in the living room by then and, almost unthinkingly, Nemo leaned over and kissed her. It was a friendly, casual kiss, but after a moment their mouths opened at the same time and their tongues met.

30

Nemo was the first to pull away. 'You are a lovely woman, Sam Barry. Not what I expected.'

'Thank you, sir,' she said, then asked, 'What did you expect?'

'Some large, masculine lady. I mean, they proliferate in your field, don't they?'

'Are you disappointed?'

'No, I'm not into masculine ladies,' he said. He got up then. 'I must go.'

Again the panic seized her.

'You're still afraid, aren't you?' he said, looking down at her.

'I don't want him to call again,' she said.

'Change your number.'

'I mean tonight.'

'Tell you what,' he said. 'I'm going to write down my phone number for you. I want you to call me in a few minutes. You have a phone next to your bed?'

She nodded.

'So do I,' he said. 'Call me, and we'll keep an open line all night. Or is that a closed line? Anyway, nobody will be able to call you, and if you need me, you can just yell. I'll wake up.'

'Really?' she asked. 'You don't mind doing that?'

'Not if it would make you feel better.'

'I think it would,' she said gratefully. 'It's silly, I know, but I'd feel a little more secure knowing that someone can hear me.'

'It's not silly,' he said. 'Call me in ten or fifteen minutes.'

After he left, she cleaned the kitchen and then called from the phone beside her bed.

'Sam?' he answered.

'Yes,' she said.

'I enjoyed being with you tonight.'

31

'Me too,' she said.

'Well, I'm going to get ready for bed. The phone will be on the night table, right beside my head.'

'All right. And thanks, Nemo.'

'No problem,' he said.

She had a quick shower and then climbed into bed. She lay there and stared at the telephone on the table beside her.

'Goodnight, Sam,' she heard it say.

'Goodnight, Nemo,' she said.

She was asleep in minutes.

A man's voice: 'We are dancing in the ballroom of a large house. She is the most beautiful woman in the room. She is wearing a diamond tiara in her hair and a burgundy gown.'

A woman's voice: 'What's happening now?'

'The dance ends and we go outside. We stand in the glow of the moonlight, and then I kiss her and tell her I love her.'

'And then . . .'

'She thanks me and says she is honoured. We go back inside. The orchestra is still playing. We dance until the small hours of the morning. I am the envy of every man in the room.'

The man leaned forward and switched the tape recorder off. He had heard enough for now.

He took a cigarette from a silver case and put it in an ivory holder. He lit it and took a deep drag. Then he put his head back and closed his eyes, picturing the scene: dancing with the most beautiful woman in the world.

She loved him, she truly did. All he had to do was make her remember.

Given enough time, he would.

Chapter Three

Nemo Riley spent the morning unpacking boxes, putting things in their proper places, and trying to decide where the proper places were. He performed his chores absently, his thoughts on Sam Barry.

Beautiful, intelligent, talented, able – and very scared. Why, he wondered? In spite of his consoling words to her, it was likely that she was overreacting to the attentions of her secret admirer. It was a puzzle. And yet, what he had told her about his little voice was absolutely true. He did believe in intuition – his intuition. Her's was something only she could judge.

More than her problems, however, his attention was on her attributes. Beautiful, beautiful, beautiful! he told himself. He hadn't really intended to kiss her, but when he did, he felt an affection he hadn't experienced in a long time. He had been too busy for women lately. Add to that a couple of very unsatisfactory love affairs in the last five years, and you found a man who wasn't particularly interested in developing a close relationship with a woman. Until now.

Sam Barry was something else: independent, competent, probably a tough businesswoman, yet desirable and feminine. You didn't run into too many like her. Not with all those qualities.

And yet . . . his last affair was with a woman much like her, he reminded himself. Anne Fleming was an executive in a large cosmetics firm his office represented. Their relationship was essentially physical. 'No strings,' they had both agreed at the beginning. Anne was a beautiful and sexy woman with brains to spare, but she was undoubtedly married to her job and intended to be for a long time to come. It held top priority in her life. And Nemo wasn't used to being second banana. The conflict brought problems.

He was the one who broke the agreement. He could see that more clearly now. At the time, however, his demands seemed more than reasonable. He wanted to see more of her, to build a long-term relationship, to, at least, discuss the possibilities of marriage and children. Anne would have none of it. 'We agreed, no strings,' she said one night. 'These are strings and, as of now, I'm cutting them. This is getting too messy. Goodbye.' And she walked out of his life, leaving him to lick his wounds, which he did for a couple of months until the taste grew too bitter even for one enjoying the morsels of self-pity.

That was two years ago. Since then he had thrown himself into his business with renewed vigour. If career was where it was at, then goddamnit, career it would be. At first it had been nothing but some kind of childish reaction, but after some time the rewards were enormous. He expanded his business tenfold, thriving under the added responsibilities, becoming both successful and sought after. And with increased business power, came increased social exposure. Women, beautiful, bright and wealthy women were increasingly available. But all to no avail. Apart from the odd frustrating casual liaison that led nowhere, he was married to his business – just like Anne.

Nemo smiled wryly as he hung his paintings in the living room. He wasn't normally given to introspective thought, but Sam had apparently triggered off an onslaught. When all was said and done, in spite of money and success and reputation in high places, he needed more. Beneath it all, he was just like any other man. He wanted a relationship, a companion, and one day he wanted a family. It was a desire beyond thought, as automatic and basic as a tree that sends its roots into the earth to seek sustenance and to anchor itself. He too needed that stability.

He hammered the last nail into the wall and hit his thumb a glancing blow.

'Damn!' he said. Then he laughed.

Was that a reminder not to get involved with Sam Barry? Not only was she devoted to her business, but she was practically an industry herself. More than likely, she would lead him down exactly the same path as Anne Fleming – a path leading nowhere.

He finished putting the hook in and hung the painting. He lifted the bottom right corner to straighten it and stepped back for a critical view. It was a portrait by the American Impressionist Robert Henri, and it had cost a great deal of money. Sam, too, enjoyed the Impressionists, he discovered when they had talked last night.

Funny how his thoughts kept returning to her. Perhaps it was too late to consider not getting involved. All signs seemed to indicate that he was *already* involved on an emotional level.

He looked at his watch. Noon. The urge to speak to her tempted him. Unfortunately, he didn't have her telephone number. They had agreed that she would hang up her phone after getting up in the morning. She must have risen first, because he had been woken by the telephone company's whining signal that his phone was

35

off the hook. Too bad the line still wasn't open.

The hell with it, he thought. He washed his hands, combed his hair and walked over to her house.

She answered the door and beamed when she saw who it was. 'Hi! Come in,' she said.

A denim shirt hung loosely over blue jeans and her feet were bare. She looked much better than she had last night. She was, he noted again, beautiful.

'I just wanted to see how you were doing,' he said, stepping inside.

'I'm doing fine. Would you like some coffee?' she asked.

'That'd be good,' he said, following her into the kitchen.

She poured the coffee and said, 'I want to thank you. I had the best night's sleep I've had in days. I've woken with a new perspective on things.'

'I'm glad.'

'One sugar and cream, right?' She glanced at him.

'Yes.'

She handed him the cup. 'Come and sit on the patio. It's beautiful outside today.'

An untidy stack of drawing pads and materials covered the table. She pushed them aside as they sat.

'What are you doing?' he asked.

'I'm working on a new line for children, girls. I was just getting some concepts down.'

'You really do love this part of your work, don't you?' he said.

'Yes, I do. I've always loved designing things, particularly clothes. I remember what you said about luck last night, but I often think I'm one of the luckiest people in the world to get paid for doing what I love.'

'You probably are,' he said. 'I love my job when I win, hate it when I lose.'

'I guess I haven't lost too much,' she said thoughtfully. 'Things have gone very well.'

'So what's your new perspective?' he asked.

She looked puzzled, then smiled. 'Oh. Just that whatever is going on with this guy, I don't have to let it get to me. I've dealt with worse.'

'Very good,' he said.

'I'll get my telephone number changed tomorrow, for a start.'

'You have a maid that lives here?'

'Yes. She has a room above the garage. She's visiting relatives. She'll be back tonight.'

'And you have my phone number.'

'Bless you for it,' she said. 'That was very kind of you.'

'I'm happy to help.'

'I like you,' she said forthrightly. 'I'm glad we met.'

'I lied when I said I came over to see how you were,' he said.

'Oh?'

'Yes. I just came over to see you. I've been thinking about you all morning.'

'I'm flattered. At least, I hope I will be when you tell me what you've been thinking.'

'I've been thinking how beautiful you are and how I feel this overwhelming attraction towards you, something I haven't felt for anyone for a while.'

For the first time, Sam looked flustered. 'Oh,' she said.

Nemo touched her hand, resting his fingers on it. 'Do you think two people who work as hard as we do have a chance with each other?'

'You pointed out that we make our own chances,' she said. 'If it's something we both want, we have as good a chance as anyone.'

'Do you think it's going to be something we both want?'

'It seems to be heading in that direction, doesn't it?' she said. 'I've been thinking about you too.'

They looked at each other for a long moment and then he wrapped her hand in his and lifted it up and kissed her in the hollow of the palm.

He stood, still holding her hand. 'I want to make love with you,' he said. 'More than I've wanted anything.'

'This is moving fast,' she said cautiously.

He smiled down at her. 'If it's too fast, say so. But think of all the time we've missed already.'

She threw her head back and laughed. Then she got up and said, 'You've talked me into it.'

They kissed, tentatively at first, but with a rising passion. When they parted they were both breathing hard and their eyes shone like lights, flooding each other with desire. He took her hand and led her into the house.

'What's happened?' Maddy said when she saw Sam at the office on Monday morning.

'What do you mean?' Sam asked innocently.

Maddy snorted. 'You look beautiful. You're different. You look as if you – ah.'

'Ah?'

'Ah. Let me guess. A man. It has to be a man. You met someone. What did you do on the weekend?'

'Maddy, you're the nosiest friend I have,' Sam said, unable to hide a slightly smug smile.

'I'm the only friend you have,' Maddy said, unabashed. 'Come on, give. Who was it?'

Sam almost danced over to her desk and flopped into her chair. 'You're right. It's a man. I met a wonderful man and I'm having a wonderful affair.'

'Who?' Maddy persisted.

Sam shook her head.

'Come on, tell,' Maddy said. Then her hand rose to her mouth. 'Oh, no. I know who it is. You didn't. Not him. Not that delicious man.'

'What man?'

'Your neighbour. What's his name? Nemo? Nemo Riley. Tell me it wasn't him.'

'I confess. It was. It is,' Sam said.

'Aaah! Foiled again!' Maddy said, rolling her eyes.

'I'm sorry, first come, first served,' Sam said, and giggled. 'He wasn't your type anyway. No gold chains, no IQ of an alligator.'

'Oh, I'm happy for you,' Maddy said, dropping the pose. She came up to Sam and hugged her. 'He's a nice man. Perfect for you.'

'He's the nicest man I've met in . . . for a long time,' Sam said. She remembered the feel of his arms, the taste of his mouth, the unashamed ardour with which they had made love. Again and again. Until Margarite, the housekeeper, had arrived at five and Sam leapt up to warn her not to come into the bedroom. 'He's quite a wonderful man,' she added.

'This is not just a one-night stand, is it?' Maddy asked, looking at her carefully.

'I don't think so,' Sam said warily.

'This is great,' Maddy said. 'This is really, really great. You're a goner, I can tell. Smitten. No more cranky boss. Boss with her head in the clouds, her feet off the ground. Life around here is going to be wonderful.'

Sam laughed. 'Don't count on it. We still have a show coming up and you're still going to have to bust your butt, along with me.'

'Yeah, but at least you'll be *pleasant*,' Maddy said, determined to have the last word.

Sam spent the morning handling paperwork and answering telephone calls. It was one of those rare days

39

when all activity seemed effortless. Events moved in a straight line; barriers were absent. It was all due to her elevated mood, she knew. She was riding an emotinal high and nothing in the mundane world below her could match it.

In the afternoon, after grabbing a quick sandwich in the building's cafeteria, she walked the four blocks to her downtown studio. The building was once a warehouse. The enterprising owners gutted the inside, constructed partitions and walls, painted them bright colours, and created a trendy centre for artists and others who needed large spaces. Rents were minimal compared to the high-rise buildings just blocks away. Here, Sam employed a full-time staff of six – patternmaker and seamstresses – to produce the first finished products of her designs. She and Maddy jokingly called the studio her 'sweat shop,' but in fact, conditions were good and her employees well-paid.

After meeting with her head patternmaker and solving a few problems on-the-spot where design and reality did not exactly meet, she went back to the office. There would be phone calls to answer, and then she could return home to work more on the drawings for her Dallas meeting.

Maddy dogged her as soon as she entered the office. 'I have the reservations. We leave at eight a.m. and have a flight back at four.'

'Package came for you,' Sam's secretary called out. 'It was marked personal, so I didn't open it. It's in your office.'

Sam entered her office with Maddy on her heels, took off her jacket and slung it over a chair. 'What time's the meeting?'

'Eleven, then lunch, then another hour with them before we come back.'

'Do we have an agenda?' she asked, moving around her desk and sitting.

'You can start off talking about your latest ideas for the line and then we'll sit down and talk money. Or the other way around, whichever you prefer.'

'Let's talk money first,' Sam said. 'I want to make sure we have a firm deal we can all live with. Then the new ideas will be the icing on the cake for them. Make them feel they've made a good decision.'

'Right,' Maddy said.

'Where's the –' Sam said, looking around. 'Oh, there.'

The package sat on a chair beside the wall. Maddy got up and brought it over. 'No return address,' she said, handing it to Sam.

The size of a dress box, it was wrapped in plain brown paper. The label was neatly typed on a plain label, as was the *Personal* instruction. It had been delivered by the Post Office.

Sam found a paper cutter in her drawer and sliced one side of the package. It was, indeed, a white dress box. She lifted the lid and saw the card.

The familiar black ink made her stomach lurch. She picked it up with trembling fingers, all her well-being of the day deserting her like spilled water.

Lela, it said. *I'm returning this to its rightful owner. Remember it? T.*

She drew back the tissue paper and looked at the dress.

'It's a dress,' Maddy said unnecessarily.

Sam stood and lifted the dress out, holding it up.

It was a full length dress with a three-tiered skirt of pale peach chiffon. The bodice had a low-cut neckline and hung straight to the hip, where the skirt started. A five-inch wide heavy dark peach satin ribbon circled the hips and came together over the left hip to form a large

41

satin rose. The lining was a pink silk. Hand-stitched crystal bugle beads totally covered the bodice.

The bodice shimmered with movement as she held it, and the skirt seemed to float.

'It's beautiful,' Maddy said. 'Who's Lela?'

'Don't you recognise it?' Sam asked, her voice like ice. She ignored Maddy's question.

'What? It does look familiar, now that –'

'I designed a dress exactly like this about eighteen months ago,' Sam said.

Maddy looked blank, then said, 'Why would he send you a copy of a dress you designed?'

'You don't understand, do you? Sam said as calmly as she could. 'This dress is probably sixty years old.'

'What?'

She picked it up again and pointed. 'The beadwork has been done by hand, see? And these beads are real crystal, unlike anything done today. Mine were glass. Look at the underslip. This lining looks like fine Chinese silk. And the hand-rolled hems are stitched in silk thread. And look how age has worn the material here. This dress was made in the 1920s.'

'You mean that you copied this design?' Maddy asked.

'I've never seen it before in my life,' Sam said.

'Uh . . . I don't get it. What does this mean?'

'I've absolutely no idea,' Sam said.

She knew only that if she didn't sit down she was likely to fall. The blood thumped in her ears and the dress in her hands began to blur.

That evening, over dinner at La Serre, Sam told Nemo about the dress.

'Is there any way the dress could have been made now to look old?' Nemo asked.

42

Sam shook her head emphatically. 'No way. Absolutely not. The thread is rotting in places, the material, the – no. That dress is from the Twenties, I swear it.'

The waiter came and they stopped talking. Nemo ordered *medaillons de veau* – thin slices of veal with zuchinni, lemon and butter – for them both, and another bottle of wine.

When the waiter left, Nemo leaned forward. 'All right, let's assume the dress *is* old. What then? You must have copied it when you designed your version.'

'I'd never seen it before.'

'Maybe you saw it in a photograph years ago, forgot about it and then when you remembered it thought the idea was yours.'

'No. I'd never seen it. And besides, if I had, how would he know? It's crazy.'

'Well, then maybe it's just a coincidence.'

'And a coincidence that he had it and sent it to me.'

'Stranger things have happened.'

'Not this strange,' Sam said. It was too strange. It had bothered all her day. Finally, unable to concentrate on her work, she had left the office early.

Nemo looked around the room. There were plants everywhere, helping to create the French country-garden atmosphere that was the restaurant's trademark. At the table beside them, a bald, older man was complaining loudly to his wife about the size of his portion. 'You think they'd feed you for this price,' he said.

'I don't know what to think,' Nemo said, turning his attention back to Sam.

She fiddled nervously with her cutlery. 'Me neither.'

Nemo tried another direction. 'Do you remember designing that dress?'

'Yes. It was a year or two ago.'

43

'How did it happen? I mean, was there anything un-usual about it?'

'The design just came to me. Popped into my mind. Sometimes it works that way. It was beautiful, I thought. Then, after I did the dress, I hated it.'

'Why?' he asked, surprised.

'I don't know really. I usually like everything I do. There was just something repugnant about the finished product to me.'

'Did you market it?'

'I didn't want to, actually, but a client persuaded me.'

The waiter returned with their meal. Nemo commented that it was delicious, but Sam half-heartedly picked at her food.

'What do you think about the design of the dress now?' Nemo asked a short while later. 'I mean, based on the one you got in the mail?'

'I feel ambivalent about it,' she said, after thinking for a moment. 'I mean, I can look at it and logically see that it's beautiful, but at the same time there's this sense of repulsion.'

She put her fork down and said, 'Look. Whenever I get a card or something from this guy, I react. I break out in a sweat, I find it hard to breathe, I get scared. I feel the same way when I look at that dress.'

'And the dress you made?' he asked. 'After you made it, how did it make you feel?'

Sam stared at him. 'Yes,' she said finally. 'It's the same. It wasn't the same intensity, but I felt the same after I made it. I felt dislocated, nervous, threatened. Why, Nemo? What's happening to me?'

He put his hand over her own. 'I don't know, Sam. Maybe nothing. Whatever it is, we'll find out.'

She pushed the remains of her food aside. 'I want to go, Nemo. Do you mind?'

44

'Come on,' he said, rising. 'It's fine. Whatever you like.'

The *maître'd* rushed over to them. 'Is everything all right?' he asked. 'Was the food unsatisfactory?'

'No, not at all,' Nemo said. 'The lady isn't feeling well, that's all. Excuse us.'

When they made love at Sam's house that night, there was a kind of desperate intensity about her lovemaking. She clung to him and said his name over and over again. He was as gentle and caring as possible, sensing her need for comfort and giving what he could. But after they finally came together, he saw that she was crying.

'Sam, don't worry,' he said futilely, stroking her head as he would that of a child.

'I'm sorry,' she said, trying to blink the tears away. 'It's just that I'm so scared.'

'There's nothing to be scared of,' he said. 'Nothing has happened, Sam. Nothing bad has happened.'

'I know,' she said, and cried even harder.

When she grew calm, he asked if she had brought the dress home with her.

'Yes, I did. I don't know why. I wanted to throw it away, but I brought it.'

'May I see it?' he asked.

She walked unselfconsciously across the room, still naked, her long legs graceful, her breasts swaying slightly. So beautiful, he thought for the hundredth time, lost in admiration.

She took the dress from where it hung in the closet and brought it back, tossing it on the bed across his legs. He sat and lifted it.

'God, it's gorgeous,' he said. He looked closer. 'You're right. This is old. I think I must have seen your version of it. It looks familiar.'

She sat on the bed and looked dully at the dress. He saw that her face had grown pale.

'Sam, I want you to tell me something,' he said. 'You say this makes you feel scared. Scared of what?'

'Of what?' she repeated. 'I don't know.'

'There must be something,' he persisted. 'What does it feel like to you?'

She twisted her fingers together, looked at him and then away. 'It feels like I'm going to die,' she said, her voice almost whispering. 'If I'm afraid of something, it must be death.'

The world seemed to tilt for Nemo then. It was like taking a step into space and suddenly finding no foundation below you. The full impact of what she was going through suddenly became as real as life to him.

The thought of her absence, of her not being there for him, a concept unexpectedly vivid, carved a hole in his heart. He knew at that moment that this was no casual affair. He loved this woman.

He reached over and pulled her to him. She lay stiffly in his arms. 'It's going to be all right,' he said.

'Is that a promise?' she said thinly.

'Yes,' he said, his voice fierce. He pushed her away so that he could see her face. She wouldn't meet his eyes, awash in her misery. 'I love you, Sam. I'm not going to let anything happen to you.'

She looked up, her eyes glistening with tears and a creeping awareness of hope. 'You love me?'

'Yes, I do.'

He pulled her arms and kissed her, feeling the softness of her mouth and the salt of her tears, and a determination building in him like an iron rod. He wouldn't let anything happen to her. Nothing could happen to her. It wouldn't be fair. Not now.

46

A passion grew in them again. 'Put the dress away,' he said.

She got up from the bed with the dress. Halfway across the room she stopped and did a strange thing.

She pirouetted and turned to face him. Holding the dress in front of her body, she struck a pose. Then she smiled vacantly at him and said in a curiously mechanical voice, 'Lela.'

More than anything, she reminded him of a broken doll.

The expression left her face as suddenly as it had come. For a second she looked puzzled and then she turned and continued to the closet.

He felt a chill seize his body and pulled the covers up to his neck.

Chapter Four

The trip to Dallas was successful on a number of fronts. The moment the plane thrust her back into the seat and lifted off, Sam felt a sense of relief. Her problems were below, somewhere under that layer of smog. For the present, at least, she was beyond the reach of her persistent admirer.

And the business went well. The Huffakers people liked her new concepts and wooed her like an eager suitor. Their marketing staff made an impressive presentation to show how aggressively they would handle the new line, leaving both her and Maddy confident in their ability. By the time the meetings were over, they had agreed in principle on terms. Contracts would be drawn up and lawyers would finagle over the fine details, but to all intents and purposes the deal was made. If sales met projections, Sam Barry, Inc., stood to make a great deal of money.

They celebrated with a beer on the flight home. After clinking their bottles together, Maddy said, 'I think we're going to need a few more people on the staff.'

'Can we afford it?' Sam asked.

'At the rate we're expanding, yes. And it's a necessity. I'll work up the figures for you when we get back so that you have something to look at.'

Once again Sam realised how much she depended upon her friend. 'I've been thinking,' she said. 'You do so much, you're more of a partner than an employee. I'd like to give you a piece of the company.'

Maddy was astounded. 'Really?'

'It's only fair,' Sam said. 'You've helped me create Sam Barry, Inc. And you continue to help. You deserve a stake in our expansion, don't you think?'

'I don't know what to say.'

'First time I've ever seen you speechless,' Sam said, amusement in her voice. 'Come on, Maddy, you must have thought about the possibility.'

'Yes, I have, but you pay me well, Sam. I've been satisfied with that.'

'Well, it's time for a change,' Sam said. 'I'll talk to the lawyers in the next couple of weeks and get all the legal stuff sorted out.'

Maddy called the stewardess. 'Champagne,' she said. 'A bottle of champagne, please.'

They giggled through the bubbly like college girls. 'Who would have thunk it?' Maddy said, at least half-a-dozen times. At one point, she grew uncharacteristically sentimental. College, she said, had been an attempt to fill in time. 'All those jobs after I left – filling in time. Success was a dream, the old American dream, you know, but there didn't seem to be a way to reach it. I was like a kid without a home.' She punched Sam lightly on the arm. 'You gave me a home, Sam.'

'You created the home for yourself, Maddy. Without your help, we wouldn't be where we are now.'

'Who would have thunk it?' Maddy said.

They were both still lightheaded and in good spirits when the plane landed. It was only as they walked down the long corridor of the terminal that reality intruded into Sam's thoughts again.

They were standing on the moving escalator when a man pushed past them. He bumped into Sam's shoulder, knocking the briefcase out of her hand. After a quick backward glance, which left her with the impression of a pale face, dark eye-brows and black eyes, he hurried on without speaking.

'It's all right, don't mention it,' Maddy called out sarcastically after him.

She turned back to Sam and saw the tight, frightened expression on her face. 'Are you okay?' she asked.

'Yes, I'm fine,' Sam said. 'He just came up so quickly, I got a fright.'

The truth was different. But how could she tell Maddy of the shocking awareness of her vulnerability that struck her as the man walked away? She was open and unprotected. People, utter strangers, could come up to her, touch her. She was back in Los Angeles and nothing had changed. Somewhere in the city was a man determined to haunt her.

He wouldn't stop – she knew that with irrefutable certainty. No matter how many people told her he would just give up without encouragement from her, she knew he wouldn't. He was driven by compulsion. She had no idea what it was, but she knew it was there.

Maddy had obviously chosen not to bring up the subject of T. Since the incident of the dress, she hadn't mentioned Sam's mysterious admirer, deciding that as it obviously upset her friend, it was better forgotten. Now, however, seeing the withdrawn look in Sam's eyes, she reconsidered. 'Are you still upset about that guy?' she asked.

'No. It's all right,' Sam replied.

'Did you ever figure out what his trip was with the name and that dress?'

'No.'

Maddy shrugged. 'Just another weirdo,' she said, and let it drop.

But Sam was right. It wouldn't disappear. When they got back to the office, she found a large bouquet of flowers waiting for her. The envelope was addressed to Samantha Barry, but the card said, *Welcome back, Lela – T.*

Sam's reunion with Nemo that evening was tense. She paced the floor of his living room, a glass of wine in her hand.

'What could the significance of Lela be?' Nemo was asking. 'Maybe there's some clue there. Have you ever known anyone by that name?'

'Lela! Lela! No, I haven't. That's not important. What's important is that this freak is watching me. He knew I was out of town for the day. He's watching me, Nemo!'

Nemo was concerned by the hysteria in her voice. He spoke as calmly as he could without sounding condescending. 'That's easily explained. He could have called your office, asked for you and been told by your secretary or receptionist that you were out of town. It's no big deal.'

'He's been watching me. I know it,' she said stubbornly.

'You can't know that,' Nemo said.

'I know it!' she spat out angrily.

Nemo grew silent. There was apparently nothing he could say to console her. She had made her mind up and there was no changing it.

'For all I know, he could be watching me now,' she continued wildly. 'He may have followed me home from the office, seen me walking over here. Who knows?'

'What evil lurks within the hearts of men,' Nemo murmured.

'What?'

'Nothing. I was just finishing the quote. Who knows "what evil lurks within the hearts of men?" It seems appropriate to how you're feeling.'

'You think I'm nuts, don't you?'

'No,' he said. 'I do think you're overreacting though. Your only chance of handling this thing, whatever it is, *if* there is anything to be handled other than a persistent and slightly weird suitor, is to stay on top of it. Not to let your emotions take over and send you spinning. You must see that.'

'Easier said than done,' she said bitterly. 'My emotions seem to have a will of their own in this matter.'

'Yes, I see that,' he said.

'I feel helpless, violated, almost like a rape victim must feel. This, this, intruder is coming at me and there's nothing I can do about it. It's the most frustrating experience I've ever had. Can you see that?'

'I understand that,' Nemo said.

'Like you pointed out, he's done nothing illegal. I can't go to the police, or do anything about it. All I can do is wait until he does do something illegal, and then . . .'

Nemo poured more wine into his glass. 'Maybe there is something we can do,' he said. 'We could take the offensive and try to find out who he is.'

Sam stopped pacing and looked at him. 'How?'

'The flowers he sent you. They had to come from somewhere. I'll take a few hours off tomorrow, come to your office and see if I can track it down.'

'The florist they came from,' she said, her anger changing to excitement. 'Of course. There must be a piece of paper, a delivery slip, a label. Then we can go to the shop.'

52

'Right. He might be a regular customer or he might not. At least it's a start. I have to go to Washington the day after, so I'll come to work with you tomorrow and get going on it.'

'All right!' she said. 'I feel better already. Just to be doing something, anything, makes me feel less helpless.'

'Great,' Nemo said, grinning. 'Then how about you stop pacing the floor and come over here.'

'Am I pacing?' she asked, looking surprised.

'You've worn an inch off my carpet.'

She went over to him and sat heavily on his lap, causing him to grunt. 'My poor Nemo,' she said, kissing his forehead. 'What you have to put up with. You thought you were getting into a nice, relaxed little affair with me and here you are playing detective.'

'There are consolations,' he said, running his hands over her body.

Sam fell asleep in Nemo's arms after they made love. For a long time he stared up at the ceiling, unable to sleep. She was right: she was more than he had bargained for.

Her moods, the pressure she was subjecting herself to, concerned him. In the matter of a few days, this woman had become more precious to him than any other. She had filled the void in his life like rushing water. He hoped only that he had the strength to keep her, protect her and see her through this difficult time.

He had learned long ago that nothing seems to happen as easily as you want it to. But he also knew that nothing worthwhile could be attained without effort, or 'No pain, no gain,' as his old high school football coach was fond of saying. Loving Sam was the most worthwhile event in his life. He would do what he had to do to see that nothing happened to spoil it.

53

He fell asleep with that thought.

And then he dreamed . . .

He was standing in a large room. A ballroom? The men all wore evening dress, the women long gowns and jewels, the waiters were uniformed. A huge crystal chandelier sparkled like diamonds in the centre of the ceiling. An orchestra played music.

He was watching a woman. She was dancing with a man, but he only had eyes for her. She wore a burgundy gown and she was the most beautiful woman in the room, if not the world.

Finally he saw his chance to cut in. She was like a feather in his arms and smiled languorously up at him.

'I want to see you again,' he said. 'May I call you?'

'Of course,' she said, and his heart leapt.

The song ended and another man approached her.

'Lela,' the man said.

Nemo woke up sweating. Sam had thrown one leg over him. Her face nestled against his shoulder. Her breathing was deep and relaxed.

The most beautiful woman in the world, he thought, just before he fell asleep again.

There were uniformed policemen walking through Sam's suite of offices when she and Nemo arrived in the morning. The staff gathered in excited little knots, buzzing with speculation.

Maddy stationed herself beside Sam as soon as she entered the door.

'What's going on?' Sam asked.

'Someone broke in here last night,' Maddy said. She noticed Nemo and smiled at him. 'Hi, handsome,' she said.

'What was taken?' Sam asked.

54

'That's what's weird,' Maddy said. 'As far as we can tell, nothing. Petty cash hasn't been touched. Typewriters, tape recorders, files, everything seems in place. The police want you to check your office and see if anything is missing there. I took a look around but everything seems okay.'

Sam shot Nemo a disturbing look and went into her office. One of the policemen followed her. Nemo leaned against the door jamb.

'Anything missing here, ma'am?' the policeman asked. He was a patrolman by the looks of it, an elderly man with grey hair and a scarred face. Apparently a burglary where nothing was taken didn't rate a detective.

She opened the drawers of her desk, then examined her filing cabinet. 'Nothing that I can see,' she said.

'Could somebody have been after designs? Photographed them maybe?'

'It's a possibility, I suppose. But I do most of my design work at home. How did he get in?'

'Not very professional. Just broke the glass on your front door, reached in and opened it.'

'And nobody in the other offices saw anything? A lot of people here work odd hours, you know.'

'No, ma'am,' the officer said. 'Nobody saw anything.'

'It was him,' Sam said stiffly, sliding her eyes over to Nemo.

Nemo stepped forward quickly.

'Who?' the officer asked.

'T. The man who's been harassing me,' she said.

'Would you explain that, please, ma'am.'

Nemo interrupted. 'There's a man that's been calling and sending Miss Barry gifts and flowers. He won't give his name. Just calls himself "T." an initial.'

'What makes you think it's him, ma'am?'

55

'I don't know. It just seems likely,' she said.

'Has this person done anything illegal? Any threats? Obscene suggestions?'

'No,' she said.

'Any idea who it is?'

'No.'

The policeman shrugged. 'And you're sure nothing's missing?'

'Yes.'

He shrugged again. 'Well, if later you find anything gone, would you give us a call?'

'Is that all you can do?' Sam asked.

'At the moment, I'm afraid so, ma'am. We'll ask some more questions in the building, but it's a long shot.'

'What about fingerprints?'

The officer began to look harassed. 'We'll report it to burglary detail. But everyone who came in touched the door. Also, nothing was taken, ma'am. It won't be too high on the priority.'

'Nothing was taken!' Sam said disgustedly after the police left. 'It was him, I know it.'

Maddy looked sceptically over at Nemo then back at Sam. 'You can't know that, Sam. It could have been anyone.'

Sam's mouth tightened. 'Fine,' she said.

'Well, what about the flowers?' Nemo said.

'I'll ask out front. See if anyone knows the florist,' Sam said and left the room.

'I'm worried about her,' Maddy said to Nemo.

'Me too.'

'She's taking this whole thing way out of proportion. It's turning into paranoia.'

'That's a little strong,' Nemo said.

'No, it's not,' Maddy said. 'You don't know her as well as I do. This is totally unlike her. She's usually single-minded and calm, interested only in her work. In the last few days she's been closer to hysteria than I've ever seen her. It's scary.'

'You two are good friends, aren't you?' Nemo said.

'The best.'

'Ever known anyone named Lela?'

'No. I've thought about it a lot. I once knew a girl by that name in high school, but that was before I met Sam. We met at UCLA, you know.'

'Yes, she told me.'

'What do you think is going on here?' Maddy asked. 'I mean, do you think this guy is dangerous at all?'

'He's bizarre, I know that, but dangerous? I don't know.'

Sam returned. 'The first stroke of luck,' she announced. She held a card in her hand. 'The delivery man left a card with the receptionist. She admired the flowers and asked for it.'

Nemo took the card. 'It's not too far.' He looked at her. 'Shall we?'

'What's going on?' Maddy asked.

'I'll tell you later,' Sam said hurriedly. 'I'll be back in a little while.'

The florist had a small shop in the Arco Plaza. As they walked on the hard tiled floor, their footsteps clattering in the near empty corridors, Nemo told Sam what he wanted her to do. 'He may get up tight if we're both there snooping around, so here's your story . . .'

Sam went directly to a young woman behind the cash register. 'I wonder if you could help me?' she said. 'Someone has been sending me flowers, but he's too shy to give his real name. I need to find it out so I can thank him properly.'

'Well . . .' the woman said doubtfully.

'Oh, please help,' Sam said. 'This is the most romantic

57

thing that's ever happened to me. I mean, it could go on forever like this unless I do something.'

An older woman at the other end of the counter nodded at the shopgirl and smiled at Sam.

'All right, what's the name?' the clerk said.

'Barry, Samantha Barry.'

'Oh, I remember that. We've sent you a lot just in the last few days. Expensive bouquets too. Let me look.'

She scanned through the order book. 'Here it is,' she said. 'I'm afraid it's not much help. There's no name. Just an initial – T.'

'No name, no address?' Sam said anxiously.

'No.'

'How about a cheque or credit card. I mean, how did he pay?'

'Cash.'

'Do you remember what he looked like?'

The older woman moved along the counter. 'I handled that. I remember it because he payed all cash for a number of deliveries. He even wrote the cards beforehand and told us what days to send them. Then yesterday he came in with another card, wanted to exchange it for the one he'd already written.'

'Do you know what was on the one he took back?' Sam asked.

The woman shook her head.

'Are there more deliveries planned?'

No. Yesterday was the last one.'

'What did he look like?'

'A very well-dressed gentleman,' the woman said. 'Tall, good-looking, dark hair, dark eyes.'

The description would fit every fifth man on the street. 'Anything unusual about his looks, something specific?' Sam asked.

The woman thought for a moment. 'No, not really.

I'm not very observant about people. I remember his face, it was very pale, like he hadn't been in the sun much, like someone from Oregon, you know. That's the only thing.'

'Nothing else,' Sam said disappointedly.

'No. Oh, yes. Wait a minute. I noticed when he was writing the cards that he wore beautiful black leather gloves. Kind of unusual to see that.'

Not if you don't want to leave fingerprints, Sam thought.

'Listen, I'm dying to meet him,' Sam said. 'If he comes in again, could you call me? I'll leave my card. Or if you see him anywhere. I'd really appreciate it.'

She handed her card to the woman. The younger girl looked over the shoulder of the owner and said, 'Oh, you're the fashion designer. I love your clothes.'

'Thank you,' Sam said. 'Please call if you see him again.'

The woman promised she would and Sam left the shop and joined Nemo at the bookstore next door, where he had been waiting.

'Any luck?' he asked.

'Not a whole lot. I have a vague description. Tall, dark and handsome with an unusually pale face. Paid in cash, in person. No address, no cheque, no credit card.'

'Not much help,' Nemo said.

'I asked her to call me if she saw him again.'

'That description could fit almost anyone,' Nemo said.

'I know,' Sam said, as they walked away. 'You see men like that all the time, except for the pale face. I mean, this is Southern California and –'

She stopped in midstride. 'Oh, my God!' she said, lifting her hand to her mouth.

'What? What's wrong?' Nemo said.

'I saw him. I did see him,' she said.

59

'You saw him? Where?'

'It was him. I know it. At the airport yesterday.'

She told him about the man who had bumped her on the escalator. 'It fits the description exactly. I swear it was him.'

'How can you be sure?' Nemo asked. 'You just said that you see men like that all the time.'

'I'm just sure, that's all.'

'But it's such a general description.'

'I'm positive it was him, Nemo,' she said, voice brittle now.

'Maybe you're grasping a little,' he suggested.

She gripped his arm tightly with her hand. 'Nemo, don't you sometimes just know things? Doesn't your little voice tell you? Not through logic, but just through *knowing*? Well, I know it was him. Believe me.'

'All right, Sam. Did you notice anything else about him?' Nemo asked.

'I didn't even look at him. Not really. I just got a vague impression, a quick glance.'

'Sam, would you be able to draw the face, just a quick sketch based on what you saw?'

'I don't think so,' she said uncertainly. 'I didn't see him closely enough to get a good look.' She put her hand on his arm. 'You believe that he's the man I saw at the airport?'

'It could be,' Nemo said. 'I don't know. But if he knew you were out of town, it's not that difficult to find out what flight you were on. The airlines aren't supposed to give out that information, but if you know the ropes it's easy to get.'

'God!' she said. 'He actually touched me. He bumped right into me.'

'Maybe that's all he wanted to do,' Nemo said. 'Some sort of sexual buzz. You're sure you'd never seen him before anywhere?'

'Never.'

'Well, why don't you try and draw the face as best you can?'

'I don't think it would help.'

'Just give it a shot. Did Maddy see him?'

'Only his back, I think. She was looking back at me when he turned.'

Nemo looked at his watch. 'I've got to head back. I'll take you back to your office first.'

'Sorry I have wasted your time,' she said.

'Hell, that wasn't a waste. We got a dead end on the flowers, but at least we have a vague description and you know you've seen him. We're ahead of the game. I'll see what else I can dream up.'

He double-parked outside her office and kissed her. 'Don't worry, Sam. We'll get to the bottom of this.'

'I appreciate the help,' she said. 'You want to come over tonight? Dinner?'

'For a little while,' he said. 'My flight to DC leaves pretty early tomorrow morning, so I've got to get some sleep.'

'I'm thankful for the crumbs you hand out, kind sir,' she said. She got out of the car. 'See you after work.'

Back in the office, things had calmed down. A workman was replacing the glass in the front door and the staff were back to normal.

'You got a call from that guy again,' her secretary told her as she passed her desk.

'What did he say?'

'Nothing. I told him you weren't in.'

'Good,' Sam said. 'Keep on telling him that when he calls again.'

Maybe he'd get the idea, she thought. But even as she wished for it, she knew it wouldn't be that easy.

*　　　*　　　*

61

Nemo told Sam over dinner about his desire for a family. They were sitting in the dining room. Sam's housekeeper Margarite, an elderly Frenchwoman with strong ideas about men in general and Sam's suitors in particular, was thrilled about her affair with Nemo. She prepared the meal and garnished the table with candles and flowers. After serving them, she winked at Nemo and disappeared.

'She likes you,' Sam said. 'It's the ultimate compliment.'

'I'm honoured.'

'She's lived over here for thirty years. Her husband was an American, but he deserted her. She went back to France for six months and then came back here. She said she couldn't stand it there after California.'

'Does she have a family?'

'No. I think it's her one regret in life.'

'I regret not having one too,' Nemo said. 'I'm thirty-five already and nothing to show for it.'

'I know what you mean,' Sam said. 'I'm thirty and beginning to worry.'

'You'd like children?'

'I would *love* to have children.'

'What about your career? Your time?'

'Lots of women have careers and families. I could work it out.'

'I hope so, Sam, because sooner or later I'm going to ask you to marry me, you know that, don't you?'

She smiled at him, her face soft in the flickering flames of the candles. 'I think I've guessed it,' she said.

'I'd want to have a family,' he said.

He told her about his affair with Anne Fleming, the cosmetics career woman. 'Things tend to work out,' he concluded. 'We weren't really right for each other. I wasn't in love with her. I was in love with the idea of being married and having a family. And, the big AND, if it had worked out, I wouldn't have met you.'

'Are you still in love with the idea of being married?' she asked.

'I'm in love with you,' he said.

'Will you spend the night with me?' she asked.

'I can't,' he said. 'I still have packing to do and some paperwork to prepare for these meetings in DC.'

'I wish you weren't going away. I don't like the idea of being alone right now.'

'Margarite's here. And I'll call you every day. Twice a day. Even though I'm only going to be gone for two days.'

'You're laughing at me,' she said.

'I love you,' he replied.

'I love you too, Nemo,' she said for the first time. 'But I wish it wasn't happening now.'

'Hey, it'll pass,' he said lightly. 'And you and I will still be here.'

'I hope so,' she said sadly.

'I don't have to go home yet,' he said, pushing his chair back. He wanted to eradicate the cloud of sadness that had encompassed her, to hold her and reassure her of his love in the safety of his arms. He came around the table and kissed her neck. 'Shall we?'

'So soon after dinner?' she asked in mock horror.

'Absolutely,' he said.

'Oh, Nemo,' she said. 'If only we could shut out the world.'

Sam was watching Nemo dress when the telephone rang. Wonderfully fulfilled by their lovemaking, she lay half-propped up by a pillow, her eyes languorous, her body as relaxed as a cat. He dressed with a grace that encompassed all his movements, she thoughts.

On the third ring she lazily reached over to the bedside table and picked up the phone.

'Lela?'

She shot up and Nemo stopped what he was doing to watch her.

'How did you get my phone number?' was all she could think to say.

'Have you been thinking about who you are?' T. asked, ignoring her question.

'What do you want?' she asked, her voice rising.

'I want you to remember,' he said.

Nemo came to the bed and sat beside her. He bent his head to the telephone, trying to hear the man. His presence calmed Sam, and she lowered her voice.

'Remember what?' she asked.

'To remember us, you and me,' the man said.

'I don't know what you mean,' Sam said. 'Look, I want you to stop bothering me. I don't want anything to do with you.'

'You can't change the past, Lela,' the man said, his voice almost sad.

'Goodbye,' she said.

'Wait! Listen to me carefully, Lela. Didn't the dress mean anything to you?'

'No,' she said, but her voice lacked conviction. The dress was still a source of confusion and upset.

'You wore that dress when we loved each other, Lela. Remember?'

'I don't know what you mean.'

'Think, Lela! Think of reincarnation. Think of the past life when you loved me. Remember it. It's there, in your mind, just waiting for you to see it again. Remember, Lela.'

'You're crazy,' she said in a shaken voice.

64

Nemo took the phone from her and spoke, his voice harsh with anger. 'She doesn't want to talk to you, to have anything to do with you. The police have been informed of your harassment. I suggest you –'

There was a click on the other end of the line.

Nemo looked at the phone then replaced it on the receiver.

'Did you hear what he said?' Sam asked.

'No. Just a bit of it. Something about remember.'

'He told me he knew me in a past life. A past life! Reincarnation! He wants me to remember,' she said. 'Do you believe that? He said I wore the dress in my past life. Jesus!'

Nemo shook his head. 'Well, at least we know the guy's not rowing with all his oars in the water. Did you try doing that drawing, as I suggested?'

'It came to nothing. I couldn't do it,' she said absently.

She was more angry than upset, he was pleased to see. She coiled her hand into a fist and hit it against the bed.

'I just got this new number two days ago. How did he get it?'

'That's easy,' Nemo said. 'The burglary in your office. Your home number is probably in at least three Rolodex's.'

'How dare he! How dare he do this to me,' she said.

'It ties him into the break-in. At least this is something you can tell the police.'

Her anger dissipated. She put her hands over her face and said in a muffled voice, 'Oh, God! Why is this happening to me?' Nemo began to remove his shoes. 'What are you doing?' she asked.

'Staying,' he said. 'I'm not going to leave you alone tonight. And I'm going to cancel my DC trip. I can do it later.'

'But wasn't it important?' she asked, concerned for him now.

'Not as important as you are,' he said. 'I don't think this is a good time for me to be out of town. I can put it off for a week or two.'

'I feel guilty about it,' she said, eyes downcast.

'Don't. It's my decision,' he said.

Later, when they lay in bed, he said, 'We're going to track this guy down and find out what all this is about. Obviously, we're dealing with a lunatic here. He shouldn't be too hard to find.' But even as he spoke, some doubt nagged at him.

It wasn't until later that it crystalised. Sam was already asleep, and he was almost there, falling into a light doze.

The dress, he thought. The one thing they couldn't explain was the beautiful antique dress that Sam had somehow redesigned sixty years later without ever seeing the original. There was no logical explanation for that. None that he could think of, at least. There was only – no, he thought. It's insane and impossible.

Insane, he thought again, and finally fell asleep.

Chapter Five

Nemo's presence had a relaxing effect on Sam. Breakfast, catered by Sam's housekeeper on the patio, was leisurely and lighthearted. Sam was intent only upon displaying her affection for Nemo and acted as if nothing had happened to upset her. She touched him at every opportunity and watched him lingeringly during the silent moments.

'What are you thinking?' he asked her, during one of her reflective pauses.

She flushed as if caught. 'How foolish I've been,' she said.

He asked what she meant.

'Work. I've been so heavily into my work, I haven't thought of developing a real relationship with anyone. And I've been cheating myself. I had no idea it would be so – so like this.'

'Has there been anyone recently you'd want to have a relationship with?' he asked.

'No. That's probably why I haven't made the time for it. The right guy never showed up and demanded I do.'

'And now?' he asked.

'Fishing, fishing,' she accused playfully, then touched his hand. 'The right man came along.'

'Talking about work,' he said, looking at his watch. 'Don't you have to go to your office?'

'What about you?' she countered.

'I'm the boss. I can show up when I like,' he said.

'Me too.'

'Wanna play hookey today?'

'Love to,' she said. 'What do you want to do?'

He looked at her through half-closed eyes. 'I thought we could start off by going back to bed, then get up and go play somewhere.'

'That sounds quite wonderful,' Sam said. 'Only one problem. If we get back into bed, do you think we'll make it out?'

'Who cares?' he asked.

They left the house at noon. By then, Nemo had worked up an appetite and insisted they stop for lunch at Weby's Dely.

'Best damn bagel chips in LA,' he said. 'They sell them through Neiman–Marcus as well. Baked with garlic butter and Parmesan cheese.' He also had a pastrami sandwich, pickles and latkes, while Sam barely made it through a large bowl of matzo ball soup.

'God, you eat like Hun,' Sam said admiringly.

'Did Huns eat a lot?' he asked.

'I don't know. I always thought so. Whenever I heard of Huns it was in the context of raping and pillaging and that sounds like hungry work.'

'Well, I've been indulging in half their activities. The pillaging comes later.'

'I can hardly wait,' she said.

They spent the afternoon walking, something people rarely do in Los Angeles, a city so spread out the automobile is like a second home. In fact, some people spend more time on the freeways that criss-cross the basin than they do in their homes. Still, more than three miles of

Ventura Boulevard stretches through Studio City. From a car it looks like a jumble of billboards and gas stations, but on foot it offers surprising treasures if you wander down the side-streets within a block of the boulevard. Strange little stores carry everything under the sun, ranging from doll collections to movie wardrobe clothing to outright junk.

Sam was captivated by a doll store that sold Madame Alexander dolls. 'Oh, I had two of these when I was a child,' she cried when she saw them. 'Do you know how much they're worth now? The old ones?'

'Do you still have them?' Nemo asked.

'No,' she said wistfully. 'When my parents died, there was a lot of my old stuff that I couldn't find.'

She moved across to a row of modern dolls. 'I'd love to design clothes for dolls. Fashionable, quality clothes, not these prissy things, and not the junk they put on the Barbies. You know, elegant stuff.'

'That's not a bad idea,' Nemo said. 'I'm sure if you approached one of the manufacturers you'd –'

Sam put her finger on his lips. 'Sssh!' she said. 'This is how I get into trouble. I get ideas like this and suddenly I find I have yet another project and even less time.'

'And you find yourself richer,' he said.

She linked her arm in his. 'I've found something else. There are other kinds of riches. Come on, let's get out of here before I have any more ideas. This is our day, right?'

'Right,' he agreed.

And it was. They wandered uncaringly through the day, stopping when they felt like it, covering miles of streets, as carefree as youngsters. In the evening they had dinner at a Sushi bar, and finally reached his house at ten.

'I'd better call Maddy,' she said, suddenly growing conscientious.

'Use the phone in the study,' he said, and poured wine while she talked.

When she returned he handed her a glass and clinked his against it. 'To a wonderful day,' he said.

He sat on the couch and kicked off his shoes.

'Maddy was amazed. She said I should do this more often,' Sam said. She mimicked her friend, 'You mean you did absolutely nothing?'

'You didn't even call in during the entire day,' Nemo said approvingly.

'Neither did you,' she said.

'I know. And, you know what? I don't feel an iota of guilt. I think we've both been suffering from the same disease: all work and no play.'

'We'll make up for it,' she said, swivelling around to put her feet up and her head on his lap.

'Sure,' he replied. 'We're young, strong and healthy.' He stroked her hair and became serious. 'I'm glad I found you, Sam. My life has been . . . I don't know. I was going to say empty, but that's not true. I do happen to love my work. But work for its own sake hasn't been enough. There has to be a reward.'

'And I'm the reward?' she asked with mock indignation.

'The best,' he said.

She reached for his hand and kissed the palm. 'It's amazing, isn't it, how we both fill exactly the same need for each other? Before we met, we had the identical problem with life. Success, money and a gaping big hole where other people have love and family and children. If there's such a thing as fate, it's made itself visible.'

She ran her tongue over his palm. 'How young and strong and healthy are you?' she asked.

'Are you trying to test my mettle?'

'You never answered my question.'

70

He ran his other hand down her body. 'Enough,' he said. 'I'm all of those things enough.'

Mmm,' she said. 'Prove it.'

Later, just before they fell asleep, she rubbed her face into his neck. 'You proved it,' she murmured. 'More than enough.'

The real world caught up with them the next day. He had to go to his office and she to hers. However, both tore themselves away soon enough to meet at six, enjoy a couple of drinks and make it to the opening night of a new Neil Simon play starring Richard Benjamin.

Afterwards they had supper in a small Chinese restaurant specialising in sea food. It was tucked away on a side alley at the edge of Chinatown and they were only one of two Caucasian couples. 'Place hasn't been discovered yet,' Nemo said with satisfaction.

'You have to order for me,' Sam said. 'I used to think all Chinese food was like chop suey, then I discovered Mandarin and Sezchwan food, but this is all new.'

'You want to go messy or delicate?' Nemo asked.

'I don't know. It depends how good it is.'

'Tell you what. I'll go messy – crab in black bean sauce – and you go delicate – sole in plum sauce. Then we can share.'

They talked about the play. 'Benjamin is so droll,' Nemo said. 'He's never disappointed me. He always gives a good performance.'

'I've only seen him in movies,' Sam said. 'God, I've just been missing so much. Until I met you.'

'You didn't go out often?' Nemo asked. 'There must have been men.'

Sam shrugged. 'There've always been men, but I didn't go out much. It seems like a waste of time when

71

you don't really care much about the person you're with. You play these silly boy-girl games, and there's all this anticipation, and hurt feelings when you decline, and all the rest that goes with that. My work seemed so much more important than that. So satisfying compared to that.'

'Come on, Sam. You must have fallen in love before,' he said, smiling.

She raised an eyebrow. 'Fishing again?'

'Of course,' he said. 'I want to know everything about you. But if you'd rather not talk about it . . .'

'No, no,' she said quickly. 'It's no big deal. There've been a couple of guys. I lived with a guy before I met Maddy. At college, you know. It didn't last long. It was just a sexual thing, I guess. We were so young and so hungry and wanted to experience it all. He wanted to experience even more. He started playing around. I left. Simple.

'After that, I was gunshy for a while, but then met this really nice guy, which I guess I needed at the time. But his niceness kind of covered a big blank nothing. There wasn't much of him. I guess he bored me, when it gets right down to it. And then, lately, I've been on a few dates, but nothing sparked. It was an exercise in futility, so I gave it up.'

'What do you want in a man?' Nemo asked.

She pointed a finger at him. 'You. You fit the bill perfectly. Sharp and intelligent, which are two different things. Kind, compassionate, tough, successful, handsome and a great lover. What more could I want?'

'Absolutely nothing,' he said.

'What about you? What were you looking for in a woman?'

'Sharp and intelligent, kind, compassionate, tough, successful, handso– no, beautiful and a great lover. What else?'

'And?' she asked, unable to prevent a coy note from appearing in her voice.

'And what?' he asked innocently.

'And . . .' She glanced away. 'It's embarrassing to have to say. Forget it,' she said tartly. She looked back at him and saw a broad grin on his face.

'You bastard,' she said.

'. . . And I found you,' he conceded.

'I almost had to wring that out of you,' she said.

He laughed loudly, then took her hand in his. 'You know what? It's all I can do to stop myself telling everybody. I want to stand on street corners and shout it out, jump on restaurant tables and sing it, get on the telephone and tell all my friends. I love you, Sam. You're my missing piece.'

Sam melted. A blush crept over her cheeks.

'And I love a woman who still blushes,' he added.

Their main course came and within minutes his hands dripped with sauce. 'Mmm. This is what I mean by messy,' he said. 'You've got to eat this with your fingers to get the flavour.'

'It looks good, but this is wonderful,' Sam said.

'Here, taste.' He picked up a piece of crab and popped it into her mouth.

'More,' she demanded.

'Sam . . .' he began when they finished eating. But changed his mind and said instead, 'Do you want dessert?'

'Not another bite,' she said. 'You keep up like this I'm going to look like a sow.'

He had intended to ask her if she had heard anything else from T., but she hadn't mentioned him for two days now, and he didn't want to create an upset where none existed. He loved her like this, lighthearted and enjoying herself, he didn't want to see the worry cloud

73

her face again. He was also curious to know if she had ever called the police after the la.t telephone call from the man. It was circumstantial, but it did appear to tie him in to the break-in at her office. He decided to leave it, however. There was time enough later.

Maybe the guy has dropped it, he thought optimistically. After all, the last time T. called her, he had got on the phone and warned him off. Maybe that had been all that was needed – for the guy to know there was a man in her life.

Yet even as he thought it, another little voice in his mind told him his optimism was foolish. The man was obviously unbalanced with his talk of reincarnation and past lives. It would probably take more than a simple warning to scare him off.

'What are you thinking?' Sam asked for the second time.

'Oh, just work,' he said with a smile. 'I just remembered something I was supposed to do. I'll get to it tomorrow. Now, what do you want to do?'

'Go sit in the hot tub and then crawl into bed with you,' she said. 'I feel sated.'

'Are all your appetites sated?' he asked, disappointment crossing his face.

She squeezed his arm. 'All but one,' she said.

Sam called him at the office the next morning. He was going over a brief with two assistants, pointing out a few legal points they had missed and telling them where to find the information when the call came through.

'It's Miss Barry,' his secretary said.

'Good, I'll take it,' he said, and waved for the two young men to leave the room.

'Hi, Sam!' he said. 'Are we still on for tonight?'

74

They had decided on a quiet evening at his house. He had promised to cook dinner.

'Nemo. He called again,' she said. Her voice quivered on the edge of tears.

Nemo moved the receiver to his other hand and leaned on his desk. 'What happened? What did he say?'

'He said it was dangerous for me to keep seeing you. Dangerous for you,' she said. 'Oh, God, Nemo, it was terrible. I was so scared.'

'What did you say?' he asked.

'Nothing. I hung up.'

'Where are you? When did this happen?'

'I'm at the office,' she said. 'It was ten minutes ago. I'd left orders with my secretary not to put his calls through, but she is sick today and we have a temporary on.'

'Look, I'm coming over there right away. I want you to call the police. No, I'll call the police for you, okay? Then I'll be there, all right?'

'All right,' she said.

'Did you call them after the last phone call?'

'No,' she said. 'There didn't seem much point. I mean, they didn't seem to be able to do much when they came to the office and, I don't know, it didn't seem worth it.'

'Those were just patrolmen,' he said. 'I'll make a couple of calls to people I know. And then I'll be over. Are you okay, Sam?'

He heard her take a deep breath. 'Yes, I'm fine,' she said. 'I feel better hearing your voice. It just shook me up, you know?'

'It's understandable.'

'Listen, don't bother coming over. I don't want to take you away from your work,' she said apologetically. 'I'm okay now. Much better.'

'I'll see you soon,' he said firmly, and hung up.

Nemo had a couple of friends in the LAPD, one of

75

them, Alan Wisdom, he had even gone to law school with. Alan was now pretty high up in executive rank, and very public-relations conscious. They had kept in touch casually through the years. He called him and told him the story.

'You mean Sam Barry the designer?' Wisdom asked.

'Yes. Very important person,' Nemo said. 'High publicity profile.'

'I'll have someone there right away,' Wisdom said. 'Give me the address.'

Nemo gave him the address and said, 'I owe you one, Alan.'

'And I'll make sure you pay,' Wisdom said.

Nemo asked his secretary to cancel his appointments, left a couple of confused young lawyers holding a brief they didn't quite understand, and headed downtown for Sam's office.

'You shouldn't have come,' she said, meeting him in the reception area.

'Yes, I should have,' he said, taking her arm and going into her office. 'I called the police. Anyone come yet?'

'No,' she said.

They sat on a small couch and he held her hand. 'Tell me exactly what he said on the phone.'

'He said, "This is me again. Have you thought about what I said? Have you remembered anything?" Something like that. Then he said, "Your boyfriend, the lawyer. Stay away from him. End it now. It could be dangerous – for him. He could meet with an accident. I know who he is." I think those were the exact words. I hung up on him then.'

She squeezed his hand. It sounds like a B movie when I say it now, but I was so scared then. His voice. It just seemed so menacing. All I could think about was you – something happening to you.'

76

'Nothing's going to happen to me,' Nemo said. 'He was only trying to scare you, Sam.'

'He succeeded,' she said.

The buzzer on her telephone rang and she got up to answer it. 'Yes, send him in,' she said. She turned to Nemo and said, 'The police.'

Lieutenant Marshall was a thin, dark man with a balding head. The left side of his face was twisted into a scowl, giving him a permanently disapproving expression. He wore a grey sports coat and slightly grey slacks.

'Miss Barry,' he said, shaking her hand. He glanced over at Nemo and his scowl seemed to deepen.

'This is Mr Nemo Riley, a friend,' she said.

'You have friends at Parker Center too, don't you, Mr Riley?' he said, not shaking hands with Nemo.

Parker Center was LAPD headquarters. It was where Wisdom worked. Apparently the officer was displeased at the intervention. Nemo thought he'd better soothe the waters and get things off to a better start.

He held out his hand, forcing the issue. The policeman shook it grudgingly.

'What would have happened if we had called this situation into the desk sergeant?' Nemo asked.

'You would have been asked to come down to the station,' Marshall said. 'Like everyone else.'

'And then the case would have been put on a pile to be looked at, maybe, a few days later.'

Marshall shrugged. 'This is life,' he said.

'I'm sorry if it offends you that I use my contacts,' Nemo said pleasantly. 'But I'm concerned for Miss Barry's welfare. If you have a choice of rowing a river with your bare hands or with oars, which would you choose?'

Marshall stared back at him for a beat, then shrugged again. 'You've got a point. But I thought the threat was against you.'

77

'I'm not worried about my safety. I've been threatened before. It's Miss Barry who's being harassed.'

'All right, Miss Barry, suppose you tell me what's been happening here,' Marshall said.

'Would you sit down?' Sam said, indicating a chair opposite her desk.

While the policeman sat, she went around her desk and sat behind it. Nemo took a chair beside the policeman.

'It started with flowers . . .' Sam began.

Marshall listened politely, interrupting every now and again with a question to clarify a point. Nemo watched his face, unable to read his thoughts.

'And the last contact with him was the phone call today?' Marshall asked when she finished.

'Yes.'

Marshall rose to his feet. 'Well, we'll look into it, Miss Barry. In the meantime, I wouldn't worry too much about it. Sounds like the man has a crush on you. It doesn't sound as if he intends to do more than bother you on the phone.'

'What about the threat against Nemo?' she asked, irritation entering her voice.

'Sounds like an empty threat to me. I wouldn't worry about it either. This kind of thing happens all the time. There are some guys out there who get their jollies by carrying on a romance this way. It seldom becomes more than that.'

'That's it?' Nemo asked, standing up. 'You're going to go back, write up a report and file it?'

'I said we'd look into it,' Marshall said, his voice neutral.

'How?' Nemo snapped. 'What exactly are you going to do?'

'Well, there aren't exactly a luxury of leads, but I'll

78

start by looking at the report on the break-in here.'

'You won't find out any more than we've already told you by doing that,' Nemo said.

'What would you suggest I do, Mr Riley?' Marshall asked.

'I'm not going to tell you how to do your job, Lieutenant,' Nemo said. 'But I'd like to see some action here. You may think this is some harmless prankster, but I'm concerned.'

Marshall's voice grew tired. He did everything but yawn. 'Mr Riley, do you know how many complaints of telephone harassment we get a day? This town is filled with freaks. This talk of knowing you in another life just shows we're dealing with another one. Believe me, I've had a lot of experience with this. Nothing will come of it.' He turned to Sam. 'Did you change your home phone number again?'

'Yes,' she said, coming around the desk to Nemo.

'Well, if he gets it again and calls again, don't change it. We'll get the phone company to put a trace on the guy. That's really all we can do right now.'

'Marshall,' Nemo began, growing angry. But Sam put her hand on his arm.

'Thank you for your time, Lieutenant,' she said. 'I'm sure you're right.'

'I hope so,' Nemo said darkly.

Marshall took a card from his pocket and handed it to Sam. 'If anything else happens, call me, day or night,' he said. 'A message will reach me if I'm not in.'

'Mr Riley.' He nodded to Nemo.

'Goddamn!' Nemo said when he left the room. 'The trouble with the police is they're never there until *after* the crime has been committed. Patronising bastard.'

'Be realistic, Nemo,' Sam said practically. 'What else could he do right now? Nothing's happened yet.'

'A threat's been made.'

'Right. But how could they find this guy anyway? It looks impossible to me.'

Nemo shook his head angrily, then he looked up and saw the concern on Sam's face. He suddenly grinned, amused at the reversal of roles. 'Hey, I'm supposed to be comforting you,' he said.

'I'm all right,' Sam said. 'He's probably right about this guy anyway. Just you be careful.'

Nemo looked at his watch. 'I guess I'll go back to my office. You'll still come by my place after work?'

She kissed him on the cheek. 'Yes. And thanks, Nemo.'

'Wasn't much help,' he said grudgingly.

'Just having you here when I need you is help enough,' she said.

'I'll always be around when you need me,' he promised.

'I count on it,' she said.

He kissed her then, hoping while he did that the cop was right and that she was right. He wouldn't allow anything to happen to her. He'd do anything to see she was safe.

There was a sound in the doorway and they parted. Maddy stood there, an amused smile on her face.

'There's a rollaway bed in the back room, kids,' she said. 'Let me know if you need it.'

Nemo returned to the office just in time to prevent his young geniuses from entirely ruining the case they were working on. After handling that, he met with his partner, Peter Stokes.

Peter was a cheerful, ruddy-complexioned man, the same age as Nemo. They went to college together and,

80

after graduation, worked in the same firm. Dissatisfaction struck them simultaneously and they joined forces. Nemo had the brilliant legal mind and Peter, who came from a wealthy Pasadena family, had the contacts. It was a workable combination. Their firm had gone from success to success.

'Getting any lately?' Peter asked when Nemo came into his office.

'Enough,' Nemo said obliquely.

'I figure the only reason you haven't been putting in your usual hours is that there must be a lady in your life.'

'How kind of you to notice,' Nemo said.

'I've been telling you for years to take it easier. Look at me.'

Peter was a notorious bon vivant, dedicated to the gratification of his indulgences. If Nemo had concentrated as heavily on self-fulfilment, the firm wouldn't have enjoyed its successes. But he never complained. He knew Peter's strengths and weaknesses and the strengths tipped the scale. Furthermore, he enjoyed his friend tremendously.

Peter's desk phone buzzed. He picked it up then held it out to Nemo. 'For you. Your secretary.'

Nemo took the phone. 'There's a man who's calling for Miss Barry,' she told Nemo.

'I'll take it.' The call came through and he said, 'Nemo Riley.'

'Mr Riley, I am a friend, a very old friend, of Miss Barry's and I want you to stay away from her,' the voice said.

All of Nemo's senses snapped to attention. It was Sam's admirer. The man had a deep voice. East coast but maybe just a trace of a foreign accent.

'Who are you?' he asked calmly. Keep the man talking. Learn as much as you can, he told himself.

81

'It doesn't concern you,' the man said. 'But my warning should. It is not given idly. You must understand that.'

'Miss Barry is a good friend,' Nemo said. 'I have no intention of stopping our relationship.'

'I know who you are,' the man said, 'even if you don't. I'm not going to let you ruin us again, Mr Bates. You stay away from her.'

'Bates?' Nemo asked. 'What are you talking about? Ruin you again? I don't even know who you are, mister. But I want to tell you something. Miss Barry wants nothing to do with you and the police have already been informed of your harassment. For your own welfare, I suggest you stop.'

'You're a fool,' the man said disdainfully. 'But for your sake, I hope you're not too much of a fool to ignore my warning. Death is remorseless. It comes again and again and again. Think about it.'

He hung up before Nemo could say anything. He looked quizzically at the receiver and then replaced it.

'Trouble?' Peter asked casually.

'Minor,' Nemo said. 'Now, let's talk business.'

When he returned to his office, he looked indecisively at his own telephone. Should he call the police? He decided against it. What was the point? They wouldn't do anything until they tripped over his dead body.

He also decided not to tell Sam about the call. She would only worry, and she had enough on her mind already. It was probably nothing anyway. The cop was undoubtedly right about it being only another empty threat. But he would be extra careful. No harm in that. He didn't like to admit it, but the truth of the matter was that the threat hadn't sounded empty. The man sounded as if he meant exactly what he said.

Chapter Six

Nemo confided in his partner during lunch the next day. It wasn't entirely a matter of choice. Never one to allow his curiosity to go unsatisfied, Peter brought the subject up.

'That phone call you had in my office. Are you sure it isn't anything serious I should know about?' He was drinking a Bloody Mary after complaining about his revelries the night before.

'It's nothing to bother you with,' Nemo said. 'Just something personal.'

But Peter wouldn't let it pass. 'Personal?' he said expansively. 'What are friends for?'

So Nemo explained. When he told him about the man claiming to know Sam in a previous lifetime, Peter burst into unrestrained laughter.

'Ha! Ha! Hoo! Hoo! I love it. It's just too LA for words,' he said.

People at nearby tables turned to look at the source of the noise.

'Yeah, it's real funny,' Nemo said.

'I'm sorry. Carry on,' Peter said, wiping his eyes. 'It's just too much.'

When Nemo reached his finale – the threats against

83

him – Peter grew more serious. 'There are a lot of whackos around,' he said. 'I'd be careful if I were you.'

'You think I should take it seriously?'

'Not really. I think the guy's probably just a flake. But it can't hurt to be careful. You never know what people will do these days. I don't mean you should get paranoid, or anything. Just keep your eyes open, that's all.'

'Well, I intend to do that,' Nemo said. 'It's probably not worth worrying about though.'

Peter agreed. He tapped Nemo's hand with a finger. 'Now, what I want to hear about is the lovely Sam Barry. I saw her at a party once and, man, she lives up to her name. Are you two cohabitating?'

'I love her,' Nemo said simply.

Peter raised both eyebrows and formed an O with his mouth. 'This is serious?'

'That's one way of putting it. I'm going to marry her.'

'You've asked her?'

'Not officially, not yet. But it's kind of understood. It's just that this other thing is hanging around. It's hard on Sam.'

'Hey, I'm really happy for you,' Peter said with a trace of sincerity. 'Me, I don't know why anybody would get married with all of this free stuff around.'

'Different strokes,' Nemo said.

'Like that,' Peter said, inclining his head at a booth near them. 'Excuse me a second.'

He went over to two young women, leaned on their table and began to talk animatedly to one of them – the more attractive of the two, naturally. After two minutes or so he came back.

'Ah,' he said, rubbing his hands together. 'That takes care of tomorrow night.'

'Did you know those women?' Nemo asked, amused.

Peter looked hurt. 'What do you take me for? Some kind of promiscuous, undiscriminating low-life? Of course I knew them . . . kind of. I met the girl at a party in our office building once.'

Nemo shook his head. 'Herpes City,' he warned.

'I always ask first,' Peter said.

When they got back to the office, he called Sam who was working at home this afternoon.

'Miss me?' he asked.

'It's only been five hours, but yes, I miss you,' she said. 'When are you coming back?'

'Make the invitation attractive enough and I'll be right there,' he said.

She breathed into the phone and said in a heavy accent. 'Come at vunce. I vant your body.'

'Can't stand Yugoslav women,' he said. 'But I'll be there by five. I want to go home first, take a shower and change, then I'll walk over.'

'Oil be waitin', mate,' she said.

'Maybe sooner,' he said. 'I love Australian sheilas.'

He left his Century City office at four, took Laurel Canyon Boulevard into the Valley and reached his house at 4.45. Traffic was light for a change.

He stopped at his mailbox and emptied it, then drove down the driveway and parked in front of the house. He scanned through the mail as he walked to the house. Mainly junk. Sweepstakes offers and other promises of instant wealth.

He unlocked the front door and made it to his burglar alarm in time to adjust it before it went off, something he didn't always remember.

The telephone rang.

'I saw you drive up,' Sam said. 'Don't be long.'

'I'll come over wet,' he said, and hung up.

He showered quickly and changed into jeans, T-shirt

85

and sneakers, the clothes he preferred to wear. In fact, he had been known to wear them to the office, but in matters of appearance Peter was uncharacteristically decorous and pleaded with him to keep up the three-piece suit corporate image.

He reset the alarm and locked the front door on the way out, slipping the keys into his pocket. The hard cinders of the driveway crunched beneath his feet as he strolled towards his fence. He'd taken to climbing into Sam's yard these days, rather than go back out to the road.

Just as he passed his front windows, he heard, almost all at once, a bang, the whistle as something passed him, and the sound of shattering glass. He swung his head to the side and saw a hole in the large front window, swung it back towards the road, still not quite realising what was happening.

Another bang. This time dirt kicked up at his feet. Another. And a sprinkle of glass from his window again.

He was being shot at.

A shot sprayed cinders a foot to his right.

Without even thinking now, he saw there was no cover nearby. The shots were coming from his fence near the road. The closest tree was fifteen or twenty yards away.

He took off with a springy jump then, running low and fast, heading directly for the plate-glass window. Six feet from the house, he left the ground, curled himself into a ball, turned in midair and hit the glass back first.

He landed in a pile of broken glass on his living room floor.

One more shot pounded into the wall behind him.

He stumbled through the hall to the dining room which also faced the road. Cautiously drawing aside the curtain, he saw movement at the fence. There was the sound of a car's engine and a glimpse of red on the road.

He called the police.

Sam arrived first. He had already unlocked the front door and she charged in, her face white.

'Are you all right?' she cried, running to him. 'I heard the shots.'

'I'm fine,' he said. 'You shouldn't have left your house.'

She put her arms around him and then drew away. 'You're bleeding. Did you get hit? My God, Nemo, are you all right?'

'It's just from the glass. I got cut a little bit. I'm okay.'

Without hesitating she went to the bathroom and came back with a towel. She dabbed gently at the cuts on his back and arms.

'Those were shots I heard, weren't they?' she asked as she worked.

'Yes, they were,' he said. He looked at his hands. They were still shaking.

'It's him,' she said grimly. 'I knew he wouldn't leave us alone.'

'It seems that way.'

'Do any of these cuts hurt? I mean, do you think there's glass in any of them?'

'Yes, they hurt a little, and no, I don't think there's any glass in them.'

'Oh, Jesus,' she said, putting her hands on either side of his head and kissing his forehead. 'Thank God nothing happened to you. I don't know what I would have done, Nemo.'

She began to cry then and he kissed her eyes. 'It's okay, Sam. I'm fine. The guy missed me by a mile.'

'The window,' she said between sobs. 'What happened to the window?'

'I jumped through it. I had to get into the house,' Nemo said.

The sound of a police siren intruded. Tyres skidded in the drive and the siren wound down like a man losing his breath.

'Come on,' Nemo said.

There were two patrolmen at the door. They looked at him and then at the window. 'Gunshots were reported here, sir,' the older man said.

'I called it in,' Nemo said. 'I also asked for Lieutenant Marshall. Where is he?'

'Wouldn't know about that, sir. Could you tell us what's been going on here?'

Nemo pointed at the road. 'The shots came from over there. The man was firing from my fence. Then he drove away.'

'Didn't see anything when we drove up,' the cop said. 'Do you have a description of the suspect or his vehicle?'

'No,' Nemo said. 'I just caught a touch of red, which I think was his car.'

'Were you hit, sir?'

'No.'

The policeman pointed at his shirt. 'The blood?'

'He jumped through the window,' Sam volunteered.

'Look, I need to sit down,' Nemo said, feeling suddenly weak. 'Come inside and ask your questions.'

Ten minutes into the futile round of questions, Lieutenant Marshall arrived.

'What happened?' he asked, coming into the living room.

'That harmless freak, you know, the one who was just likely to give up bothering us? He tried to kill me,' Nemo said acidly, and then immediately regretted it. Marshall wasn't the right target for his ire.

'Are you hurt?' Marshall asked, coming closer.

88

'No he isn't, and no thanks to you,' Sam said.

Nemo waved his hand at her. 'Let's give it a break. It's not his fault this guy went crazy.'

'Tell me about it,' Marshall said.

Nemo ran down what happened.

'You jumped through the window?' Marshall asked, a trace of respect in his eyes.

'I had nowhere else to go,' Nemo stated.

Marshall spoke to one of the patrolmen. 'I want forensics here. Go out to the road and see what you can find. Look for shell casings.'

He turned back to Nemo. 'Why didn't you tell me about the phone call you got?'

Sam cut in: 'And why didn't you tell me?'

'I didn't want you to worry,' he said to Sam. And to Marshall, he said, 'It didn't seem worth it, based upon your previous attitude. What would you have done about it?'

Marshall looked uncomfortable and murmured, 'Probably nothing.' A slight plea entered his voice. 'You have to understand our limitations in cases like this.'

'Believe me, I do,' Nemo said. 'That's why I didn't call.'

Marshall scratched his head. 'Bullets went through the living room window, you said. If you don't mind, I'll look around. See if I can find any of the slugs.'

'Here, I'll show you,' Nemo said, getting to his feet.

'We should get you to a doctor to have a look at those cuts, Sam protested.

'I think they're just scratches,' he said. 'Don't seem to be any deep cuts.'

'How high was the bullet hole you saw in the glass?' Marshall asked as they walked into the living room.

'About halfway up over there,' Nemo said, pointing. 'And there was another about there.'

Marshall walked to the opposite wall. Dark knotty wooden panelling made it difficult to spot holes.

'I wish you'd have told me about that call,' Sam complained.

'What good would it have done?' Nemo asked, spreading his palms out.

'I'd like to think we can share things, even if it does no good,' Sam said petulantly.

It was an unreasonable attitude, Nemo thought. But under the circumstances, he could understand it.

'I'm sorry,' he said.

'Here we go,' Marshall said. He took a penknife from his pocket and began to pry at the panel.

'Looks like a 30.06,' he said, holding the lead in his hand. 'Very common. Too common to be of much help, I'm afraid.'

'Unless they match something already on record,' Nemo suggested.

'Unlikely. I think this is our man's first venture into violence of this type. His infatuation seems to be with Miss Barry here. Because she's not returning his attentions, he feels driven to it.' Marshall pointed at another spot on the wall. 'There's the second one. I'll leave it for the others. It'll go to ballistics, of course, but I don't think they'll be able to do much more than confirm the calibre of the gun.'

'So once again we're left with nothing,' Nemo said.

'Something could turn up,' Marshall said. 'Forensics, maybe something out on the road, maybe a witness. We'll be questioning the neighbours.'

'It's unlikely they saw anything,' Sam said. 'This is a quiet street with trees and hedges and people who like their privacy.'

'We'll see,' Marshall said.

'And you come with me,' Sam said to Nemo. 'I'm

90

going to wash those cuts and put some antiseptic on them.'

'I'll take a walk to the road and see what I can find,' Marshall said. 'When the forensic boys come I'll bring them into the house for that bullet, if you don't mind.'

'Make yourself at home,' Nemo said.

'Maybe we can work together on this thing instead of being at odds,' Marshall said. It was the closest he came to an apology.

'Yes, that would be better,' Nemo agreed.

'Come on, medicine time,' Sam said, tugging his arm.

'Will it burn?' Nemo asked. 'I'm in enough pain as it is.'

'Just grit your teeth,' she said unsympathetically.

The police were there for hours, it seemed. They did find some shell casings, confirming the weapon was a 30.06 rifle, but that was all. No witnesses, no prints on the shells, no evidence left at the site where the marksman stood or parked his car.

When they all left, Sam collapsed on the couch and said, 'Thank God that's over.'

'Let's go sit in the hot tub,' Nemo said. 'My legs and arms feel like they're hanging in their sockets by thin threads.'

'We have to talk,' Sam said, ignoring his suggestion. She swivelled herself upright.

'About what?'

'About what we're going to do,' she said. 'I mean, somebody just tried to kill you and all the police can do is ask a lot of pointless questions and tell you to be more careful in future.'

'There's not much more they can say, Sam.'

'It's not enough. Your life's in danger.'

91

'Maybe. Maybe he was only trying to scare me away. You should be able to hit a man with a rifle at that range.'

'Maybe he's a bad shot,' she said. 'Or maybe it was just a warning. But what'll happen next time if you ignore it?'

'What are you saying?'

'I don't know,' she said, getting to her feet. 'I just feel that you're a sitting duck, Nemo. That someone, unseen by you, can put you in the sights of a rifle . . . It scares me. Maybe we should just cool it for a while, not see each other for a few days, let him think we've stopped.'

'You mean we should succumb to his pressure?' Nemo said, his voice suddenly cold.

She moved close to him and took hold of his arms. 'Nemo, I love you. I don't want to see anything happen to you. Couldn't we just give the police time to get a line on this guy?'

'They won't,' he said emphatically. 'He hasn't left a line for them to trace. I don't think they'll get anywhere. But that's not the point here, Sam. The point is, I'm not going to let myself be scared off by threats. No way. That won't solve anything.'

'These aren't threats,' she said. 'This was an attempt to murder you. What does he have to do for you to take it seriously? Kill you?' She pushed him away and turned, tears shining on her cheeks.

Nemo put his hands on her shoulders and pulled her back to him. 'I understand how you feel, believe me. I know how tough this is on you and how badly you want it to end. But, trust me, Sam, you don't solve problems by not facing up to them. You know that as well as I do. If we give in to this guy, it won't end there. It will just give him power and we can't do that.'

'I'm afraid for you,' she said softly.

He turned her so that he faced her. 'I know you are.

But nothing will happen to me, I promise. I'm going to be careful from now on.'

She rested her head against his chest. 'When I ran over here, I had this picture in my mind of you lying on the ground, shot, dying. The feeling that went with that picture was just too awful to bear. If anything should happen to you, I don't know what I'd do.'

'Nothing will happen to either of us,' he said, and kissed the top of her head. 'Now what about a hot tub for my war wounds?'

'All right,' she said, but he knew the conversation was far from over. She would mull on it, turn it over and over in her mind and come up with some other solution, maybe in an hour, maybe in a day. The attempt on his life had left her shaken but determined not to let it happen again. The sad truth was that it wasn't in her hands. Not anymore. In spite of his reassurances to her, he too felt like a sitting duck. The man did have him in his sights today. Perhaps he felt mercy, or perhaps his hand merely shook as he pulled the trigger. Neither scenario made him feel safer. Mercy could be strained and hands could be steadied. It was not a thought to dwell on.

When Nemo lowered himself into the tub, he groaned enthusiastically.

'Are you okay?' Sam asked.

'Every muscle in his body is thanking me,' he said. 'They aren't used to flying through windows.'

'When are you going to Washington?' she asked.

It appeared a non-sequitur remark, but he knew it was a continuation of their conversation in the living room. 'In a couple of days,' he replied.

'Good,' she said.

'Anxious to get rid of me?'

'It will get you out of town for a couple of days,' she

said with a smile of victory. 'You aren't running away, you aren't not facing the problem, you're just going on a planned business trip. It won't hurt your pride.'

'Do you think my pride is the issue here?' he asked, irritation showing on his face.

'Isn't it?'

'No, it isn't. It has nothing to do with it. There are two factors. One is the principle involved. I'm not going to let myself be railroaded by violence or fear. The other is purely practical. If I give way to this person's insane demands, he won't stop there. You'll be next on the list. He'll think that with me out of the way, you'll be available for him. Is that something you want?'

'Of course not,' she said, her turn to be irritated. 'I'm only thinking of your safety.'

'Well, then don't make ridiculous remarks about my pride.'

'It wasn't that ridiculous. I still think your pride is involved.'

'So what if it is? Is that so bad?'

'Yes,' she said heatedly. 'If it gets you hurt or killed, it's very bad.'

'Jesus,' he said, sinking until his chin rested on the water.

'Oh, hell,' she said.

'Closest we've come to an argument.' He glanced up at Sam.

'I'm sorry. I'm worried about you.'

'I'm sorry too,' he said.

She slid along the seat until she was beside him. Putting her hand on his chest, she rubbed it. 'Water help?' she asked.

'Yeah, my body likes it.'

'What are we going to do?' she asked.

'We're going to carry on,' he said.

94

'That's it?'

'We love each other. Nothing's going to change it and nobody's going to stop it,' he said.

She kissed him on the mouth.

'There is one thing,' he said, moving back. 'When I leave town, I'd like you to get someone to look after you, a bodyguard. There are outfits that specialise in it. I can fix it up for you, okay?'

'It's you that was shot at,' she said. 'I'm not the one who needs a bodyguard.'

'I'm not convinced of that,' he said. 'This man may be crazy, but he's also dangerous. And it's you he wants.'

'What about you?' she said. 'What about you getting a bodyguard too.'

'When I get back, I'll think about it,' he said.

'You think about it now, and do something about it when you get back.'

'Only if you do as well.'

'All right. It can't hurt.'

'Good,' he said, relieved at her acquiescence. 'I'll call them tomorrow and have somebody round at your house on the morning I leave.'

It made him feel better. True, he had been the target, but that was merely an apparency. Sam was the real target and he was just someone standing in the way.

They both took the afternoon off on the day before Nemo was due to leave town. 'Your choice,' he told Sam. 'Anything in the world you want to do today, and we'll do it.'

She opted for a visit to the LA County Art Museum. 'I never have the time to get there,' she complained. 'It's like this treasure chest I'm always walking past without sticking my hand in.'

It was a hot day. Smog choked the air and irritable drivers clogged the streets, Nemo and Sam ignored the liabilities and concentrated on each other, determined to gain the most out of their time together.

'I want to see the Asian section and some of the Impressionists,' Sam said when they arrived. 'It's too overwhelming to try and do more in one afternoon.'

They held hands and browsed through the Asian collection with its Tibetan thangkas, Cambodian bronzes and multi-armed Indian gods. Sam stopped before an enormous bronze figure of Bhuddha and stared at it without speaking for a long time.

'What are you thinking?' Nemo asked finally.

'How serene that face is. It sees the world as illusion and is unaffected by it,' she said, and there was a wistful longing in her voice.

After a while, they went outside and sat on the grass. They had hardly spoken of the shooting incident since it had happened, but now Sam asked, 'Have you heard anything from the police?'

'I talked to that cop Marshall this morning,' Nemo said. 'It was as he predicted – no leads. No record of the gun. He assured me that he was continuing the investigation. Wants to talk to you about the stuff T. sent you. He'll call you.'

'Better late than never,' Sam said derisively.

Nemo was more philosophical. 'Old Indian saying that if no tracks it hard to find buffalo. I don't know what else they can do.'

'I think they're useless,' she said.

'Listen, I did call some people though, a firm we work with. They're sending a man to your house tomorrow morning. Your bodyguard. Sounds very competent.'

Sam shrugged. She still thought it an unnecessary gesture, but they had made a deal and she intended to

96

stick with it. 'When are you leaving?'

'Tonight. Late.'

'I thought you were leaving in the morning?'

'I decided to take the red-eye. I have an appointment first thing tomorrow.'

'Oh,' she said.

'Disappointed?'

'Yes. I thought we'd have tonight together.'

'I'm sorry. I should have told you, but it just happened this morning. The senator can only see me tomorrow. I had to change the flight to get there earlier. But, we still have half the night. I don't leave till late.'

'I suppose half is better than nothing,' she said.

'Right,' he said. 'Besides, we have a whole life together. What's a few hours?'

Later that evening he decided to make the question of their lives official. After an early dinner, they sat in his living room and listened to an old Dinah Washington album he had rediscovered.

Sam leaned against him appreciatively and complimented him on his cooking.

'How would you like me to cook for you always?' he asked.

'Is this a proposal?' she asked sitting upright.

'Yes. I think we should get married when I get back.'

'So soon?' she asked.

'Well, I think we should start planning it then. We can do it when you like.'

'It's so busy now,' she said hesitantly. 'The show coming up and everything. Maybe we should –'

'We can make the time,' he said. 'It doesn't have to be a big deal. The honeymoon can wait. I'm the one who doesn't want to wait.'

Sam looked troubled. 'I don't know,' she said.

'You do want to marry me, don't you?'

97

'Yes, of course I do. I love you, Nemo. It's just that . . . I don't know. With what happened, it just doesn't seem the right time.'

'You mean your friend T.?' he asked.

'Wouldn't it be better to wait until the police find him and this whole thing is over?'

'No, it wouldn't. It's the same thing I was saying before, Sam. We can't allow this person to direct our lives or influence our most important decisions. That's what he wants, and we can't let it happen. If we do, we become victims. I've no intention of letting us become victims of this situation.'

Sam sighed. 'I know,' she said. 'I understand what you're saying, but I can't help but feel that it would be better to wait.'

'I don't think so,' he said stubbornly. 'I love you and want you to be my wife. Just because there's some weirdo out there, I'm not going to change my mind about that.'

'It's just the timing I'm concerned about,' she said.

'All right,' he said. 'All right. I didn't want to put it this way, but I have to. After he took those shots at me, you know what I thought? I thought, "My God, I could be dead." I got this appreciation of my mortality, Sam. I realised that things can happen to us, no matter how in control we try to be. And I realised again that I love you and that I want to be married to you. If anything ever happens to me again, I want it to happen to me as your husband.'

She touched his cheek softly with her hand and felt his face from top to bottom. 'You're right,' she said. 'Time is too precious, my love. All right. As soon as you get back we'll talk about it and make the arrangements.'

He kissed her and pulled her close to him. 'I love you, Sam,' he said.

'And I love you.'

He snuck a glance at his watch. 'And time *is* precious,' he said, moving away and standing. 'Why are we spending it in the living room?'

She smiled and took his outstretched hand.

They made love and reached a depth of tenderness neither had ever attained before. It was a passion so sweet it almost hurt. Nemo fell asleep thinking he was the luckiest man in the world.

The man walked slowly across the thick Persian carpet and listened intently to the tape recording of the session.

'She thanks me and says she is honoured. We go back inside. The orchestra is still playing. We dance until the small hours of the morning. I am the envy of every man in the room.'

'All right, is there any more to this?'

'After I take her home, I am the happiest man in the world. My life has new meaning. I finally have someone I can love and I know everything will change.'

'Anything else?'

'No, I fall asleep.'

'All right. Now give me the date this happened.'

'April 16, 1924.'

'Good. When I count to three and snap my fingers, you will wake up. You will —'

The man stepped over to the tape recorder and switched it off. He stood and looked at it, as if waiting for it to tell him something.

'It's time to do more,' he said finally. 'She must remember. She must.'

The man parked his car in the shadows of a large Moreton Bay fig tree. He was dressed in black – gloves, shirt, trousers and shoes, all darker than the night. In his hands he held a bottle and a brown handtowel.

He got out of the car and closed the door silently. He glanced left and right and then slipped over the low stone wall, hugging the dark patches, moving swiftly along the edge of the lawn, past the rose beds, to the side of the house and then around it.

It was a hot night and he was sure there would be open windows. He found one at the back and quietly pushed it up. Another quick look around and then he was inside. There were no lights on and he stood there a moment, his eyes growing accustomed to the gloom.

Then, moving carefully but quickly, he glided into the hall and up the stairs, staying close to the edges to avoid creaking them.

The door was slightly ajar. He pushed it with one hand and looked in. She was sleeping soundly, curled up, her hands under her cheek. She wore only a thin nightgown.

He poured liquid from the bottle into the towel, turning his head away as he did so to avoid the strong smell of chloroform that suddenly filled the room with sweetness. He went to the bed and held the towel an inch away from her face. He knew that chloroform didn't work in seconds as the movies showed. It would take a minute or two for her to go under. Then, to be sure, he would press the towel against her face. There would be no struggle, no awareness on her part.

Soon you will be with me, my lovely Lela, he thought. He looked fondly down at her as she slid deeper and deeper into darkness.

Chapter Seven

Sam woke slowly and lay still for a while in that jumbled state between sleep and wakefulness. Her head was heavy and her mouth felt filled with fluff. She opened her eyes and stretched, pushing her muscles against the bed.

She looked up at the ceiling. Its heavy moulding swirled in art deco patterns.

What? she thought, still confused by sleep.

She looked down at her body then. At first she only blinked at what she saw, but then it was like jumping into ice cold water. She sat up, her heart thumping, adrenalin rushing through her body.

She was wearing the dress T. had sent her.

'What?' she said aloud, touching it.

The rest of what she saw finally hit her.

This was not her bed! This was not her room!

The room was large, dominated in its centre by the canopied four-poster bed in which she was lying. Red and purple satin hung from the top of the canopy. An ornately carved oak vanity with a diamond-shaped mirror dominated one wall. Across the room was a dresser, a tall closet, Beardsley prints of graceful, wan women on the walls.

She got up then and ran to the window, pulling the

101

curtains apart. Ironwork protected the glass from out-side intruders. She saw green lawns, a high wall, a driveway. In it sat a gleaming old cherry-red car from the 1920s. Sunlight reflected like blades from the brilliant chrome.

She ran to the door, gasping now, not knowing what to think, She turned the handle and pulled, but the door was locked.

Sam leaned against the door and looked wildly around the room. She had been transported to another time and another place. Was this a dream? It couldn't be – she was awake. But she did not understand, could not comprehend. All she knew was that she was alone and that this was her prison.

She began to scream.

Nemo returned to his hotel room after yet another meeting, switched on the television set, went to the bathroom and splashed water on his face. It had been a long morning. He had arrived at dawn after barely sleeping on the plane, checked into the hotel, and left immediately for his first appointment. There were more to go before the day would be over.

He came back into the bedroom and was about to lift the phone to call room service for coffee, when the announcer said, '. . . Designer Sam Barry.'

It didn't sink in until too late. The news item, whatever it was about, was over.

Quickly he changed channels.

Then heard it again.

'The mysterious disappearance this morning of fashion designer Sam Barry,' the announcer called it. 'Police believe she has been abducted, but say there has been no ransom demand.' There was a little more background on Sam, but no details about what happened.

Nemo reached for the telephone.

He called Sam's office and asked to speak to Maddy. She wasn't there, he was told. He tried Sam's house.

'Yes,' a male voice answered.

'Who is this?' Nemo asked.

'Who are you?' the voice said.

It had to be the police, Nemo thought. He told him who he was, what he had heard and where he was calling from.

'I'm a police officer,' the man said. 'Do you have any information that might help us?'

'What happened, for chrissakes?' Nemo asked, almost shouting his frustration.

'When are you returning to Los Angeles, sir?' the policeman asked.

'Immediately. As soon as I can get a flight. Listen is Miss Shapiro there? I want to speak to her.'

'Yes, I'll get her.'

'Nemo?' Maddy's voice trembled. 'Is that you? Where are you?'

'I'm in DC. What the hell happened?'

'Somebody kidnapped Sam last night. The maid went into her bedroom this morning and she wasn't there.'

'How do they know she was kidnapped?'

'There was a towel in her room that had chloroform on it,' Maddy explained. Nemo heard a male voice in the background and Maddy said, 'Just a minute.'

'But he's her boyfriend,' he heard her say to someone.

She came back on the line. 'I'm sorry, but the police don't want me to talk about the –'

Nemo cut her off. 'Has a Lieutenant Marshall been there?'

'Yes, but he left already.'

'I'm getting the next flight. I'll be there before the end

of the day. Give me a phone number where I can reach you and get a number where I can get Marshall, okay?'

'Okay,' Maddy said.

He scrawled the number she gave him on a matchbook. 'All right. See you soon,' he said and hung up.

He began to throw clothes into his suitcase. Should he call and get reservations? No time. He would drive to the airport and just get on the damn plane.

Oh, God! he thought desperately. I shouldn't have left you, Sam, I should have stayed.

He blamed himself on the way down to the desk to check out. He blamed himself in the cab on the way to the airport. He should have taken it all more seriously, particularly after the guy took those shots at him. Above all, he shouldn't have left Los Angeles while she was going through such stress. He was selfish, negligent, opinionated, insensitive. What a jerk! And what a fool! He had heard the man, his wild and obviously insane claims. How could he have flown blithely off to the other side of the continent to take care of business of such insignificant importance compared to Sam?

By the time he reached the airport he had subjected himself to a beating as severe as any he had ever given himself.

He managed to get a flight leaving in twenty minutes. For almost six hours he sat on the edge of his seat, willing the plane to fly faster through the air.

Maddy met him at Sam's office soon after he landed. Gone was the cheerful wisecracking woman he remembered. This Maddy twisted her hands together and balanced on the verge of tears. He hugged her and patted her back and told her not to worry, even though his own worry was verging on the uncontrollable.

104

'So they found a rag with chloroform,' he said when they sat down in the reception area. 'What else did they find?'

'Nothing. A window was open and they figured he got in through there. That's all. No fingerprints, except maybe yours and Sam's and the maid's.'

'Nobody saw anything? No neighbours?'

Maddy shook her head. 'I think the police assume it's the guy who's been calling and who shot at you.'

'Seems logical,' he said.

Maddy looked at him and then began to sob. 'I know the guy shot at you and everything. But I didn't think Sam was in danger. I don't know why. Up until that point I thought she was overreacting about the whole thing. It just wasn't real to me. Oh, God, I should have believed her.'

'What would you have done if you had believed her? How could you have changed things?' Nemo said.

'I don't know. Nothing, I suppose. I would have been more supportive, more helpful, stayed with her, perhaps.'

'Maddy, I've been travelling this route almost all day. I should never have gone to Washington until this thing was settled, no matter what precautions we took. But there's no point to it. It doesn't help her and it doesn't help us. Right now, we have to figure out how to help her.'

'Yes, I know you're right,' Maddy said unhappily. 'It doesn't make me feel any better.'

'Well, luckily, your feelings aren't what's important right now,' Nemo said harshly.

Maddy looked up sharply. He stared back at her unblinkingly. 'You're a real tough asshole, aren't you,' she said.

'That's better,' Nemo said. 'Have you got the cop's phone number for me?'

Maddy pulled a small telephone notebook from her bag and handed it to him, marking the page with her finger. 'It's Marshall,' she said. 'Douglas Marshall.'

Nemo went to the telephone and dialled the number. Funny, he'd never thought of Marshall as having a first name. He was one of those guys who would have been called Marshall by his mother when he was in diapers. When someone answered, he asked to be put through to Marshall. He wasn't in, the man told him. But he could get a message to him.

'Tell him I'm Nemo Riley and I'm on my way to Sam Barry's house. I'll either meet him there or be at my house next door.' He left his phone number with the man and hung up.

'Come on,' he said to Maddy.

'I think I'll just go home,' she said.

'Come on. I need to talk to you more and, besides, you're too miserable to be left alone. I'll cook you dinner after we see the cop.'

Maddy mustered up a weak smile. 'My Galahad,' she said.

Before, they left for Studio City, she told him more of what had happened that morning. 'Sam was going to be working at the house this morning, so I got there about nine-thirty to go over some things with her. Margarite was there, but Sam wasn't. She thought Sam had left early for the office. Her nightgown was on the floor.

'Anyway, I saw Sam's car was still there. I called the office to make sure she hadn't got there somehow, but, of course, she hadn't. I looked around her bedroom and found this towel on the floor beside the bed. My father's a doctor, I know the smell of chloroform. That's when I called the police.'

'Shit! I wonder what happened to the security guy we hired. He was supposed to start in the morning.'

106

'Oh, he arrived later. Too late.' She forced a smile. 'Sam told me about this guy who's been calling. Past lives. Reincarnation. The guy sounds nuttier than a fruitcake. You do think he's the one who has her, don't you?'

'Who else?' Nemo asked.

When Nemo reached Sam's house, closely followed by Maddy in her car, a grey Ford sedan was already parked in the driveway. He got out of his car and met Maddy. 'Is that Marshall's?' he asked.

'I guess. I saw the car here before.'

They found Marshall sitting in the living room. He shook Nemo's hand, but the persistent scowl still shadowed his face.

'Where were you?' Marshall asked, coming immediately to the point.

'I called your people here this morning from Washington, DC. Don't they tell you anything?' Nemo said irritably.

'Have any witnesses? People you met there?'

Nemo rolled his eyes up. 'Sure,' he said, and gave the policeman the name of a senator.

Marshall was unimpressed. 'When did you leave for Washington?'

'Last night's red-eye on United. I checked into the Dawson Hotel after arrival there,' Nemo said. 'You'd do better asking questions that'll help get Sam back.'

'All right,' Marshall said, satisfied for the time being. 'Did you or Miss Barry hear anything more from this guy since we last spoke?'

'No. Not by the time I left, which was about nine. You do think he's the one, don't you.'

Marshall shrugged. 'Maybe, but at this stage it's strictly guesswork.'

'Anything better to go on?' Nemo asked. 'I mean, the

107

guy thinks he knew her in another life, for godsakes. He takes a few potshots at me, either to kill me or warn me off. He's obviously mentally unbalanced. Just as obviously, he's the one who abducted her.'

Marshall shook his head. He seemed to have made some decision about Nemo and opened up more now. 'Perhaps, but we know nothing about him. The towel the chloroform was on could have been bought anywhere. I need your prints to see if they match those found on her door and in her room. I'll bet they are. Whoever this guy was, he was cool. Nobody saw him, nobody heard anything.'

'It's got to be the same guy,' Nemo said. 'There are no other motives, no ransom demand, right?'

'No ransom demand,' Marshall said regretfully.

'So?'

'Look, it seems that way, but there's really nothing to go on here. A vague description . . . What about that dress you mentioned? Let's go and see it.'

Nemo opened the closet in the upstairs bedroom. He had seen her take the dress from there and put it back. Now there was no sign of it. He scrambled through the hanging clothes and checked a pile on the closet floor.

'Gone,' he said, turning back to the policeman.

'Any place else it could be?' Marshall asked.

'I'll check the laundry room and ask Margarite if she sent it to the cleaners or anything,' Maddy said, leaving the room.

'Where did you find prints?' Nemo asked.

Marshall pointed. 'On the door jamb, the table here, the telephone.'

'Mine,' Nemo confirmed. He sat heavily on the edge of the bed. 'Jesus,' he muttered.

'Any other information that could help?' Marshall asked.

'No. Have you guys come up with anything at all?'

Marshall looked uncomfortable. 'Not really. Not yet.'

'Shit!' Nemo said.

Maddy came back into the room. 'Nothing,' she said. 'She doesn't know anything about the dress.'

'The guy must have taken it with him,' Marshall said.

'But why?' Nemo asked. 'Perhaps there was some clue to his identity there.'

'Her nightgown was on the floor,' the policeman said carefully.

Nemo looked at him and then away. He swallowed. 'You mean, the guy dressed her in that dress before he took her?'

'It's possible.'

Nemo was afraid. He had come across unbalanced, unpredictable minds when he did some criminal work early in his career. Their very unpredictability was dangerous. They were the kind of people who murdered senselessly, compelled by some inner logic only they could see. What sort of man carried fantasy to this degree? Who were they dealing with?

Marshall's thoughts on the subject didn't help. 'If it's the same guy, he's a real weirdo,' he said.

'Maybe there's something about this past life stuff that could lead us to him,' Nemo suggested vaguely.

'What? Find everyone who believes in reincarnation, palmistry, spiritualism, psychics and the I Ching? I'd have to talk to half the city. Forget it.'

'Right,' Nemo said wearily. The long day was beginning to catch up with him. 'Well, if there's nothing else, Miss Shapiro and I are going to have some dinner.'

'Nothing else,' Marshall said, 'but if you think of anything, here's my card. My home number's on it too. Give me a call, anytime.'

'Hmm. He didn't give me his home number,' Maddy

complained as they walked out of the house.

'Probably doesn't want any obscene phone calls,' Nemo said, attempting a joke.

'He's safe from me,' Maddy said. 'Cold as a fish, that one.'

'It's the job, the people he has to deal with.'

Which brought them right back to the subject and an uncomfortable silence.

Maddy decided to leave her car there and walked over to his house while he drove. Once inside, he showed her into the living room and poured them each wine. He slumped into an armchair and realised that every muscle in his body ached. The tension of the day had taken its toll.

'I'll cook us something,' Maddy said. 'You look wiped out.'

Nemo didn't argue. He followed her into the kitchen, pointed to everything she needed and, from a comfortable vantage point on a barstool, watched her cook a quick cheese omelette.

'I keep thinking there's something I'm missing,' he said.

'Like what?'

'I don't know. Something he said or did, some clue as to who he is or what he's really about. Something.'

'What's going to happen?' Maddy asked, her face suddenly vulnerable and frightened.

Nemo just shook his head. There was no point in repeating the inchoate thoughts tumbling through his mind. Every fearsome conclusion you could think of had been imagined by him – death, torture, sexual assault, everything. Sam was in the hands of a madman and anything could happen.

'Something will turn up,' he said finally.

'I'm not filled with confidence that the police are going

110

to turn anything up. They have nothing,' Maddy said.

'Well, I'm not going to stand by doing nothing. I'll turn something up,' Nemo said.

'How? What are you going to do?'

'I'll let you know when I think of it,' he said. 'For starters, I'll hand my case load over to my staff and take some time off.'

They sat at the bar and picked half-heartedly at their food. Nemo finally pushed his half-eaten omelette aside.

'I'm sorry. It's good, but I'm not hungry,' he said.

'I'll have some more wine,' Maddy said.

He poured them each another glass.

'Did you guys talk about marriage already?' Maddy asked.

'Yes, we talked about it,' he said.

Nemo gulped his wine.

Marriage had been a preordained fact since the moment they met. they were like two magnetic bodies lost in space. When they got close enough to each other there was no alternative but to meet and join. There was nowhere else to go, nothing else to do.

There were tears running down Maddy's cheeks. 'I was so happy for her when I heard about the two of you,' she said. 'Sam needed a man and I didn't think she could have made a better choice. I kidded her about it, but I was so happy for her.'

Maddy began to ramble. She told him how she had forced Sam to show her work and encouraged her. She talked of college days when they lived together and about the men they had dated. 'It was funny,' she said. 'I used to bring guys home and they always fell in love with Sam. I was never jealous, not really. It was like she deserved it. It had to be that way. She was so beautiful, men just couldn't help themselves.'

'Stop talking about her in the past tense,' Nemo said.

111

'I was?'

'You were, and it's inappropriate. Wherever Sam is, I know she isn't dead,' he said, forcing the word out.

She began to cry again. Nemo put an arm around her shoulders. 'I have a guest room upstairs,' he said. 'I think you'd better spend the night here.'

'Yes,' she said. 'I'm too tired to drive. In fact, I think I'll crash now if you don't mind.'

Nemo showed her to the room then came back downstairs. He was near exhaustion himself, but he doubted that he'd be able to sleep. He refilled his wine glass and went out to the back patio. He sat in a deck chair, cradled the glass in his hands and looked up at the sky.

It was a clear, warm night. Only a lonely handful of the larger stars were visible in the reflected light of the city.

For the first time he felt an urge to cry himself. It was so unfair, he thought miserably. They had just found each other only to be torn apart. As a lawyer, he knew there was no assurance of justice in the world. There were winners and losers, there was compromise, and there were also the smart and the dumb. Justice wasn't doled out as a birthright. It was created by will and intent and it was rarely satisfactory. But even so, you'd think the gods would smile on lovers.

Cut it out, he told himself. Self-pity wasn't even a tempting luxury, it was simply destructive. There was no time for it now. He needed to act. What, for instance, was it that had been bothering him? The fact he had overlooked?

It came to him five minutes later. The picture! The clipping from a newspaper or magazine. He'd forgotten about it. Sam had mentioned it briefly. T. had sent a clipping of a woman's face to her. What was it the card had said? *Who is this?*

112

He would ask Maddy about it first thing in the morning. It could be important. Perhaps there was a clue there. At this stage, anything was worth checking.

Encouraged by the fact he now had something constructive to do, Nemo went inside, took a hot shower and went to bed. For a long time he stared into the dark, disturbed by the realisation that somewhere a frightened Sam was also staring into blackness. Finally he fell asleep.

He was sitting with her in a restaurant. The soft lighting illuminated her face and eyes.

'You're even more beautiful than when I first saw you,' he said.

'Thank you, sir,' she said.

'Is there another man? In your life, I mean?'

Was that a troubled look in her eyes? But then she said, 'No. Not really.'

He was too pleased to query the qualification. 'I'm glad,' he said and reached across the table to take her hand.

Dissolve to:

They were parked above the city. She had asked him to stop there before driving home, and now she was staring down at the lights, her profile magically still and calm. He wanted to kiss her more than anything then, but it would have been sacrilegious in some strange way, an unwanted disturbance.

Dissolve to:

He opened the door for her and then followed her in. She closed the door and leaned against it and watched him. He kissed her then and their lips were like molten metal.

'Do you want a drink?' she asked.

'No,' he said.

She took his hand and led him into the living room. He kissed her again, standing in the middle of the room.

And then they were in the bedroom:

Her clothes were falling to the floor in slow motion, floating down to reveal her beauty. She stood there and looked at him while he undressed and then they stood an inch apart and felt the heat rise from each other.

'I love you, Lela,' he said.

She put her hand on her mouth and said, 'Sssh. Not yet, Phillip.'

And they were on the bed:

He was seeing it as if watching from the ceiling. Two bodies grappling with tenderness, hands exploring gratefully, the gasps of wonder, the rhythm of motion, the cries of delight that grew as passion mounted. And then the movement became a blur and blood boiled and shouts as natural as those of animals joined to make a single sound with the power and majesty of thunder.

What on earth was that, Nemo thought, waking from the dream? Lela again? Phillip? What did it mean? How real it had been, how intense the emotions. Bizarre, he thought, dismissing it. His mind was playing tricks on him, twisting the events of the past days into narrative form.

He realised he was wet then and felt mildly embarrassed, a residue of sensation from the guilty nights of adolescent longings.

Whatever the dream was about, his body had believed it.

114

Chapter Eight

'I'm telling you, I'm sure she would have thrown that
stuff away. She wouldn't even accept the guy's flowers,'
Maddy said for the third time. She opened the office
door and ushered Nemo in.

It was only seven-thirty. Nemo rose at six, waited half
an hour until he couldn't stand it any longer, woke
Maddy up and hustled her to the office. She grumbled,
but didn't resist.

'All right, I heard you,' Nemo said, more patient than
he felt. 'Let's start with her desk.'

They entered Sam's office and Nemo went directly for
the letter trays on her desk.

'I'll make us some coffee while you do that,' Maddy
said with a yawn.

Letters, memos, telephone massages. Nemo sorted
through them quickly, then attacked a tray marked
'Pending' on the other side of the desk.

Nothing there either.

He opened the top left drawer and saw the casual pile
of cards immediately.

Lela, I'm returning this to its rightful owner. Remember it? T.

With deep respect and love, T.

Welcome back, Lela – T.

And the one he was looking for: *Who is this? T.* She had kept them all, tossed them into the drawer.

But no magazine or newspaper clipping. And then he saw the envelope. He opened it and found the small piece of yellowing paper. Carefully, he took it out and looked at the picture.

It was a picture of the woman in his dreams.

Nemo felt his pulse beat against his temples. His throat was dry. Tiny droplets of sweat beaded on his forehead. He forced himself to swallow.

He looked again, not believing it.

The clipping was old, the details faded, but there was no mistaking the face, the same beautiful lines and wide, curved mouth. There was no doubt – it was the woman he had dreamed of only the night before. Lela.

Yet even as he thought he had no doubts, his certainty faltered and he looked again. The clipping was only about an inch in size. The head filled most of the picture, but it was still a small view. Could he be imagining the likeness? No, damnit, it was the woman.

He turned the paper over. No other pictures, no name of the newspaper this had come from, no dates. He tossed the clipping on the desk and leaned back in the chair.

What could it mean? How could he dream a face he'd never seen? It was impossible.

Nemo wasn't used to thinking in these concepts. He was a pragmatic man who thought in practical terms. He believed only in the here and now, what he could see and touch. There was no time in his life for fanciful flights into grey areas of speculation, no time for visits to *The Twilight Zone*.

Maddy came back with two mugs of coffee.

'What's the matter?' she asked. 'I told you we should

116

have had breakfast first. Here.' She handed him his coffee. She looked at him again. '*Is* something the matter?'

'I don't know,' he said. He took the coffee and gulped at it. His dry throat needed it. He had no idea what the rest of him needed, but it could have used something.

Maddy narrowed her eyes and came around the desk. 'What is it?' She saw the clipping and picked it up. 'Oh, you found it.'

'Yes. Does it look familiar to you at all?'

'No. It looks old though.'

'It looks familiar to me,' Nemo said nervously.

'It's someone famous?'

'I don't know,' he said. It was too crazy, he thought. Maybe he should just shut up now while he was ahead. But no, he had to tell someone. 'I saw this face in a dream last night,' he said.

'A dream?'

'Twice,' he said, feeling foolish. 'Last night was the last one.'

'You're putting me on,' Maddy said, a small smile creeping onto her mouth.

'I wish I was,' he said. 'I wouldn't be sitting here feeling like an idiot.'

'You really dreamed about this woman? In living colour? In your very own bed?'

'Read my lips,' Nemo said irritably. 'I dreamed about this woman.'

Maddy went back around the desk and sat opposite him. She cocked her head to one side. 'What does that mean?'

'How the hell do I know,' Nemo said, wishing now that he had never mentioned it.

'ESP,' she said. 'You have psychic powers, O Mighty Karnack the Magnificent. Hold an envelope up to your

117

temple and tell us what is in it.'

'Ha, ha,' Nemo said dully. 'Your ridicule doesn't change the facts.'

'I suppose not,' Maddy said, becoming serious. 'Is there any clue on the back of the picture as to where it came from?'

Nemo picked it up again. 'The words don't make a whole lot of sense. *Gershwin last night,* Rhapsody, *Aeolian.* Seems to be a revue of some kind. A concert?'

'1924. George Gershwin first performed *Rhapsody in Blue* with Paul Whiteman in New York.'

'What?' Nemo asked. 'How the hell do you know that?'

'Jazz. My second love. I'll bet you that's what the article was about. All we have to do is get the exact date, then find out what newspaper that came from. Bingo!'

'At least that'll tell us who she is, and maybe there'll be something significant about the story accompanying it,' Nemo said. He got up and added, 'I'm off to the library.'

'It's only eight o'clock,' Maddy reminded him. 'Let's go downstairs and have some breakfast. The library won't open till nine or ten.'

'How can you think of food at a time like this?'

'It won't help anyone if I starve,' Maddy said defensively.

'You want to help me with this research?' he asked.

'Can't. The phone's going to be ringing off the hook with anxious clients who've seen the news reports. Not to mention the media.'

Maddy had regained her appetite. She ate a breakfast large enough for two men while he picked moodily at his food. She spoke no more of his dream and neither did he, but every now and then she gave him an odd speculative glance.

118

She's wondering what sort of a weirdo Sam has fallen in love with, Nemo guessed. A guy who claims to see things in his dreams. A week ago he would have laughed out loud at what was happening to him. But now? There was no denying the facts. He had seen the woman in his dream, known her intimately, in fact. It hadn't even been like a normal dream. Too vivid, too intense. Normally his dreams were vague, illogical, lacked continuity, and he could never remember them properly. This was different. Every detail was still in his mind. But what it meant, he couldn't guess.

'Keep me posted on your progress,' Maddy said when they separated. He promised he would and went to stand outside the library doors until they opened.

He started by showing the clipping to a librarian in the reference section. 'Is there any way to tell which newspaper this came from? It would have been in 1924,' he asked.

She was a dark-haired woman in her late twenties who had already developed the habit of peering over the top of her spectacles. She frowned doubtfully at the small piece of paper. 'If it was a Los Angeles paper, you might be able to tell by comparing the typefaces.'

It hadn't even occurred to him that it might not be a Los Angeles paper. The thought made him cringe. 'Well, I guess the first thing I should do is find out what date this would be. I assume it's the night after George Gershwin performed *Rhapsody in Blue* for the first time, in New York, I believe.'

'Oh, that one's easy,' the woman said with a relieved smile. 'Hold on a minute.'

In literally a minute she returned to the desk with the information. 'That was February 12, 1924 at the Aeolian Hall in New York with the Paul Whiteman Orchestra,' she said.

'Amazing,' Nemo said. 'Now what about the newspaper?'

'It's only available here on microfilm,' she said. 'That's something you'll have to do and it'll take you a little longer.'

There were more than a dozen newspapers in Los Angeles in 1924. The dailies included the *Los Angeles Times*, the *Examiner*, the *Herald*, the *Mirror*, the *Illustrated Daily News* and the *Record*. Nemo decided to start with the LA *Times*. After all, it had outlasted them all, which was as good a reason as any. To save himself time, he got the microfilm for February 13 for all six papers.

He loaded the film and scanned through at high speed. After overshooting the mark once, he went back.

The article on Gershwin was on page three of the *Times*.

Excitedly, he scanned to the next page.

And there it was.

The picture was almost black on the microfilm, but still recognisable as the one he held in his hand. The story was headlined, *Fashion Stars Attend Benefit*. And there was a caption below the picture.

It said, *Top fashion model Lela Edwards makes her entrance with friend actor Terry Jones.*

Lela. Lela Edwards.

There really was a Lela – the Lela of T. and the Lela of his dreams.

He quickly scanned the story, but there was no further mention of her or her boyfriend.

Now what? he thought, moving back from the machine. How could the information help? Obviously, he needed to find out as much as he could about Lela Edwards. Whatever was happening now had something to do with what had happened then, although he had no idea exactly what the connection was. But he was looking at a major research task. A search through magazines and newspapers of all kinds.

He spooled the microfilm back, took it out and repacked it in the box. He was tempted to stay in the library and continue the search, there and then, but it wasn't the type of task he excelled at. He had people on his own office staff who were trained researchers. He'd turn it over to them. They'd be quicker and more thorough. Speed was important now. Every minute lost placed Sam in greater danger.

His mind made up, he handed in the boxes of microfilm at the desk and asked the librarian if there were any books dealing with reincarnation.

'Have a look under the subject heading in the catalogue,' she said, pointing to a scanner. 'You want non-fiction?'

'I suppose so,' he said.

'Well, they should be in that category. There's also a novelist who sort of specialises in the subject. He's done a number of novels with that theme. Let's see . . . oh, what's his name? Hazel, right, William Hazel.'

A short time later, Nemo left the library with five non-fiction books and a novel in his arms.

Reincarnation was a common belief in many cultures, Nemo discovered. In fact, more people on earth seemed to believe in it than those who didn't. He still wasn't sure why he had decided to research it, except that T., whoever the hell he was, seemed hung up on the subject and 'Know your enemy' seemed as good a rule as any to follow. To be honest, all Nemo knew about the subject was what he had read standing in line at the checkout counter of his local supermarket.

Reincarnation, the belief in past lives in some form or another, was the backbone of a number of major religions – Hinduism, Bhuddism and, in its early days, even Christianity before it was declared heretical by some special interest group within the Church. The Greeks, the Egyptians, Australian aborigines and even the Jews accepted the idea. The number of people throughout history, even in the West, who subscribed to the theory was impressive. People as diverse as Einstein and General George Patton, not to mention Ben Franklin and some of the other Founding Fathers.

Basically, from what Nero could understand, when the body died, the soul did not. Instead it found a new body and began life all over again. And yet, doctrines of reincarnation varied widely. To some, reincarnation was a chance to improve one's lot, to others it was a form of endless hell. The beliefs were as diverse as religion itself.

As far as science was concerned, the subject hadn't been researched much. The most impressive study was conducted at the University of Virginia by a man named Ian Stevenson who documented hundreds of cases involving people who claimed to remember past lives. From what Nemo could gather, these were not psychologically unstable people, but people from all walks of life. Children apparently found it easier to remember past lives than adults.

Nemo found this all interesting, but there was nothing among the reams of available data that helped him. At least, he couldn't see it. He decided to get smart and talk to someone who had already done all the research. The novel *The Wings of a Dream* by William Hazel, mentioned on the dustcover that the author lived in Los Angeles. Perhaps it would be easier to track him down and talk to him than continue this aimless search.

After six phone calls, Nemo had Bill Hazel on the

122

telephone. When he explained he wanted some data on reincarnation, Hazel didn't sound too excited. When he said it had to do with the disappearance of fashion designer Sam Barry, Hazel grew intrigued.

'Come on over,' he said; and gave Nemo directions.

Before leaving he called Lieutenant Marshall. 'Have you turned anything up yet?' he asked.

'We have no new information,' Marshall said.

'What the hell are you guys doing? Sitting with your thumbs up your asses?'

'We're doing what we can,' Marshall said stiffly. 'And I don't have to listen to this. The city doesn't pay me enough.'

'I'm sorry,' Nemo said immediately. And he was. He didn't have the right to take his frustrations out on the cop. 'I'm just terribly worried. I hope you understand.'

'Yeah, I do,' Marshall said, his voice a little warmer. 'I don't suppose you've heard anything?'

Nemo debated whether to tell him about the picture. Not yet, he thought. He should find out as much as he could first. 'No, nothing,' he said.

Marshall said he would be in touch and hung up. Nemo chided himself for his outburst. No matter what the pressure, it would be better for him and everyone else if he stayed cool. He resolved to try harder.

Hazel lived in a large Mediterranean style house in Brentwood. Apparently the man was successful, Nemo thought as he drove through the large iron gates. But he wasn't pretentious. Hazel strolled out of the house to meet him with a warm greeting.

He was about Nemo's age, a short, balding man, slightly overweight, with a quick smile and alert grey eyes. His wife, a pretty brunette, said hello to Nemo and then left on a shopping trip.

Hazel took Nemo into his study, a large, comfortable

123

room with oak panels and book cases on every wall. Aside from the desk where he obviously worked, there was also an armchair and a couch. They sat on the couch, after Nemo refused the offer of a drink.

'I didn't remember who you were until my wife reminded me,' Hazel said with a smile. 'Being one of the city's most eligible bachelors gets your name out in certain circles.'

'It seemed like a good idea at the time,' Nemo said with a grimace of regret.

'All right,' Hazel said, 'enough small talk. What's all this about?'

'Whatever I tell you has to be in confidence. That's very important,' Nemo said.

'Of course.'

'Well, we believe Miss Barry has been abducted by a man who has been harassing her for some time. Apparently, this man believes he knew her in a past life.'

Hazel shook his head sadly. 'I'm afraid the subject can attract some strange people.'

'Apparently so,' Nemo said grimly.

'Well, what can I do to help?'

Nemo spread out his hands. 'I really don't know. I felt that I needed to find out as much about the subject as possible. Maybe I'd learn something that could help me in some way. I thought, as you've obviously done a lot of research, that I could just ask you some questions.'

'Shoot.'

Nemo shifted uncomfortably on the couch. He hadn't thought it out, didn't really know where to start. 'I read your novel *The Wings of a Dream*. It was . . . interesting. Different.'

'I take it you're not a believer,' Hazel said.

'I've always believed that when you die you die,' Nemo said. 'Do you believe in reincarnation?'

124

'I didn't start out that way,' Hazel said, 'but the more I researched the subject, the more sense it made to me. You know, it takes just as much logic to support a theory of extinction as it does to support reincarnation. In fact, there's probably more proof that reincarnation exists.'

'You mean Stevenson's studies?'

'And others. Children often talk about past lives when they're very young. It's natural for them to do so. It's only the disbelief of adults that makes them doubt their own knowledge.'

Hazel named a number of studies and situations where memory of past lives had been substantiated. He talked also of the many different forms a belief in the subject took.

'All right,' Nemo said. 'How do people find out about their past lives? I mean, say I wanted to find out if I lived before, how would I go about it?'

Hazel shrugged. 'There are a lot of avenues. Some people see past lives during meditation, others in trances, visions or dreams. Hypnotic regression is a method used with some success. A philosophy called Scientology uses a questioning process where a person's attention is directed to areas of stress or confusion, and past lives often pop up, even though it isn't the primary intention. Some people remember things when they see something familiar – that old phrase déjà vu that I'm sure you've heard of.'

Nemo was disappointed. 'So I couldn't track this guy down to some place locally that believes in rein-carnation.'

'I doubt it,' Hazel said. 'There are just too many. God knows how many people practice hypnotic regression. Probably dozens. Some are private practitioners, psychologists and the like, others do it as a game. A dangerous one, I might add, particularly where hypnotism is involved. Then there are so-called psychics who do psychic readings. They tell their clients what part of their past lives they've seen. Stuff like that. It's a pretty wide field.'

'You said it could be dangerous. How?'

'Well, with most religious or philosophical groups, it would be done within strict ethical parameters. Also the person wouldn't remember this type of stuff until he was able to handle it, so to speak. Now someone who learned about this before he could handle it, could go off the deep end. Which sounds like your boy.'

'But why? I mean, why would it be dangerous?' Nemo asked.

'Because people can get stuck in roles. A psychotic, for instance, is someone who cannot escape the role he is playing. He isn't doing it on a knowing level, it's compulsive. A case could be made that psychotics, the type who are institutionalised, are simply replaying, on a compulsive level, some past life, or an incident, something that happened in a past life. It's as good a theory as any I've heard.'

'So this guy, thinking he knew her in a past life, could be completely out of control?'

'I don't want to frighten you, but it could be possible.' Hazel scratched his chin and tried to explain. 'Obviously, if he abducted her, there's something wrong with the man, right?'

Nemo nodded.

'Well,' Hazel continued, 'if he's been messing with past lives, a little bit of knowledge can be a dangerous thing. Without fully confronting and accepting responsibility for that life, without seeing all that he had to see, it could have a bad effect on him. In hypnotism, in particular, the person is not doing or seeing or knowing on his own volition. Traditionally, in religion, a person has to

126

earn his right to increased awareness. And then he does it of his own free will. That isn't the case where a hypnotist is involved. If he was crazy to begin with, which was probably the case, it wouldn't help.'

'Oh, God, how do I find him?' Nemo said, unable to keep his pain hidden any longer.

'I'm afraid I can't help you there,' Hazel said calmly. 'If I could, I would.' He hesitated, then said, 'I gather you and Miss Barry are close friends.'

'I love her,' Nemo said.

'Well, then, perhaps love will find a way,' Hazel said gently.

'I wish it were that simple,' Nemo said.

'I didn't say it was simple,' Hazel said with a cryptic smile.

'Could I call you if I have more questions?' Nemo asked.

'Anytime, and I mean that. This is a terrible thing and if there's any assistance I can give, I'd like to.'

'One last question,' Nemo said when they reached the door. 'You mentioned dreams. People can dream about past lives?'

'Well, you know people have a lot of barriers against this, particularly in the West where the belief system is so different. This is just my theory, mind you, but I think we can tell ourselves things in dreams which we might not be willing to do in a wakened state. So, yes, people can dream about past lives. And I think that's the reason they do.'

Hazel patted Nemo on the shoulder. 'Don't hesitate to call me, okay? And don't lose heart. You'll find a way, I know it.'

Nemo left feeling more confused than when he had arrived. Oh, he knew a lot more about reincarnation. More about the theory, more about the traditions of belief and the religions going back thousands of years that accepted this as a truth. He had more data than he needed.

It was himself he was confused about. Dreams. Was that what he had been doing? Dreaming about a past life? If that were the case, then T. wasn't the only one who had known Lela in a past life – *he* had known her as well.

He shook his head. No, it was impossible. Not only was it impossible, but he didn't believe in the entire thing. It was just so much mystical gobbledy-gook. A ridiculous theory dreamed up by people who couldn't face the fact of their own mortality. It wasn't for him, that much was certain. Put it all out of your mind, he told himself. The only thing he should be thinking about was how to find Sam.

A reporter from the *Times* was waiting for him when he arrived home. A tall, thin man in his mid-twenties, he rose from the front step where he had been sitting and met Nemo as he got out of his car.

'Mr Riley?'

'Yes?'

'I'm Phil Stinger from the *Times*. I wonder if I could have a few words with you about Sam Barry?'

Shit! Nemo thought immediately. But another idea followed. Nothing was happening – no trace, no clues. Perhaps he could generate something with a little publicity.

'Sure,' he said, 'Come on in.'

Stinger wore blue jeans, sneakers, an open-necked shirt and a leather jacket, standard attire for a reporter in this day and age, Nemo had previously discovered. At Nemo's invitation, he sat in the living room and pulled a

128

notebook from his jacket pocket.

'I understand that you're a good friend of Miss Barry's,' Stinger said. There was a rosy-cheeked open-ness about him, an image he tried hard to project, Nemo thought cynically. He'd had dealings with the Press before and knew their priorities.

'Who gave you that information?' he asked curiously.

Stinger looked hesitant, then said, 'The police.'

'Yes, I am. A friend and neighbour,' Nemo said.

'I was given to understand that you were better friends than that,' Stinger said. 'You were going out together, weren't you?'

'Yes.'

'Do you have any ideas about her disappearance?'

This was one area Nemo didn't intend to get into. It wasn't the kind of publicity he wanted. 'No, you'd better talk to the police again about that,' he said.

Stinger looked disappointed. There was no story here.

Nemo said sympathetically. 'Look. Let me make a statement about this. All I want to say is that Miss Barry and I were very good friends. I want to make a plea to whoever abducted her to release her unharmed. I will pay any amount of money if a ransom has been request-ed, or meet any other terms. All I want is her release. That's it.'

'Has there been a ransom request?' Stinger asked when he finished scribbling in his notebook.

'Not that I know of,' Nemo said.

'Any messages at all from whoever abducted her?'

'Not that I know of.'

Stinger got to his feet. 'Well, if I have any other questions, may I call you?'

'Leave a message at my office. I'll get back to you,' Nemo said.

Stinger looked at him hard, the innocent expression

129

leaving his face. 'There's got to be more to this story than I'm hearing,' he said. 'People don't just disappear for no reason.'

'If you find out the reason, let me know,' Nemo said.

After the reporter left, Nemo called his office and spoke to his secretary, Marion. A middle-aged, married woman with adult children, she was as efficient as a storm-trooper.

'Marion, how's the research going on Lela Edwards?'

'You only asked for it this morning,' she complained.

'Who've you got on it?'

'Kelso and Morer.'

'Not enough. I want every available person on it,' he said. 'I want them working on it day and night. They'll get double pay for overtime. I want a full report on her by tomorrow morning, okay?'

'I'll put a couple of the law clerks on it as well,' she said.

'Good. I want it delivered here by ten tomorrow morning.'

'Yes, boss.' She must have been burning with curiosity, but he knew she'd never ask why it was so important. It was one of the reasons she was so good.

He went back to his reincarnation books, drawn to them with the hope that something would turn up in the pages to enlighten him, some piece of information that would point him in a direction. Right now he was sailing without a rudder.

Tomorrow the article would appear in the newspaper with his plea. Nothing would come of the plea, he knew. But whoever had Sam, if he didn't know it already, would now know that there was still a serious rival for her affections. Perhaps that would lead to something.

He read late into the night, but nothing jumped from the pages to help him. It was difficult to concentrate. His

130

thoughts kept turning to Sam. Where was she? What was being done to her? How was she holding up? He finally fell asleep at about three in the morning, his thoughts filled with worry.

Lela screamed, her face twisted with fear, as the attacker approached her.
  'If I can't have you, nobody else can either,' he said.
  'No!' she screamed.
  He lifted his hand and light gleamed on the silver blade.
  'No!' she screamed again.
  The hand plunged down. Again and again and again, until the white sheets were crimson with her spreading blood.

Oh, my God, what have I done? Nemo thought as he awoke. My stupid ploy in the newspaper only incensed him.

The sun was streaming through the bedroom window. The telephone was ringing.

He picked it up and held it to his ear without speaking. He couldn't say anything.

'Hello?' came the man's voice. 'Hello?'

'Yes,' he said finally.

'This is Lieutenant Marshall. Is that Mr Riley?'

'Yes,' Nemo said, almost whispering. 'You found Sam? You found her body?'

'Found her body?' Marshall said.

'Did you find her?' Nemo said.

'No, we haven't found anything,' Marshall said, his voice puzzled. 'I'm calling to find out if you've heard anything.'

131

Relief washed through Nemo. 'No,' he said. 'Nothing, nothing at all.'

'Are you all right?' Marshall asked.

'I'm fine,' Nemo said. 'I had a bad dream. I just woke up, I'm sorry.'

'Oh,' the policeman said.

Just a bad dream. That's all it was. The world hadn't lost all acceptable meaning. There were still such mundane events as bad dreams, plain old nightmares. Thank God for that, at least.

Chapter Nine

The man smoked a cigarette as he listened to the tape, twirling the ivory holder in his fingers.

'April 16, 1924.'

'Good. When I count to three and snap my fingers, you will wake up. You will –'

The hypnotist's voice was interrupted by a series of painful groans.

'What's happening? Is there more to this life you want to reveal?'

'No! No! I don't want to reveal it! No!'

'Tell me, did something bad happen?'

'Bad. Yes, bad.'

'Tell me about it.'

'No! I can't . . . I can't see it. I don't want to. I don't want to. Please! Free me, let me go. Please. I didn't do it, I didn't. I didn't hurt her. I didn't –'

'All right now. Take a deep breath . . . good . . . now another . . . Good, now you feel relaxed. You feel calm. Everything is fine. Everything is –'

The man switched off the recorder. Then he stubbed his cigarette out fiercely in the pewter ashtray.

It was time to see her. It was time to make things right.

*　　　*　　　*

Sam opened her eyes. She must have fallen asleep.

It was still the same canopied bed, still the same room. The same prison.

She rubbed her face. She had slept, but fatigue still drained her. What had happened? Nothing. She had lost track of time. She had slept once before, she knew. When she awoke a tray was sitting on the floor inside the door. There were a couple of sandwiches, a thermos of coffee. She had eaten in spite of her fear.

The fear. She had never known fear like this. It had eaten its way into her until now it was a part of her. She was even growing used to it. It was like a second skin.

Another tray at the door. She got up from the bed and walked over to it. Sandwiches and coffee. She wasn't hungry now, but thirst prodded her to pour the coffee and drink it. She enjoyed the warmth, the feel of it. This was something real, something she could touch and taste. Nothing else about this room was real. It was filled with props. It was theatre. A night in the 1920s.

Where was Nemo? Was he looking for her? Were the police looking for her? Was anyone? How had she got here? All she remembered was going to sleep in her own bed in her own home. Who had brought her here? Was any of this real?

The questions! Like the fear, they were always there. She would give anything to have just one of them answered, just one. One answer, one truth was all she needed to hold on to. It would become a source of stability, a reference point.

Since being in this room she'd done nothing but think. And think. The results of her efforts were meager. T. had brought her here. She knew that much. Who else? The dress added to her conviction. How had he brought her? She must have been drugged in some way, or she would have remembered. Something in her food that

134

night perhaps? But why? Who was he? What did he want with her? Above all, what did he want with her? What was he going to do? When she sought answers to this question it condemned her to flights of uncontrollable imagination.

She'd had time to think too about her life. About her work and about Nemo – the man who had become so dear to her in such a short time.

Her work: what would happen to the show that was coming up? How could it happen with her not there? What would happen to her career? It was important, yes, but insignificant compared to what was happening to her now. Her life was at stake. She was certain of that.

And Nemo: He was trying to find her. She was certain of that too. He loved her and she loved him. It had happened in some miraculous fashion that defied understanding. He saw her, she saw him – they fell in love. The simplest event in the world.

Bad timing, she thought at first, with some bitterness. But then she considered that if she had not met Nemo recently, perhaps there would be no one who cared enough for her to seek her now. There was Maddy – she cared. But Maddy hadn't believed her fears. Maddy thought she was overreacting to T.'s attentions. What was Maddy thinking now?

When you have nothing to do but think, your thoughts repeat themselves in endless cycles. Their very repetition trivialises them; you grow suspicious of their validity. It is a tiring process. Sam wanted nothing more than for her mind to fall silent, but she knew it was the one thing it could not do.

She tried diverting herself at times by examining the room or looking out of the window to try and locate this place. There was nothing to be seen though. Just the car in the driveway. Beyond was a wall and trees that obscured vision completely. She could be in the city or on a country estate – she had no way of knowing at first. Except for the helicopters. Their frequency overhead, particularly at night, told her she was in the city somewhere. As for the room, it had been exquisitely modelled. Every piece of furniture was a genuine piece of the period – no copies here. The fabric on the bed and the curtains was new, however, although it too was a perfect replica of the period. She listened for noises in the house, but there were none. Whoever lived here moved silently or while she slept.

What else occupied her? Unbidden memories came. She thought of her childhood a lot for some reason. It too had private and silent moments like these, although without the fear; still, the similarity existed. As a child she had always been fascinated by the fashions of the Twenties and the illustrations of the time. Those men in white suits and lithe women in long gowns and short skirts. Dancing, dancing madly to an economic crash at the end of the decade that changed their lives forever. There was something about that frenetic, grasping time that had saddened her as a child.

Now that she thought about it, there had been fear associated with it as well. She thought of it as a decade of loss, and perhaps it was a fear of loss that had affected her. Many of her childhood drawings were of that time. They showed women sitting on lawns under umbrellas, sipping languidly on tall drinks, while attentive men hovered nearby. Strange, how completely she had forgotten those memories.

There was a period of a year or two when she was about ten, during which the Twenties had fascinated her. She had found a collection of old *Ladies Home Journals* and devoured them, page by flimsy page. Photography was still a dubious art then and the maga-

136

zines were lavishly illustrated. She remembered the dresses with their low waistlines and gay fluttering ribbons, the pictures of corsets, an indignity inflicted upon women that was on its way out. There were advertisements for films starring Gloria Swanson, Marion Davis and Mia May. Wallace Reid was a big star, as were Jack Holt and David Powell. Oh, yes, and the stage was sneering at the films. She vividly remembered an article by actor Otis Skinner: *The Motion Picture Not an Art*.

Curious how the names popped into her mind now, in spite of the fact that her infatuation with the Twenties had gone the way of other infatuations. No doubt it had left its imprint on her.

Life had gone full circle. Here she was, trapped in the Twenties.

An endless stream of thought. And yet . . .

What was going to happen to her? It always came back to that.

She went into the small bathroom, hardly more than a closet really.

When she came out, a man was sitting on her bed.

He was tall and well built, with broad shoulders and large hands. Dark hair and eyes and pale face.

He was the man who had bumped into her at the airport.

He smiled at her with thin lips, a slightly mocking expression on his face.

'Lela?' he said.

The fear was stronger now, but she was determined not to show it. She continued into the room and stood a few feet away from him.

'My name is Sam Barry and I demand that you release me,' she said.

He ignored her comment. 'I thought I would give you some time to get used to your surroundings before I

137

visited you,' he said. 'I hope you haven't been too uncomfortable.'

'I've been kidnapped and scared, what do you expect me to feel like? Of course I've been uncomfortable,' she snapped back.

'Abducted,' he said.

'What?'

'You have been abducted, not kidnapped. I am sorry for the discomfort, but it had to be done.'

'Who are you and what do you want?'

'The name you remember me by is Terry Jones,' he said. He rose from the bed and half-bowed at her. 'You have known me as your admirer, T., of course. And as for what I want, I want you to remember.'

'I do not remember you, Mr Jones. I have no idea what you are talking about, and all I know of you is that you are a criminal who is holding me prisoner here.'

'I'm sorry you feel that way, although it is quite understandable. You will change your mind.' He did his strange little bow again. 'Now, if you will excuse me, I must go. I shall call for you in an hour and escort you to dinner.'

He walked towards the door. 'Oh,' he said, 'there are more dresses for you in the closet. I would prefer it if you wore the burgundy gown this evening.'

And then he was gone.

There was a click as the door locked behind him. She stood speechless in the centre of the room.

The man was insane. She was the prisoner of a madman.

She remembered hearing or reading somewhere that it was best to humour madmen. She wasn't sure how true it was, but for the time being, until she found out what was going on, it was as good a strategy as any. There was nothing to be gained by antagonising him and, possibly,

138

much to be lost. Her first priority was to discover the man's intentions. Once she knew that, she could then figure a way to get out of here. In the meantime, she had to be calm. She reminded herself that he hadn't hurt her yet and, perhaps, had no intention of doing so. Perhaps.

She wore the burgundy gown. It was beautiful and fit her perfectly. It left her arms bare and swept down in long folds from the waist.

There was a knock at the door, the sound of the key, and then it opened. Terry Jones wore an elegantly cut dinner jacket with a bow-tie and black shoes.

'Good evening,' he said. 'How lovely you look.'

He took her arm and led her from the room.

They walked down a long corridor, rounded a corner and came to a curving balcony. Below was a hall, dominated by a sparkling crystal chandelier. The floor was tiled in black and white, the furniture that lined the sides of the room and the pictures on the walls were all from the Twenties. The entire house was a museum, she realised.

After descending the stairs he took her into a room leading off the hall. There was a long dining table, with two places perfectly set with china and silver with crystal glasses. Candles burned in tall crystal holders. Wine chilled in a pewter bucket.

He pulled out a chair on the right side and said, 'Please be seated.' Then he sat at the head of the table beside her.

He poured the wine expertly. 'This is a Sauterne from 1917. I hope you enjoy it,' he said.

Sam fought an urge to scream at the incongruity of it all. He was acting as if he had invited her to his home for a romantic evening, as if they were the best of friends, not captor and victim. He was endowing it all with a sense of ease and normality and he was doing it chillingly well. Her resolve to stay calm, to humour him, began to seep away.

'How long are we going to continue this charade?' she asked tautly.

'Please taste your wine,' he said evenly. 'I assure you, it's excellent.'

She tasted it. 'The wine is wonderful, the table is wonderful and I'm sure the food will be wonderful, but why am I a prisoner here? What do you want?'

He raised his eyebrows. 'Lela! You are my honoured guest here.'

'In that case, if I am merely a guest, I'd like to leave.'

'You cannot,' he said calmly.

'What do you want?' she asked, dropping her voice, trying to regain her equilibrium.

'I want you to remember, Lela. I told you that before. After you remember, you will not want to leave.'

'Remember what?'

'Why, to remember us, of course.'

He picked up a small golden bell and tinkled it. An elderly woman came into the room, pushing a wheeled trolley. Her face was harsh and lined and her grey hair was tied back in a severe bun. She wore a black apron and her sleeves were pulled back to reveal strong arms.

Jones spoke to her in some strange language Sam couldn't recognise. The woman nodded and put the appetisers on the table. There were snails in garlic butter and cucumber slices adorned with cream cheese, all superbly prepared.

'Who is that?' Sam asked.

'My housekeeper,' Jones said. He smiled. 'Unfortunately she does not speak or understand one word of English.'

The smells tempted Sam. She realised that she was

140

immensely hungry. 'Eat', Maddy would say. 'If it's your last meal, enjoy it.'

She nibbled at the appetisers. He drank some of his wine and peered approvingly at her over the rim of the glass. She felt like a schoolgirl on probation.

'Do you remember how we met?' he asked, lowering his glass.

Sam looked at him blankly.

'Let me tell you,' he said. 'Perhaps it will refresh your memory. A touch more wine, perhaps?'

He refilled her glass and then leaned back. 'We met at a party being given by Gloria Swanson,' he said. 'She lived in that lovely old house on the hill, remember? I was only a relatively unknown young actor then, of course, but I wangled an invitation, hoping to meet people who could further my career. Instead, I met you. You already had your fame well in hand.

'I remember vividly how beautiful you were. You were standing on one side of the room, talking to a man and a woman, and then you looked over and saw me. Your conversation faltered, as did my heart, but you turned back and continued talking to the couple.

'A short time later I was introduced to you and we began to talk.'

Sam found herself intently following his every word. His eyes gazed at some distant point while he spoke. His voice was soft and his expression tender. She started to feel like a child listening to a bedtime story.

He spoke of how they talked and discovered a hundred things in common, how they couldn't keep their eyes off each other. She was a famous fashion model by then, the toast of the country, but she had come as he had, from a small town in the midwest.

'What charmed me more than anything, I think, was that you couldn't understand your celebrity status. At

141

heart, you were still a small-town girl who just happened to be endowed with extraordinary beauty. There was no arrogance about you at all,' he said.

They were interrupted then by the return of the trolley. The woman dished veal, creamed peas, potatoes and asparagus in aspic.

As soon as she left, Jones continued his monologue, pausing occasionally to eat.

'You were there that night with some actor, but we arranged to meet the following day. It had to be a secret meeting you said, because your publicist arranged all your dates for you, part of an overall strategy to introduce you to the Hollywood crowd and, hopefully, a film career. You couldn't be seen with a nobody like me. I understood and I agreed.'

They met, he said, and soon became lovers. At the same time, his career received a boost – a co-starring role in a major film was offered. 'It changed everything,' he said. 'We could see each other in public. I was now an up-and-comer. We were very much in love and no longer had to keep it a secret.'

Sam grew mesmerised by his voice, the setting, the exquisitely prepared food, the wine. He spoke so calmly, so rationally, it sounded as if he were talking about an event that happened last month or last year.

'Do you remember that time at the beach?' he asked, turning his gaze on her. 'We went to a party and afterwards drove to the beach. It was deserted then. There were very few houses. The moon was out. We stripped and swam nude out beyond the breakers and cavorted like children. We swam back to shore and made love on a blanket.'

Remember? It reminded her of the reality of what was happening. This was *her* he was talking about – her in another life and him in another life. This was no innocent bedtime story. The man obviously believed

142

every word of what he was saying and just as obviously, he was completely insane.

'How did you remember all this?' she asked, speaking for the first time.

He looked surprised, as if interrupted in the middle of a sentence or disturbed from a dream. 'What?' he asked.

She repeated her question.

'Oh,' he said, 'it began with hypnotism. Regression. I discovered my past lives through hypnotism. It was all recorded, of course, and after the sessions I would listen to them. What was different about this particular life was that I began to remember it while not hypnotised. I listened to the session and as I did, bits and pieces of it came flooding into my memory – as clearly as if it had all happened yesterday – which, in a way, it did.'

'Fascinating,' Sam said, but she also couldn't help shaking her head. Illusion and reality had merged in his mind to form an entirely new reality. Wasn't that a definition of insanity, a singular new reality that overcomes the common realities we all agree on?

'Oh, indeed,' he said. 'And yet, why shouldn't we remember all that has happened to us? After all, it is our right. It is a wonderful thing to know where you have been, what you have done and who you are.'

'And me?' she asked. 'How do I fit into this?'

'I saw you about six months ago. I attended your Spring show in Beverly Hills. The moment I saw you I recognised you. I knew you were Lela.'

'But how can that be?' she asked. 'If I died and came back, surely I don't look the same.'

'Of course not,' he said. 'Not physically, at any rate, although as Lela you were beautiful and you are now. No, bodies change in every life. But the person never changes – the personality, the spirit, the soul. I recognised that part of you immediately. It's as unmistakable as a fingerprint.'

'I think you've made a mistake,' she said.

His mask dropped for a moment. The smile writhed on his face like a serpent. 'I do not make mistakes,' he said finally. 'You are Lela. I'll stake my life on it – and yours.'

And then the pleasant smile was back on his face. 'Lela, you will understand, I promise. Once you remember how we were together, you will forgive my imprudence.'

Imprudence! Drugging, kidnapping, a captive in his house, and all he called it was imprudence. It was almost too much for her. But she stifled the angry retort and said instead, 'And how are you planning to help me remember all this? As of now, it's all a blank.'

Again the smile. 'It would spoil it if I told you. This –' He waved his hand at the table and around the room, 'is a beginning.'

'Look,' she said, attempting a friendly smile, 'why don't you just let me go? We can get together for lunch or dinner of my own free will and discuss it then. I'm much more likely to listen when I'm not being held a prisoner.'

'I think not,' he said. 'This is better. And, by the way, I'm sorry you consider this captivity. As I said, you are my honoured guest, Lela. You are the woman I love. And, whether or not you know it now, you are with the man you love. The fact that I am forced to take precautions to ensure your stay here, is entirely your fault.'

'My fault? What do you mean?' she asked.

'My flowers, my calls. Perhaps if you had been more receptive, this wouldn't have been necessary. But it became obvious that you are too engrossed in this life for normal measures to succeed.'

'Look, now that we've met, it can be different,' she said. 'Let me go and we can meet. We can talk about all

144

this. You can tell me your story.'

Anger entered his voice for the first time. 'Do you think I'm a fool?' he said. 'Don't you think I know what you're doing, trying to humour me as if I was some kind of mental case?' He took a breath and calmed. 'Like it or not, in the eyes of society I have committed a crime by bringing you here. We are going to have to see it through to its conclusion.'

She couldn't hold back any longer. 'You're utterly insane,' she said bitterly.

'Don't say that!' He slammed his fist against the table.

The housekeeper scurried into the room and looked at the table. He muttered a word to her and she left immediately.

'Please restrain yourself,' he said stiffly, 'from judgements on something you don't yet understand. You'll save yourself embarrassment.'

Sam decided not to back down. Appeasement wasn't going to get her anywhere apparently, perhaps confrontation would be more successful. 'All I understand,' she said, 'is that I am being kept a prisoner here against my will by a man who is suffering from delusions and who is obviously mentally ill. You don't need *me* here, you need help, Mr Jones, if that really is your name.'

'Don't speak that way!' he shouted. He reached over, grabbed her wrist and squeezed it, his face contorted.

'You're hurting me!' she said. The fear was back now. She had overstepped the boundaries and gone into dangerous territory.

The housekeeper returned, carrying coffee on a tray. Jones released Sam's arm, his face still flushed. He started to speak, then changed his mind. The woman put the tray on the table and Jones poured them each a cup, without asking Sam if she wanted any. By the time he handed her the cup he had recovered his composure.

'My name is, indeed, for all intents and purposes, Terry Jones,' he said. 'Terence W. Jones. In this life I am a novelist. Perhaps you have heard of me.'

'The historical novelist?' she asked incredulously.

'Yes,' he said.

Almost everyone had heard of him, she thought. He was one of the top selling writers in the country. Each year one of his historical novels sat on the bestseller lists, both hardcover and paperback. He was rumoured to be immensely wealthy and something of a recluse, foregoing the usual media blitz greeting the new release of a major author's work.

'I've read some of your books,' she said stupidly.

'I hope you enjoyed them,' he said.

'Look,' she said, attempting a return to reasonableness, 'you didn't have to do any of this. All you had to do was call me, tell me who you were, and I would have been honoured to meet you. I still would be, under different circumstances.'

'I don't think so,' he said. 'You are a busy and successful woman. Men must be calling you constantly. No, I think my plan is best.'

'But can't you see that it isn't working?' she beseeched. 'I'm not happy to be here. I'm afraid. I want nothing more than to leave and never see you again.'

'It'll work, given time,' he said, finality in his tone.

Sam withdrew. She sipped at her coffee. Reason didn't work, confrontation didn't work. What else was there? Deceit? Violence? She looked at the knives on the table. Could she? Could she pick up one of those knives and plunge it into the body of the man beside her? It was doubtful. For one thing, she was not a violent person, for another, he was stronger and probably faster than she. What would his response be if she attempted and failed?

She glanced around the room. Large French windows led to a porch. Could she run? He would catch her before she got ten yards. Even if she made it out of the house and into the grounds, it was a long way to the fence. And she had no idea what was beyond the fence. Probably a quiet street in a wealthy neighbourhood where people minded their own business.

She would have to wait for either opportunity or rescue, whichever came first. Rescue looked dim. Who would suspect a famous writer of such bizarre behaviour? How could anyone trace her to him when their only connection was in a 'past life' for godsakes? It was hopeless. She would have to wait for the moment and grasp it. It was her only chance.

For now, there was nothing to be done. She wanted only to end the charade and gain the respite of sleep.

'I'm tired,' she volunteered.

Jones looked at her with apparently genuine concern in his face. 'How inconsiderate of me,' he said. 'I should have realised. Please allow me to escort you to your room.'

They went back upstairs and when they reached the door, he opened it. He took her hand and kissed it. 'Thank you for a delightful evening,' he cried.

The door closed behind her and the key turned.

'Screw you,' she said.

She leaned back against the door, suddenly weak. Tears pricked at her eyes in a surge of self-pity. What have I done to deserve this? she asked herself. My life was going so well, and now this horror story. Why?

She walked across the room and sat on the bed. She had to fight self-pity; it wouldn't help. Her only chance was to keep alert. The indulgence of self-pity would only slow her down, lower her awareness. She couldn't succumb to either sorrow or fear. She had to maintain her sense of self and develop a certainty that somehow she would get out of this.

A haze of anger enveloped her. God damn you! she thought. I will get out of this. Somehow I will. I'm not going to lie back and take it. I'll fight, I'll scheme, I'll do whatever I have to do to survive this.

She finally fell asleep, holding onto that thought like a life preserver.

Sam had been dreaming of a ball and a man who swept her across the floor again and again. And then the lights went out. And then they came on again.

She opened her eyes.

Candlelight?

He stood beside her bed, a candle in his hand. He was looking down at her. The reflected flame flickered in his eyes.

'What do you want?' she asked, drawing the blankets up to her neck and moving to the other side of the bed.

'Good night, Lela,' he said. 'Sleep well.'

He turned and walked out of the room, closing the door behind him.

She lay in the dark for hours, unable to reach the sanctuary of sleep.

Chapter Ten

Promptly at ten o'clock, one of his law clerks brought Nemo a large brown envelope. He hurried out to the back patio where he was drinking his coffee, opened it and pulled out a ream of paper.

The research consisted almost exclusively of xerox copies of newspaper and magazine articles, taken from both microfilm and paper. He began to scan through, skimming the unessential in the hope of finding the significant. Unfortunately, he had no idea what the significant would be and so, after a few minutes he changed tactics and began to read closely in order to learn everything he could about Lela Edwards.

She was, he learned, one of the most famous fashion models in the country. She began her career in New York City after a move from the midwest, and in a relatively short period of time became the darling of the fashion world. By the time she was twenty-two, coincidentally in 1922, she was at the top of her profession. Late that year, at the invitation of a number of movie makers, she came to California to investigate a career in the burgeoning art of film. Unfortunately, she died 'tragically' in 1924, before her beauty could be imprinted on celluloid.

Now Nemo had something to skim for. How did she die? He found the answer in a magazine article.

Lela Edwards was murdered. It made juicy headlines at the time. Not only was she stabbed to death by a former lover, but it happened on her honeymoon. He also murdered her new husband, one Phillip Bates. The murderer, ex-boyfriend Terry Jones, was captured, convicted and hung in 1925.

Nemo's dream of the night before came back into his mind. Lela. Stabbed. 'If I can't have you, nobody else can either.'

My God! he thought. I did it again.

How could he deny it now? The proof stared at him from the printed page. *He was dreaming this woman's life!*

And then, with even more impact, he remembered something else. In the earlier dream in which he and Lela had made love, she had called him by name: 'Not yet, Phillip.'

Her lover then was Phillip Bates, a name he had never heard of until reading it just moments before.

Wait, he thought. Bates?

Then he remembered the time T. had called Sam and he had taken the receiver from her. What was it he had said? 'I'm not going to let you ruin us again, Mr Bates.'

Nemo put the papers down and rubbed his face. This was becoming too bizarre, too confusing to get a handle on. He shook his head. It couldn't be. And yet the conclusion seemed inescapable and obvious. But it was impossible! Wasn't it?

Quickly, he examined other alternatives. Nothing seemed as logical or right as the one that stared him in the face.

He was not only dreaming the life of Lela Edwards, but he was dreaming his life as well – his past life. He,

Nemo Riley, had been Lela's lover and husband, Phillip Bates!

Impossible! Impossible! Impossible! He wanted to scream it, to deny it to himself and the world. Christ, he didn't even believe in reincarnation. How could it happen? What would author Bill Hazel say to that? Probably something like, 'You may not believe in gravity, but it's still there.'

Was he making a quantum leap from one fact to another to the wrong conclusion? Perhaps through some kind of extrasensory perception he was 'picking up' these events in his dreams. And yet, in the dream in which she called him by name, it had been him. It wasn't a dream about someone else. He was the one who had made love to her. He was Phillip.

Three dreams, and here he was thinking he had lived before. Maybe he was as crazy as T. A dream of a dance, another of a lover and a third of a murder. Yet two of the three proved to be of real events. What were the odds against that happening? Astronomical, no doubt. Lela had been murdered, and there was a lover named Phillip. In his dream, he had been Phillip, *ergo*, he was Phillip in a past life.

Ridiculous, he thought.

Maybe he should find out more about Phillip Bates.

He found another magazine article, this one longer than the previous. It was in a category called *Crimes of Passion*. It didn't say much about the background of Bates, but what it said was enough to make him put down the paper and rise to his feet.

'The other victim was Phillip Bates, a young business lawyer . . .'

A lawyer.

He needed to get out, to do something that would stop him thinking. Quickly, he went into the house and

151

changed into jogging clothes. He ran along the long tree-lined street and pounded the pavement, concentrating on the movements of his body, the rhythm, his jagged breath, the feel of the air, the smells of the neighbourhood – anything to still his boiling thoughts.

But instead, it released them.

It happened in the strangest way.

At one moment he was running fiercely, feeling the air tear at his lungs, his emotions plundering him, close to tears of frustration and worry. And then it was as if his body had turned to cool liquid and he was floating three feet behind it, as calm as moonlight, watching it move ahead of him like a graceful puppet.

His thoughts were lucid then. He thought not in words or pictures but in entire concepts. It was a kind of knowing, something beyond normal thinking.

He knew that Phillip Bates was born in Philadelphia in 1892, that his father was a wealthy banker, that he studied law at Harvard and then was taken into the firm of his father's best friend.

He knew that both his father and the man he worked for, expected him to marry the man's daughter.

He knew he was sent out to the West Coast by the firm to represent some of the vital new companies that had developed out of the motion picture business. Although the firm sneered at the Jews who ran this upstart new industry, it was still willing to take their money.

He knew he met and fell in love with Lela Edwards.

He knew he disappointed both his father and his boss.

And he knew that in a fit of jealous rage, he was murdered, stabbed again and again, by Lela's jilted lover, the young actor, Terry Jones.

He knew all this and much more as he ran past the flowering jacaranda trees and tall hedges, seeing nothing of them, caught up in the spell of disgorging memory.

152

And then, just as suddenly as he left, he was back in his body and his lungs were bursting and his legs were jelly and he stopped and doubled over to regain himself.

When he got back to the house, he picked up the morning copy of the *Times* in the driveway. He opened it as he walked inside and saw the reporter Stinger's story on page three. It was headlined, *No Leads on Abduction of Designer*, but in the fourth paragraph it quoted him, *I will pay any amount of money if a ransom is requested, or meet any other terms*.

Now, we'll see what that flushed out, he thought with some satisfaction.

The light on his answering machine was on. He played back a message to call Lieutenant Marshall.

He was put through in seconds. Marshall's voice barked at him, 'What do you mean talking to the Press?'

'I have that right,' Nemo said.

'Uninformed public statements do nothing but create problems. You're a lawyer, you should know that, pal.'

'Have you come up with anything yet, Lieutenant?' Nemo asked pointedly.

'That's not the issue,' Marshall said. 'Our investigation is proceeding. How come you didn't tell me when we talked this morning that you called the papers?'

'Because I thought you'd see it sooner or later. Apparently you did.' His tone grew conciliatory. 'Look, I don't want to argue with you. I did what I thought was best. I don't see that it will do any harm. All I did was say that I was willing to deal.'

'Any takers?' Marshall said.

'Not yet. And there probably won't be.' Nemo hesitated, wondering how to approach what to say next. 'I have some new information since then, Lieutenant. I wonder if you could come over?'

'What kind of information?' the policeman tried to

153

sound disinterested but couldn't disguise the spark in his voice.

'I'd rather not tell you over the phone. I have some stuff to show you,' Nemo said. 'Can you come to my house?'

'All right, I'll be over.'

While he waited, Nemo ran over what he had learned. It was all too fantastic to grasp at once, but he had little doubt now that he had once been Phillip Bates, Lela's lover. As stunning as it was, that wasn't what he should be examining now, he knew. The important thing was how it related to Sam's present plight. How could he use what he knew to help her? For now, he just had to put his amazement and curiosity aside and concentrate on Sam.

He still wasn't sure what he'd tell the policeman. 'You see, I was Sam's lover in a past life, so I know something about the person who has her, Lieutenant.' The guy would walk out the door and come back with the County mental health boys.

The telephone rang. It was Maddy.

'Anything new?' she asked.

'Not really,' he said.

'I saw the story in the *Times* this morning. You know we can also help with the money thing, if it comes to that.'

'I don't think it will,' Nemo said. 'That's not what he wants.'

'Well, then . . . why do it?'

'I just wanted to send a signal, let him know that I'm still here, let Sam know I'm doing something, if she gets a chance to read the paper.'

'Well,' she said doubtfully. 'I suppose it's better than nothing.'

There was a knock at the front door. 'I have to go,' Nemo said. 'I'll call you later.'

Marshall came in, his scowl more pronounced than before. 'What have you got?' he asked, dispensing with social niceties.

Nemo led him into the dining room. The papers he needed to make his case were spread out over the table.

'I know what her abductor is thinking about, what's motivating him,' he said.

Nemo moved around the table and pointed. 'These are the cards this guy, T., has been sending her. I'm surprised you guys didn't take them.'

'I was going to send a man to her office today.' Marshall said. 'I suppose you have your prints all over them now.'

'So does her office staff,' Nemo said. 'This guy's too smart to leave prints. Besides, they told me at the flower shop that he wore gloves, so I didn't worry about it.'

Marshall looked at the cards. 'Maybe the handwriting will tell us something.'

'This card did,' Nemo said picking up the one that said, *Who is this? T.*

He took the clipping of the newspaper photograph from an envelope and showed it to Marshall. 'He sent this along with it and I've identified the person in the picture.'

Marshall looked at the clipping and turned it over. 'How'd you do that?' he asked, interest creeping into his voice in spite of himself.

Nemo explained how he'd tracked the date down and found the story in the *Times*. 'It goes back to 1923,' he said. 'The woman was Lela Edwards, a famous model then. So I did some research on her and this is what I came up with.'

He told Marshall how Lela had been murdered and about the killer, Terry Jones. 'As you can see, his name starts with a "T" as well.'

155

Marshall looked sceptical. 'So what does that tell us?'

'It tells me that this T. thinks Sam was Lela Edwards and that he thinks he was Terry Jones. Real or not, he thinks he knew her in a past life.'

'The guy's obviously nuts,' Marshall said. 'It doesn't mean anything.'

'That may be,' Nemo said. 'But if he thinks he killed her in another life, where does that leave Sam now?'

'Beats me,' Marshall said, resisting it.

'Look,' Nemo explained patiently. 'I talked to an expert in this field. He told me that this stuff can be dangerous if mishandled, that people can get stuck in the roles of past lives. That seems to indicate to me that Sam could be in great danger. If the guy killed her before, or thinks he killed her before, he could do it again, particularly someone as nutty as this guy.'

Marshall scratched his chin. 'What you have here is a theory based on a lot of far-out supposition,' he said. 'I don't see how it can help.'

'From the picture he sent her and the name he called her, we at least know who *he* thinks she is,' Nemo said. 'That's more than we knew before.'

'All right, for the sake of argument, I'll grant that. But how can that help?'

Nemo sat and put his elbows on the table. 'Maybe I could leak the story to the Press and someone could come forward who knows something about this guy.'

'You've got to be kidding,' Marshall said, rolling his eyes up. 'Every freak in the city who thinks he was Napoleon in his past life is going to come forward. We'd be deluged with false leads and too busy to do any real work. No way.'

'All right. Then maybe you could start calling all the hypnotists and psychologists around who mess with past life regression and stuff like that. See if they can come up with anything or point a finger in some direction.'

'There's probably hundreds of them,' Marshall said gloomily.

'I doubt that,' Nemo said. 'More like dozens. It might turn something up.'

Marshall scratched his chin again. 'Well, it couldn't hurt. I'll have my men make a couple of calls. Problem is that it's difficult to get information out of psychologists. They claim patient privileges, but we'll give it a shot. I'll use the description we have of the guy and see where it leads us.'

'Great!' Nemo said, 'Use the name of Lela Edwards and the date we have here as well. Someone may remember a client who was fascinated by the period or something.'

Marshall shook his head. 'It's a long shot. What makes you think the guy even went to a hypnotist?'

'Like you say, it's a long shot,' Nemo admitted. 'As it turns out, there are lots of other ways people can get into reincarnation. All kinds of groups. But these are the ones that are likely to have records, like doctors with patients. We may just luck out.'

'I never count too much on luck,' Marshall warned.

'I have a feeling about this,' Nemo said.

'I don't count too much on feelings either.'

'What do you count on?'

'Hard work. And the stupidity of criminals.' Marshall walked towards the door. 'I'll get on this and get back to you if I turn anything up.'

'Thanks,' Nemo said.

'And by the way, no more statements to the Press okay?'

Nemo didn't answer. He wasn't about to close the door on his options.

When Marshall left he called his secretary and told her to research the life of Phillip Bates for him. 'I want a bio on the guy, fast,' he said. 'You'll find he went to Harvard Law School. It'd be a good place to start.'

Yes, he knew now that he had been Phillip Bates, but a little corroborating evidence wouldn't hurt. At least it would help dispel the sense of disbelief still nagging at him. He wished there was someone he could talk to about it, someone who wouldn't think he'd gone over the edge of sanity.

Bill Hazel listened to him calmly, interrupting only with questions to clarify a point or two. Nemo had called and driven over immediately at his invitation.

'It was the weirdest feeling,' he was saying. 'Almost as if I was out of my body. But my thoughts were like diamonds, sharp and clear, and I suddenly knew everything about Bates and my past life as him.'

Hazel nodded. 'I've heard of similar things before,' he said. 'I call it the Stress Syndrome.'

'Stress?'

'Well, you've heard of people who think they're going to die, their lives flashing before their eyes? It can happen with past lives when people are going through severe emotional turmoil. It's like the ninety-pound kid who lifts up a truck because is mother is trapped beneath it. Where does he get the strength? We do miraculous things when we feel we have to.'

'So you think that because of the stress I've been under because of Sam and the actual *need* to remember, I was able to?'

Hazel smiled. 'I don't want to put my ideas into your mind. What's true for you, is true for you. But it's a possible framework you could use to get a handle on what's been happening.'

'So you believe me?' Nemo asked.

'I believe that you believe,' Hazel said carefully. 'I have no reason to disbelieve you.'

'I believe it, but I'm confused. I can't see how what I believe in can change in a matter of minutes. I've never accepted anything like this before and now here I am, thinking that I've lived another life as another person.'

'Sounds to me like you were building up to it,' Hazel said. 'There were the dreams first. You weren't willing to accept them for what they were. Even the fact that you dreamed events and names weren't enough. But then it all came together and you stopped denying it.'

'It's so – so, fantastic!'

Hazel nodded understandingly. 'It may seem that way, but to a lot of people in other cultures around the world it's as natural a concept as living , breathing and dying.'

'The important thing now is how I can use this to help Sam,' Nemo said.

'Can you still remember this past life?' Hazel asked.

Nemo looked surprised. 'I don't know. I haven't had time to think about it.'

'Well, I suggest you try. There may be something back then that'll help you solve the riddle of now. This guy seems to be operating on some pattern. Perhaps that'll tell you something.'

On the drive home, Nemo tried to follow Hazel's advice. And surprised himself by remembering as easily as he remembered his activities of the week before.

His thoughts drifted to the night he met Lela . . .

The move to Los Angeles had been wise. Not only was the film industry becoming a powerful economic force, but oilfields were proliferating. About 100,000 people a year poured into the city and it was enjoying an unprecedented real estate boom. San Francisco had its Gold Rush seventy years earlier, now it was the turn of the city to the south. There were more real estate salesmen than clerks in the city. Still, Phillip concentrated on the film industry for his firm, although more clients involved in development and construction beat his door down than ever before.

He met Lela at a party given by Mack Sennett in his recently completed million-dollar mansion on top of the hill above the Hollywoodland sign.

There was no shortage of beautiful women that night, many of whom he had met before. The reigning Queens of the screen, Pola Negri, Gloria Swanson and Marion Davies were there, plus dozens of claimants for the crown. And yet it was Lela who stood out, who his eyes kept returning to.

She wore a long, high-waisted burgundy gown and a diamond tiara glowed in her dark hair. Her expression alternated between a seriousness and a brilliant smile that lit up everything around her. She was with a man, a young actor named Terry Jones, he discovered.

'She's a model. Came here from New York,' someone told him. 'Has a big career ahead of her in the movies.'

'The man you're with. Is he . . . ?' he asked when they danced.

'He's just a good friend,' she said and smiled that wonderful smile up at him.

They moved together as one. He felt the warm skin on her shoulder and wanted more than anything to bend his head and kiss her parted lips.

'May I see you again?' he asked.

'Yes, of course,' she said.

He left early, his mind filled with her. He didn't sleep that night at all, thinking of how she felt, the smell of her, the sound of her voice, the lines of her face.

The next day he called and invited her to dinner . . .

Nemo drove down Laurel Canyon, his thoughts

fixated on the past. From that point on, it had happened exactly as in the dream he had. He had taken her to dinner and then they parked above the city. At her apartment, she invited him in and they made love as naturally and comfortably as lovers of long duration. From that moment on, they became an inseparable pair.

He came into the Valley and took Ventura Boulevard. This had all been orange groves and farms back in the Twenties. Now it was billboards and skyscrapers and apartments and houses.

They drove into the Valley one Sunday and walked through the groves, revelling in the smell of orange blossoms, laying down among those that formed a perfumed carpet on the ground, joyful to be with each other.

Nemo saw his house through a haze of tears and realised for the first time that he was crying. He didn't know how long the tears had been falling and didn't care. He had loved Lela as much as he loved Sam. He had lost Lela and now he was faced with losing Sam.

It can't happen again, he thought. I won't let it.

As he entered the front door he heard the telephone ringing. He picked it up in the hall.

'Hello?' he said.

'Mr Riley?'

'Yes.'

'This is me,' the voice said, sounding familiar, and then he had it. It was T.!

'Where is she? Is she all right?'

'She is with me again and very happy,' the man said. 'I saw your pathetic plea in the newspaper. I warn you. Stay out of this. She doesn't need you.'

'You –' Nemo started to say, but there was a click and the phone went dead.

He replaced the receiver and stood in the hall, a

161

forlorn figure, his shoulders bowed, going over the conversation in his mind. No clues, no sounds in the background, nothing except a message to stay out of it. No help.

It won't happen this time, he thought again. I'll find a way. I won't lose her, not this time. Lela, Sam, whatever the name, it was the same person – the woman he loved and always had. This was their chance to finish what they had started once long before. And he would find a way to do it.

Chapter Eleven

The man hunched over a desk in the public library, leafing through the stack of magazines. He found the picture he was looking for in *Los Angeles Magazine* under a story entitled, *Most Eligible Bachelors. Nemo Riley, Corporate Law Whiz*, the caption said.

He hadn't seen him close up before, but, yes, this was her neighbour, the man she had been seeing, the man he shot at. He stared at the picture for minutes, imprinting it in his mind.

It's him, he thought. Looks nothing like him, but I know it's him again. It has to be. Same pattern. I find her, then he finds her and tries to take her away from me. Circles repeating themselves over and over. This time it'll be different. This time I'll have Lela for myself.

He read the story on Riley. Offices in Universal City, meteoric rise, unmarried and wealthy. School and other background. It was mainly a puff piece – high on PR, short on hard information. No matter. He didn't need to know any more.

Jones closed the magazine and dutifully took the pile back to the desk. He'd deal with Riley, he thought as he handed the magazines to the librarian. He'd done it before and he could do it again.

'Thank you so much,' he said, smiling at the woman.

Sam began to do exercises in her room: stretches, jumping jacks, jogging on the spot, push-ups. There was nothing else to do but think, and thinking led nowhere.

Earlier that morning, Jones brought her breakfast on a tray: eggs, bacon, English muffin, marmalade and coffee.

'Who is Nemo Riley?' he asked, as he handed her the tray.

Her heart missed a beat and the tray shook in her hands. 'Why do you ask?' she said, a coolness in her tone.

'His name was mentioned in the newspaper this morning,' Jones said. 'Who is he? Is he your neighbour, the one you were seeing so much of?'

'He's a friend of mine,' she said, thinking, be careful, be careful.

'Are you lovers?' he asked, coming to the point on his mind.

'None of your business,' she snapped.

'You've answered the question,' he said, and left.

Half-an-hour later, he returned and wheeled an ancient gramaphone into the room. He opened the cabinet and showed her a stack of heavy seventy-eight records.

'While I'm gone, I would like you to listen to these,' he said.

He took her tray, and added, 'You are looking particularly beautiful this morning, Lela.'

She looked away, not replying.

When he closed the door, she heard the key turn in the lock again. He wasn't careless. So far, there had been no opportunities.

She went to the record cabinet and thumbed through. Old songs, probably from the Twenties if Jones was being consistent.

She put one on and listened to the scratchy plastic.

Yes, we have no bananas,
We have no bananas today.
We have stringbeans and onions,
Cabbages and scallions,
And all kinds of fruits, and say . . .

Silly, but catchy, she thought. It sounded vaguely familiar.

For lack of anything better to do, she played another half a dozen records. After a while they bored her and then the tinny voices and scratchy sounds started to irritate her and she stopped playing them. The hell with him.

Her thoughts returned to Nemo. What was he up to, she wondered? Obviously, there'd be stories about her disappearance in the papers. Apparently, he had come forward and said something, or been interviewed. If nothing else, it revitalised her faith that he was looking for her. If only there was some way she could get a message to him.

Jones had said he was going out. Perhaps . . .

She went to the door and banged on it with the flat of her hand. She began to shout as well.

'Hello. Hello. Please come here.'

If the woman was here, perhaps she would come to the door. She was elderly and Sam was positive she could overpower her. She banged harder. Surely she would hear.

But there was no response.

Finally she stopped. The palm of her hand was red and beginning to swell.

A sense of desperation fell on her again. If only there

165

was something she could do to change what was happening. Throw a message out of the window? No point, there was no street out there, only Jones's property. Get to a telephone? How could she, locked in this room? She didn't even know if there was a phone in the house. He was so hung up on the Twenties, he probably used carrier pigeons. No, they had telephones then, she told herself. But it didn't help because there was no way to reach one if there was one here. The mailman? the mailbox was probably at the gates of the estate. The helplessness of her situation bothered her as much as anything. She felt impotent, useless, a victim of circumstances.

She exercised vigorously then. It didn't help her plight, but it was something to do. When she finished she was sweating, but she felt better – calmer and more in control of herself.

Control was the key. Jones was trying to work on her mind, to brainwash her in some way. She knew that. Being held a prisoner, the décor in the house, the records, his attitude, it all conspired to create a new reality for her, to make her see things his way. All she had to do was resist it, see it for what it was. It wouldn't be all that difficult but for the unreasonable fear that overcame her every now and then. Fear was a hard master; it could twist a mind and make a person choose irrational courses.

She couldn't help it. The awareness that he was mad came to her at odd moments, and with it the fear that he was terribly dangerous. He had already demonstrated the potential by abducting her, an act of unrestrained arrogance. Beneath the social veneer, the admiring words and protestations of undying love was a man waiting to explode into some destructive force. And she would be the target. She tried not to think of that, but there were times when some button was inadvertently pushed and it jumped into her mind, keeping everything else out. It was not a pleasant feeling.

Balance, she told herself at moments like these. Keep your balance. Hold onto what's real and let the rest sweep by you. It was, as the saying went, easier said than done.

He came for her at about eleven in the morning. She was learning to guess the time now, watching the shadows thrown by the avocado trees near the window.

When he entered the room, he wore an apologetic smile. 'I'm sorry to keep you waiting for so long,' he said. 'I got a little tied up.'

He wore a white suit and a brightly coloured tie. Like something out of *The Great Gatsby*, she thought.

'I understand you made quite a noise this morning,' he said. 'Please don't do that again.'

She said nothing.

'Well, please come,' he said. 'I have something interesting to show you.'

He led her downstairs, this time to a room on the other side of the hall. It was lined with shelves of dark wood and filled with books. There was a large desk, a table, an armchair and a couch.

'Please sit,' he gestured towards the couch.

Instead, she moved around, looking at the bookshelves. The bottom shelf consisted almost entirely of books by Terence W. Jones. She pulled one out and looked at the cover, feeling his eyes on her.

'You've been very prolific,' she said.

'Fourteen novels and three non-fiction books,' he said, a note of pride in his voice.

'It's easy for you to write?' she asked.

'History is simple once you know you were actually there,' he said.

'But you didn't find out about your reincarnation until recently,' she said.

'True, but it was never far below the surface. I know that now. I was always able to write historical novels as if I was there. It just came to me.' He laughed. 'Imagine my surprise to find out that I actually was there, that I had lived in all those times! No wonder they seemed so familiar to me.'

She turned away from the shelf and looked at him. He sat on the couch, manilla folders balancing on his knees.

'Come,' he said, patting the space beside him.

She sat down, careful not to touch him. Physically, there was something repulsive about him to her, an unclean feeling.

'These are pictures of you at the height of your popularity,' he said, opening the top folder.

It consisted of newspaper photograph clippings, advertisements taken from magazines and a few old original faded brown photographs. The pictures showed a dark-haired beautiful woman with a shapely mouth, wide cheekbones and large eyes. Sam had the feeling that it was someone she would have liked. There was a determination, a spunkiness to the woman.

'An interesting looking woman,' she said.

'And there is a picture of us,' he said.

It showed the woman with a tall, thin man. A handsome, intense face, although there was a sullen touch to the mouth. He wore striped blazer, white trousers and a straw hat.

'Where did you get all this stuff?' she asked.

'I'm a writer. I know how to research,' he said. 'It took a while to gather it, but it was simply a matter of finding it.'

168

'And you think this was me?'

'I know it was you,' he said, a cutting edge to his voice.

He put the folders down on the floor and looked at her. 'Don't you understand?' he said. 'I remember all of this perfectly. It's like something that happened to you yesterday. I remember it the same way. And you would too if you only opened yourself up and stopped resisting it and disbelieving.'

'To what purpose?' she said, her voice tired.

'What?' he asked, disbelief on his face, his eyebrows rising, his mouth open.

'What's the point?' she asked.

'We loved each other,' he said. 'We loved each other and it was all cut short. We all died untimely deaths. What should have been never happened. We have a chance now to change it, to live our fated lives. Together, as we should be.'

'Look,' she said, 'just for the sake of discussion, let's say that this – all this – is true. You knew me in a past life and I knew you and we had an affair, and all the rest of it. We're different people now with different lives. You have yours and I have mine. None of this means anything anymore.'

'No!' he said emphatically. 'No! It does, you see. We *are* the same people. Different names, different bodies, but we are the same people. We love each other. We can't be cheated of our right to happiness.'

There was no getting past his obsession, she saw. She could talk till the cows came home and he would persist. 'It takes two,' she said. 'There's only one. You. Do you honestly think that by keeping me prisoner here, I'm going to change my mind and suddenly love you? It won't happen, I promise you that.'

He looked at her silently, his face blank. After a while, he smiled. 'But it will,' he said. 'I can promise you

169

it will. As soon as you begin to remember how it was between us, you'll change your mind. It's easy to change your mind. People do it all the time. You will too.'

'You don't see it,' she said. 'I don't remember. I'm not going to remember. No matter what you try to do, you're not going to make me remember a past life, for Christ's sake.'

She couldn't keep the derision from her voice. Here was this unbalanced man, determined that she would remember a past life in which she loved him. She didn't even believe in reincarnation. If she weren't a prisoner here, she would be laughing out loud at the absurdity of it.

His eyes glittered and his mouth grew tight. For a moment she wondered if she had gone too far. He was standing on the edge of a pit. She had to be careful.

But he picked up one of the folders and opened it, showing her another photograph. 'This was taken by one of the studios,' he said conversationally. 'You came out here to get into the movies. They all wanted you, but you never had enough time left.'

That evening, after an early dinner, he took her into yet another room. It was large and gloomy, with dark paintings, heavy wood furniture, large china cabinets and an empty fireplace. She assumed it was the living room, although it didn't look as though it was used much.

While she sat on the couch, he poured them dessert wine and then sat opposite her in a wide armchair.

During dinner he had dominated the conversation, talking haphazardly about events in 1923. He spoke of the unexpected death of President Harding and the swearing in of Calvin Coolidge ('I never thought Cool-

170

idge had the stuff for the highest office in the land, and I was right,' he said). Of seeing Jack Dempsey fight, of the first non-stop cross-continental aeroplane flight from Long Island to San Diego, and a number of other events that didn't interest Sam in the slightest.

Now, he seemed inclined to continue. 'Probably the greatest tragedy of the period was the death of Sarah Bernhardt. She died in Paris, aged seventy-eight. I saw her you know, and she was indeed magnificent. One of a kind. Do you remember the day she died? It was near the end of March, 1923. We got into the car and drove to the beach. I wanted to walk, but it was windy and you wanted to stay in the car. So you did. And I walked – in memory of a great actress and a great woman.'

God, no wonder I dumped this guy, Sam thought. What a wimpy jerk. But she kept quiet and listened. Let him ramble, she thought. Sooner or later he would say or do something she could seize on.

'Well, enough of that,' he said, rising to his feet. 'Tonight I have a special treat for you. Come with me, please.'

He led her through a door into another room. A white screen filled one wall, a projector sat on a table at the other end of the room, and chairs in neatly placed rows covered the floor.

'This is my screening room,' he said. 'Please sit down while I set it up.'

He continued talking while he fiddled with the projector. 'We saw this film together when it first came out. I think it was in September of 1923. You – well, lights out.'

The room grew dark and the projector cast its dancing, scarred light on the screen.

It was *The Hunchback of Notre Dame* starring Lon Chaney.

She felt Jones sit in the seat beside her and moved over to avoid touching him.

171

'You know, they built the cathedral and a large section of Paris right in Hollywood for this. Thousands of people worked on this movie,' he said.

And then, as the plot unfolded, he stayed silent. She could feel him watching her, however, and kept her eyes on the screen. What now, she wondered? What was he expecting from this?

It was an amazing performance that Chaney, the master of make-up, put on as Quasimodo, grimacing and writhing his way through the story, endowing his deformed character with humanity and pathos. Through the skill of storyteller and actor, his pathetic plight demanded compassion and even pity.

Was that what Jones wanted? Perhaps he identified with Quasimodo in this situation. Blind, loyal, unrequited love?

When the hunchback was flogged with metal-tipped lashes, she couldn't help but wince. She felt Jones look at her again and stopped, determined to sit frozen in position and show no reaction.

Finally, Hollywood's customary divergence from the Hugo story came, the obligatory happy ending, and the screen flickered with blank light again.

She turned to Jones and saw him watching her. He went to turn on the lights and then came back.

'You didn't cry,' he said, sounding like a disappointed child whose toy had been taken away.

'Cry?' she asked. 'Why should I? I don't cry at movies.'

'You cried before,' he said. 'When we saw the film together, you cried and asked me to hold you in that darkened theatre. I felt . . .'

'That wasn't me,' she said.

He looked at her sadly. 'How can you forget?' he asked. 'How can you blanket out what it was like

172

between us, how it was until he came along and ruined it?'

'Who?' she asked. 'What are you talking about?'

He smiled craftily then. 'He won't do it again, not this time.'

There was a mad glow in his eyes then, and once again she felt an ebullition of fear that left her knees weak and her hands shaking.

'Who?' she forced herself to say again.

- 'Your friend Riley. He won't take you away from me again.'

Oh, my God, she thought, now Nemo is in his fantasies. No! He can't hurt Nemo. I can't let him.

'I don't understand you,' she said.

'You really remember nothing, do you?' he asked, as if he had doubted her all along. 'You can't remember your past life or me or that fellow Riley and what he did to us?'

'I already told you that,' she said. 'As for Mr Riley, he's just a good friend.'

'Ah, yes, that's what you said to me when he came along last time. Not to him, to me! You looked at me and said, "Terry, you're just a good friend, the best. Don't confuse it with anything else." I suppose you don't remember that either.'

She shook her head dumbly.

Jones moved from foot to foot while he spoke, the manic gleam intensifying in his eyes. 'God, you hurt me,' he said, anguish in his voice. 'I loved you and you loved me and then when he came everything changed and we were suddenly expected to be good friends. How could anyone have blamed me? You threw me aside, wasted me, you –'

He stopped then, clenched his fists against his breast and gradually released the pressure. Slowly his compo-

173

sure returned. He tried to smile at her and said, 'They know not what they do.'

She couldn't help herself, but she felt a stirring of pity for him then. It was a tortured soul that stood before her, a man trapped in some agony. But she stopped herself from saying any word of sympathy or making any gesture.

'It was in the past,' he said, his voice normal again. 'This is now and we can make a fresh start, Lela. A new beginning.'

'If you really want a new beginning,' she said cautiously, 'you'd forget all about me and carry on with your life and let me carry on with mine.'

He looked at his watch. 'I'm afraid I have an appointment tonight,' he said. 'Come, I'll take you to your quarters.'

They went silently upstairs. When they reached her room he put his hand on the doorknob and turned to her. His other hand touched her shoulder.

She recoiled as if burned.

'Do you remember the first time I took you out?' he said softly, ignoring her reaction. 'You had that funny apartment off Sunset? We walked upstairs and stopped outside your door, just like this. I kissed you then and at that moment I knew we loved each other and always would. Do you remember?'

'No,' she said, her throat growing tight.

'You will,' he said. 'Given time, you'll remember it all.'

He reached out for her shoulder again and inclined his head. She knew he wanted to kiss her. Any feelings of pity and sympathy vanished then. She wanted only to protect herself.

'You'll have to kill me first if you want to touch me,' she found herself saying. And even as the words came

174

out, she knew she meant them.

He judged her for a long moment and then dropped his hand. He opened the door and waved her into the room. 'Goodnight, Lela,' he said.

When she heard the door lock and his footsteps move away in the hall, she took the chair from its position in front of the dresser and propped it in front of the door, pushing it up against the handle. He wouldn't be able to open the door until she removed it. There would be no uninvited visits on this night.

She sat on the bed and covered her face in her hands. It was beginning to wear on her, the strange unreality of it all, not knowing what he'd do next, or what would happen to her.

One thing had become clear: the man absolutely believed everything he said to her. He had stepped into the twilight zone and to him it was as real as the everyday world. He had no intention of turning back, even if he could.

She had discovered something about herself tonight as well. She was willing to die if she had to.

She felt strangely ambivalent. The thought terrified her and yet, at the same time, it comforted her. It offered an alternative, something that wasn't present before. It was by no means desirable, but, if things got too bad, it was a known course of action she could take, something she could do. Like it or not, there was a choice and it gave her a sense of freedom for the first time since this horrible ordeal had started. there was an open path and all she had to do was walk along it. If things became unbearable, she could always kill herself.

Chapter Twelve

Amanda Baker was a scion of old Pasadena society. In her mid-fifties now, she still bore traces of the sparkling beauty that had attracted three husbands and countless lovers. Vivacious and gay, an unscarred veteran of two divorces and widowhood, she gained a reputation as a Patron of the Arts. In fact, she was a woman with talent only for entertaining, and she used it to collect artists of all types with the pride and greed of a true connoisseur.

When Terence Jones arrived, she swept through the crowded room, took his arm and lifted her cheek for a perfunctory kiss.

'Darling, I'm so glad you could make it,' she said. 'I was afraid you wouldn't come.'

'I was detained. I apologise,' he said, adding gallantly, 'I wouldn't miss one of your parties for the world.'

They had met two years earlier and she still considered him one of her prize catches. Although she preferred to recognise and nurture talent when it was still young and fresh and, of course, relatively undiscovered, he was, after all, a major novelist whose every book latched onto the *New York Times* bestseller lists like a leech.

'I have some fascinating people who are dying to meet you,' she said. 'What would you like to drink?' She crooked a finger as she spoke and a waiter appeared at her shoulder.

'A white wine would be fine,' Jones said.

He glanced quickly around the room. It was the usual assortment. The wealthy, the once-wealthy and those hoping to one day be wealthy. Amanda believed in mixing people like some people mixed explosives. If the ingredients were volatile enough, the results would never be boring and sometimes even detonate interesting conflagrations.

Boredom and age were her two constant foes. Most people, including Jones, admired her for the way she dealt with them. She took their admiration as her due.

'Have you been writing?' she asked.

'My fingers are worn to the bones,' he said.

'You do look a little peaked, dear,' she said solicitously. 'You really should take time off more often. God knows you can afford it.'

'I'm afraid I'm driven to work by more compelling demons than money,' he replied.

'The muse never sleeps,' she said understandingly

The waiter brought the wine and she handed the glass to him. 'Come and I will introduce you to a brilliant young artist. His work is filled with spiritual energy. In fact, I recommend you buy his paintings now. In a year, their prices will have tripled.'

Jones smiled as he followed her to the other side of the room. Outwardly altruistic, Amanda still managed to profit from her relationships. It ran in her family. Although her father ran a perfectly respectable pharmaceutical company, a little research had uncovered the amusing fact that her grandfather and father before him, had been little more than travelling pedlars, selling balms and elixirs to gullible farmers up and down the West Coast. The grandfather had amassed enough

177

money to enter the field of real pharmaceuticals.

'This is Eldo,' she said with a triumphant gesture at a pink-faced young man. 'Eldo, this is the famous writer, Terence W. Jones.'

Eldo was in his mid-twenties. He had long hair, a scraggly beard and a pugnacious tilt to his chin. He was surrounded by a knot of admirers. When Jones shook hands with him, the painter said, 'I haven't read any of your books. I'm afraid I consider literature a dead art form.'

Jones shrugged. 'I haven't seen any of your paintings. But I have heard they may be a dead art form as well.'

Amanda clapped her hands in delight. 'Oh, I knew it would be fascinating when you two met each other.'

'What kind of books do you write, Mr Jones?' the painter asked.

'Historical novels,' Jones said.

'The present doesn't interest you?'

'Not as much as the past, particularly at this moment,' Jones said unkindly.

He wished he hadn't come, but appearances were important now. He had promised months earlier to attend and his absence would have created unwanted speculation.

'Oh, excuse me,' Amanda said, and deserted him.

'I've read your books and I enjoyed them immensely,' a woman said, touching his hand.

'Thank you,' he said with a small bow. 'And you are?'

'Janet Desmond.'

She was in her late thirties and wore a gown that half-heartedly covered her breasts and dipped from her shoulders to reveal a long and shapely brown back. Her mouth was dissatisfied and her eyes bored, but she was without doubt a beautiful woman.

Jones shook her hand graciously. She held it a

178

moment longer than necessary and said, 'My husband is Gary Desmond. He's in canned foods.'

Of course,' Jones said. 'Amanda has spoken of you.'

'My husband is in Europe at present,' she added unnecessarily.

'Oh, how unfortunate,' he said.

A carnivorous glint entered her eyes. 'You don't know my husband,' she said.

Jones knew he could have her if he wanted to. Bored and jaded, she was the type who drifted from affair to affair, hoping for something new. He met these women all the time. As a celebrity of sorts, he found that unhappy women threw themselves at him, hoping some of the glow would rub off on them. He despised people like that, but took advantage of them when he wished. Why not? They demanded it.

He despised most of the people who attended Amanda's parties, he thought, as he circulated further. Soft, rich and unproductive, generally unhappy, they were frivolous wastrels, all of them. They thought themselves the cream of society, but they were little more than parasites.

Amanda dragged him to another group and then another. An overweight, elderly woman with sharp grey eyes said she had never met a writer before. She wore a diamond necklace worth six figures. Her name was Butler and her husband, she said, was a lawyer.

'I've read your novels, of course,' she said, 'but I've never read anything about you. There's never any information on the fly-leaf, no picture, no biographical details, and you never give interviews. Why is that?'

'I prefer to let my books speak for themselves,' he said glibly. 'There are more than enough publicity hounds without adding to their numbers. Besides, I prefer to keep my private and public lives on different pages, so to speak.'

179

She looked at him shrewdly and said, 'Such modesty could be grounded in arrogance, couldn't it?'

Bitch, he thought, but said, 'Arrogance is a vital quality for a writer. How else could he expect people to want to read the scribbles of his puerile imagination?'

She laughed and threw her head back unselfconsciously, showing the folds of skin on her neck. 'Come now,' she said, 'isn't that merely another pose. You don't consider your imagination puerile, do you?'

'It's what my readers consider that is important,' he said.

'Are you always this self-effacing?' she asked.

'Excuse me,' he said, 'I need another wine.'

He walked across the room, fuming. He hated people like that bitch. They thought of themselves as perceptive, but they spoke directly from the pages of some women's magazine. Amateur psychologists. Besides, he couldn't help it if he sometimes sounded pompous. If she were truly perceptive she would sense his underlying sensitivity.

Amanda intercepted him before he reached the bar. 'Darling! How goes the hypnotic regression?'

It was she who had sparked his interest in the subject. She had told him about it one night over dinner and even recommended a hypnotist. She enthusiastically claimed that her awareness of her past lives had changed the present.

'I didn't do it,' he said. 'I decided it wasn't for me.'

'Oh, dear, how disappointing,' she said. 'Do you know what I found out last week? I was a peasant in Russia in 1850. I did the laundry for aristocrats in St Petersburg. It's given me an entirely new sense of humility.'

'Humility has never been one of your vices,' he said.

'Naughty boy,' she said, batting her hand at him. 'I do

180

wish you'd see the person I told you about. You could learn all sorts of things about yourself.'

'I'll think about it again,' he said.

He finally sequestered his wine and stood near a corner, isolated from the crowd. Thank God he hadn't used her hypnotist or told her of his experiences, he thought. It would have been all over town by now.

He found himself wishing that Samantha Barry – no Lela – was with him. He would be the centre of admiration. Her beauty and her status would have ensured it. Unfortunately, events were proceeding more slowly than he had expected. Originally, he thought that simply by meeting him, the floodgates of memory would have opened for her. How could one forget feelings of such depth? Decorating the entire house in the Twenties décor should have helped as well. Not to worry, he had many other avenues to explore.

'A penny for your thoughts.'

He turned to face the beautiful Mrs Desmond.

'You are very generous,' he said ironically.

'They aren't worth that much?' she asked.

'It's a subjective matter.'

'Are you enjoying the party?' she asked, obliquely surveying the room. 'I'm terribly bored.'

'It's not one of Amanda's best efforts,' he conceded.

'Perhaps we should leave,' she suggested, turning to look at him.

She had slate-grey eyes, yet try as he did, he could read nothing in them. Were they truly vacant, or just hidden, he wondered? It didn't matter. The invitation was in her sullen and waiting mouth, not her eyes. And it was a beautiful mouth, loose-lipped and full, a mouth of promise.

Why not? he found himself thinking. Lela was a long-term project, relatively speaking. Better he should indulge these physical urges now than risk a moment of inconvenient timing with her. This would only be a meaningless substitute, of course, and it would do nothing to erode the depth of his feelings for Lela.

'May I take you home?' he asked, summoning a smile.

'Indeed,' she said.

He drove and for the first part of the journey she sidled against the passenger door and watched him, occasionally giving directions.

A mile from her home in the Glendale hills she moved closer to him and casually placed her hand on his crotch. He jumped as if shocked.

'I didn't mean to frighten you,' she said, rubbing her hand in slow circles.

'You didn't,' he said thickly, his penis hardening even as he spoke.

It was what he needed, he thought. A good, casual, meaningless roll in the sack. Having Lela in his house as an honoured guest was too much to bear. He had found himself dwelling on the times they had made love, imagining what it would be like now. The success of his strategy depended upon restraint. Better he indulge himself now and face her without these impulses. Janet Desmond would be an enjoyable surrogate.

'The servants have the evening off,' she said as she let him into the house.

It was expensive and tasteless, just as he expected. Impressionists and modernists sat side by side on the walls. The furniture was trendy and dominated by chrome and leather.

'Would you like a drink?' she asked.

'A whiskey,' he said.

She brought the drinks to the couch and sat, patting the cushion beside her. He sat obediently and took the glass she handed him.

182

'To adventures,' she said, clinking her glass against his.

'What kind of adventures do you like?' he asked. Such trite and predictable conversation. He swallowed his revulsion.

'The pleasurable kind,' she said. 'And you?'

'We have that in common,' he said.

She threw back her head and swallowed her drink. After placing the glass on the table with all the care that accompanied intoxication, she looked at him through half-closed eyes.

'Make love to me,' she said.

'Here?'

She slipped the straps from her shoulder and pushed her dress down to her waist. Her large brown nipples were hard already.

He leaned forward slightly and found his mouth clasping one of them. He rasped his teeth across it and heard her breathe sharply in response.

'I want you to do exactly what I tell you,' she said urgently, pushing her dress down below her hips.

'No,' he said, resisting. Damned if he'd let her control him.

'Yes,' she said. 'We'll play a game. You'll like it, I promise. Yes.'

He pushed her away and stood, removing his clothes while she watched.

When he was naked he allowed her to touch him. He felt her hands and then her mouth. She drew away, gasping. 'Turnabout is fair play,' she said, pulling him down.

'No,' he said.

She tugged harder. 'I want you now,' she said. 'Come on, lover.'

He lashed out with his hand and slapped her cheek.

183

Her eyes were shocked at first, but then they softened.

'You're a slut,' he said.

She looked up at him and smiled. It was a smile of agreement, of recognition. 'I knew you were right for me,' she said.

He stared back at her, disgust mounting. Lela was waiting for him at home, but meanwhile this would have to do.

'You are worthless scum,' he said. 'Slut, bitch. I'm going to make you scream for mercy.'

She smiled up at him with vacant delight. 'Come on,' she said, anticipation glazing her face. 'Do what you want, lover. You want to do everything, don't you? You want me so badly, it aches, don't you?'

He threw himself down on her with a groan of humiliation. He wanted her. Yes, he wanted her. He would use her and when he was done with her he would throw her aside.

They started in the living room and ended in the bedroom upstairs. She was everything he needed: demanding, inventive, an unscrupulous lover. She performed mindlessly, intent only upon pleasure. She was also loud and appreciative.

After two hours, he began to dress. She watched him from the bed, naked and indolent, leaning on her elbow.

'You're a cold fish,' she stated.

'Was I unsatisfactory?' he asked.

She smiled at that. 'No, you were perfect. I wasn't looking for deep emotions.'

'Neither was I,' he said.

'Yes, that was obvious.'

'You're a substitute,' he said callously. 'A machine. Little more than an animal.'

She showed no shock, but just stared blandly at him. 'A substitute for what?' she asked. 'True love?'

184

'What would you know of love?' he asked cuttingly. 'Your type is interested only in themselves, their own gratification. Love demands more.'

'Like what?' she asked.

'Some love lasts for lifetimes. I'm talking of reincarnated souls – something a person at your level of awareness wouldn't understand. But real love transcends even death. There's nothing fickle or transitory about it. It demands true faithfulness. It's selfless in its virtue.'

'Funny,' she said. 'You seem to be one of the least selfless people I've ever met. You're infatuated with yourself. You may pretend otherwise, but nobody matters to you as much as you do.'

He walked back to the bed and slowly bent towards her. He reached his hand out and caressed her throat. His fingers began to tighten around the soft skin and for the first time fear crossed her face.

'You know nothing,' he said, pushing her so that she fell.

Her eyes glinted with excitement. 'Must you leave?' she asked.

'Yes.'

'Perhaps some afternoon? I have a friend, a woman. Would you like to join us?'

'You are despicable,' he said, and walked from the room.

He was angry at himself as he drove away. He had degraded himself with that woman. Lela deserved purity from him. He shouldn't have succumbed to those physical temptations like some horny adolescent. He could have restrained himself for a few more days.

The first time again with Lela would be wonderful, he knew. A candlelight dinner, soft music and then he would carry her upstairs to the large bedroom. Their lovemaking would be both tender and passionate,

185

totally unlike the animalistic gropings of the past hours.

When they had first met, soon after she arrived in Los Angeles, he had been surprised by her inexperience. Lela had only been with two or three men before, she told him. In fact, at the time, he had been both afraid and delighted by her confession. He, of course, was extremely experienced. His sexual adventures began with the maids on his father's estate. Knowing and anxious to serve, they were only too pleased to assist his extra-curricular education. From that point, they progressed in degrees of sophistication with women of his own class, not to mention his young and desirable stepmother.

He had been afraid of Lela's inexperience because of the challenge it involved. What if he failed to please her? Or if she was one of those women who took no pleasure in sex – a holdover from an earlier era? On the other hand, he was pleased because it provided him with an opportunity to mold her into the woman of his desires.

As it turned out, she had no revulsion of sex. She was a healthy young woman and eager to learn. She gave pleasure willingly and enjoyed receiving it. Their lovemaking had been supremely satisfactory by all accounts.

When she left him – Jones' hands tightened on the steering wheel at the thought of it – when she left, she had been a different woman, a woman experienced in the arts of love. He had invested in her, and another man had gained the interest. Everything he taught her was denied him and given to an opportunistic stranger. It had been most unfair.

The headlights of a passing car swept like a searchlight across his face. His lips were tightly compressed and a pulse beat against the side of his temple.

She should never have done that. He never suspected her of ungratefulness, not all the time they were

186

together. My God, he had given her everything! Above all, he gave her his love, something he previously denied all women. And she had chewed it up and spat it back at him. How could he be blamed for reacting as he had? He was no saint. It was too much to ask of any man.

He reached his house, pressed the remote control button in his car to open the gates and drove down the long drive. The light in her bedroom was off. The only glow came from the front hall.

When he stepped out of the car, a pain shot across his head. He lifted a hand and rubbed it away before entering the house.

He stood in the hall and listened. All was well. The only sound came from the large grandfather clock.

It would be different this time, very different. No betrayals, no unrequited love. They would rediscover each other. Perhaps it would take time, but she would learn to love him again. This time they would not be cheated of the joy that was promised them.

He walked upstairs and stopped before her door. He reached out with his hand and quietly turned the handle. The handle turned, but the door didn't open. He pushed again. She had barricaded the door!

For a moment he thought of smashing it down with his shoulder, but restrained himself. Patience, he told himself. All things would come in time. They were meant for each other, he and Lela, and nothing could change that. Fate could not be disputed. Events would march to their conclusion, regardless of the wishes of the players in the games. It was one thing he had learned during the recent exploration of his lives.

'She will learn to love me again,' he murmured aloud.

And this time she would stay with him forever.

Chapter Thirteen

'I've called the police three times a day,' Maddy said. 'The lieutenant finally suggested I talk to you. He said you know as much as they do.'

'I've been bugging him as well,' Nemo said. 'He must be getting sick of us.'

They ate lunch in a small Japanese restaurant on a sidestreet near Little Tokyo, after Maddy called and asked to meet.

'So what do you know?' Maddy asked.

'Not much, really. But I've reached a few conclusions about our mystery man,' Nemo said. 'And I know who Lela was.'

He told her what he had discovered so far, carefully neglecting to mention his more subjective experiences. Maddy would laugh him out of the room if he admitted that he too remembered his past life.

'So you think that this guy thinks that he was the Terry Jones who murdered Lela – who? – Edwards?' she asked, incredulity in her eyes.

'It seems that way.'

'Maybe he thinks he was the other guy, the guy that was killed with her.'

'Phillip Bates?'

188

Maddy nodded. 'Why not?'

'Because of the initial "T" that he used. T for Terry,' Nemo said, wishing he could openly say, 'because I was Bates.'

But it wasn't necessary because Maddy nodded. 'I guess it makes sense. In a weird way. God, the guy's over the edge, isn't he?'

Nemo picked up a piece of shrimp tempura with his fingers and bit into it.

'You told the police this theory?' Maddy asked.

'Yeah, I told Marshall.'

'Oh, he must have loved it,' she said sarcastically. 'Is he doing anything about it?'

'Maybe. He says he's going to check with hypnotists and people who might have had the man as a client. It's a long shot.'

'Is there anything I can do to help?' Maddy asked. 'I feel so stupid. All I can do is try to keep the business going while Sam is God knows where enduring God knows what.'

Maddy looked as if she'd endured heavy weather as well. The dark rings under her eyes hadn't been there a couple of days before and her hands fiddled constantly as she talked.

'I'll let you know if I think of something,' Nemo said. 'In the meantime, I'm sure Sam would want you to do just what you're doing.'

Maddy beat a rhythm on the table with her chopsticks and then put them down. 'Nemo . . .' she began uncertainly.

'Yes?'

'Do you think that . . . that Sam is, well, you know?'

He chose the positive side of her question. 'Alive? Yes, I'm certain she is. Absolutely.'

'How can you be so sure?' she asked miserably.

189

'It's just something I know,' he said. 'I realise that's not much consolation, but trust me on it. Sam's alive.'

'I hope you're right. I can't help but think she may not be. Who knows how crazy this guy is or what he has in mind.'

'She's alive,' he said emphatically.

'Let's call Marshall now and see if he's come up with anything,' Maddy suggested.

'Sure,' Nemo said. 'I'll do it now.'

There was a call box at the end of the room. He dialled Marshall's number and asked to speak to the lieutenant.

'No, nothing new,' Marshall said in response to his question. 'I have a couple of men checking on the hypnotist thing, but they've come up dry so far. We also have a police artist down at the florist shop you told us about. See if we can come up with a composite drawing of the guy. Anything new on your end? No further contact?'

'You should know,' Nemo said.

Nemo had called him the previous day, right after the phone call from 'T.' Marshall had insisted upon putting an immediate tap on his line. It was now in place.

'I mean other than by phone,' Marshall said.

'Nothing.'

As he walked back to the table, something the policeman said nudged Nemo's memory. He sat down and then slapped his hand on the formica top. 'Drawing!' he said.

Maddy asked what he was talking about.

'When Sam realised she'd seen this guy at the airport, I asked her to try and do a sketch,' Nemo said. 'She said later that she tried but it didn't work. Maybe there's something around though, some record of her attempts that would help. The police are trying to do a composite.'

190

'Would she have done it at the office or at home?' Maddy asked.

'Probably the office.'

'There's a small studio off her office where she does some design work,' Maddy said. 'If she did something and trashcanned it, it's gone. The janitorial people would have taken it.'

'Let's go and look,' Nemo said.

They returned to the offices of Sam Barry, Inc., without finishing their meal. Maddy led him into the small room Sam used for design work and they began to search through the drawing pads.

Maddy found it. 'Here,' she said, an open newsprint pad in front of her.

Three quick sketches of a man's angular face filled the page. Each one looked different.

'Recognise any of them?' Nemo asked.

'From the airport? I never saw him. They're all different. No wonder she gave up. How could that help?'

'I don't know, but let me call Marshall. Maybe by putting this together with the composite they can come up with something a little more substantial.'

Marshall seemed mildly interested when Nemo told his story, which Nemo figured was about as interested as he ever got. The detective asked him to take the drawings to the florist where the police artist was and show them to him and the witnesses. 'Maybe something will come of it,' he said dubiously. 'My experience with composites though is that they hinder more than they help. Give people a wrong idea and turn up more false leads than good ones.'

Nemo arrived at the florists shop to discover that Marshall had already called ahead. The artist, a plump red-faced little man, held the pad up to the elderly lady who had served T.

'I'm terrible with faces,' she said apologetically.

She looked at them and then pointed to the one on the right. 'I think that's closest.' Then she moved her finger to the one on the left. 'No . . . Maybe this one.'

The artist pulled a wry face and said, 'Make up your mind, lady.'

'The one on the right,' she said.

The artist turned to Nemo and shook his head. 'I wouldn't hold your breath on this, pal,' he said.

'Well, I'll call your boss later and see what you've got,' Nemo said.

It looked like another useless lead, Nemo thought as he wound his way through the lunchtime crowd. Smiling people, eating, shopping, gossiping, chattering away to each other as if all was well with the world. Sam was suffering somewhere, terrified, maybe even hurt. And he was getting nowhere.

Instead of going directly home, Nemo stopped at his office for a couple of hours. Although he'd delegated most of his caseload to others, there were still cases to review and papers to sign. He attacked his tasks half-heartedly and finally gave up. His heart just wasn't in it.

As he left, his secretary handed him a manila envelope.

'The research you wanted,' she said.

'Research?'

'On Phillip Bates.'

He'd completely forgotten the call he'd made asking her to research Bates.

When he reached home, he took the envelope with him to the kitchen and put water on for coffee. While it heated, he opened the envelope. They'd come up with only two pages of typewritten information and he scanned through it quickly.

The essentials came down to: Phillip Bates, born Philadelphia, 1892, son of Angus Bates, banker of Bates & Idler; studied law and graduated from Harvard in 1915. Worked for the law firm of Jackson and Devereaux in Philadelphia, opened the West Coast branch of the firm in 1922, murdered in 1923. A brilliant career cut short.

Well, that does it, he thought. The last doubt dispelled. The data matched his memory perfectly. He had been Phillip Bates. There was no other explanation.

Curiously, the information did little to bolster his spirits. The problem was, in spite of his initial incredulity, he had already grown used to the idea of being Bates. It was amazing how easily he accepted the data once he jumped the gap between disbelief and acceptance. The question now was, how could he use his knowledge to help Sam? What more could he do?

He called Lieutenant Marshall.

'Any luck with the drawing?' he asked when the policeman came on the line.

'I don't think so,' Marshall said. 'The woman was so uncertain, it may be way off.' His voice grew cynical. 'I'm going to release it to the Press though. Not because I want to, and not because I think it's a good idea, and not because I think it will help, but because my seniors have told me to.'

'Signs of progress for the media,' Nemo said.

'Right. We have nothing else to show for our efforts, there's a lot of external pressure, and the chief is getting impatient. It doesn't make him look good, you know.'

'What about the past life angle? You haven't turned anything up?'

'Nothing. And I don't have the manpower to question every freak in LA. I'm letting it drop,' Marshall said.

'But it's all you have!' Nemo protested.

'It's a wild theory,' Marshall said, sounding tired. 'It's not going to lead anywhere.'

193

'You can't just drop it,' Nemo said. 'It's the key to the guy's motivation. I know it.'

'Maybe. But I don't think it'll lead us to him. Anyway, when that picture appears in the *Times* tomorrow morning, we're going to have our hands full of people claiming they know the suspect. Wives saying it's their husbands, shopkeepers saying it was a customer, little old ladies claiming it's their landlord.'

'Well, if it's such a waste of time, why not concentrate on the past life angle and keep interviewing these people?'

'Because that's not what my boss wants me to do,' Marshall said. 'Listen, I got to go. I'll call you if we come up with anything.'

Nemo was furious. The police were ignoring the only valid lead they had. Yes, it was a long shot and yes, it was difficult, but it did present a chance. Nothing else did, as far as he could see.

Well, the hell with them. He wasn't going to stand by doing nothing.

He opened the telephone book and found the number of the *Los Angeles Times* editorial department.

'Mr Phil Stinger please.'

When Stinger came on the line, he said, 'This is Nemo Riley. You interviewed me on the Sam Barry story.'

'Yeah, I remember. What can I do for you?' Stinger asked.

'You're going to be getting a composite of a suspect from the police department,' Nemo said. 'I have a story for you to go along with it.'

'What kind of story?' Stinger asked with interest.

'Come out over to my house and I'll tell you all about it,' Nemo said.

*　　　*　　　*

194

'You expect me to print this?' Stinger said. 'It's too far out, not to mention nuts!'

Nemo waved at the papers on the dining room table. 'We're dealing with a guy who *is* nuts,' he said persuasively. 'There's the documentation. He thinks that he was this guy in a past life and thinks that Sam Barry was this model. I'm not saying it's sane, I'm just saying it is how it is.'

'And the cops actually started to follow this up?'

'Until the heat came from upstairs. And you can quote me on that. Say I got it from a source in the LAPD. That they're putting out a practically useless composite just to look as if they're making progress,' Nemo said.

'It's too weird,' Stinger said.

'It's good copy,' Nemo said. 'Suspect thinks he was honeymoon killer in past life. Come on. It's a great story. I'm giving it to you first. But if you don't want it, I'll guarantee the TV stations will eat it up.'

Stinger couldn't help smiling at the thought of the headline. 'It's unusual,' he admitted. He looked up at Nemo. 'Why are you doing this?'

'Nothing else is happening,' Nemo said. 'This might at least turn something up or bring someone forward, someone who knows this guy, maybe even someone who's been involved with him on a professional basis in this past life stuff. The police won't do it. Too many weirdos, they say. Not to mention the fact that it'll make them look flakey. I don't give a shit.'

'Yeah,' Stinger said.

'Run it by your news editor,' Nemo said. 'He can only say no.'

'And ask me what I've been smoking,' Stinger said. He shuffled through the papers on the table again. Then he pulled a notebook from his pocket. 'All right, give me all the details again. We'll give it a shot.'

195

'Great!' Nemo said, and added deviously. 'Call me if you're not going to run the story though. I'll give it to Channel Seven.'

Stinger made up his mind. 'We'll use it,' he said. 'In some form or another, we'll use it.'

Nemo rubbed his hands together after the reporter left. He was doing something and he felt better for it. He was taking the action to T. now, splashing his bizarre behaviour all over the media. It would be up to the man to react. As a basically irrational person, he would react in an irrational way, Nemo hoped.

As long as he didn't react against Sam. That was the only danger, and one that Nemo had gone over and over in his mind. It was a risk, but a calculated one. He was betting that T. would do something stupid, that evidence of his insanity – which is surely how the media would portray it – would force the man to justify his behaviour in some way. No person likes to be called insane, not even a crazy man.

Nemo poured himself a drink and strolled out to the back patio. The stillness of dusk hung in the air now, interrupted only by the shrill cries of straggling birds and the odd automobile passing on the street. Dying streaks of magenta coloured the western sky.

Peaceful, he thought, but I am not at peace. He could see Sam's house through the hedge to his left. Empty, but for the footsteps of an aged housekeeper. What else could he do?

If the actions of the present created the future then the secrets of the past held the key to predictability. If only he could unlock them. There had to be something that happened back then to give him a clue as to what was happening now.

He leaned back in the deck chair and closed his eyes, willing himself to remember. A picture formed vaguely

196

in the distance and then moved closer and closer, gaining in clarity and brightness . . .

. . . and they were in Phillip's house in a canyon off Franklin Boulevard. Lela had just driven up and entered the living room where he was sitting. She was agitated, wringing her hands.

'I'm afraid,' she said. She stood in front of the fireplace and looked down at him. 'He's off his rocker and dangerous.'

'Suppose you tell me what happened,' he said.

'He's still following me. Every time I look back I see him, like some shadow I can't get rid of.'

'Has he approached you?'

She nodded. 'Today. I came out of my agent's office on Sunset and there he was, on the sidewalk. He held flowers in his hand and pushed them out at me. It was pitiful, Phillip.'

'So what did he say?'

'He said, "I wanted you to have these," and pushed them at me. I told him I didn't want them, that it was time for him to realise that it was over, that he had to stop following me and that I loved you. He just stared at me while I spoke, a silly grin on his face. It was scary. It was like he was looking at something else, all the time I was talking.'

Phillip rose from the couch. He took her in his arms and hugged her.

'I wouldn't worry about him,' he consoled. 'After all, he thinks of himself as an actor. He's just playing the part of the jilted lover.'

She drew back and looked at him, fear in her eyes. 'No,' she said. 'Don't underestimate him. He's crazy, Phillip. You know what he said when I wouldn't take the flowers? He said, "I'll put them on your grave." He just stood there, the smile vanishing from his lips, his voice sweet, the moonstruck expression still in his eyes and said that. It scared me, Phillip.'

'He's just talking, just trying to scare you, that's all. Don't play into his hands.'

'Well, if that's what he wanted to do, he succeeded.'

'Come on, Lela, I'm not going to let anything happen to you. In a few days you'll be my wife. We'll be married and that's something he won't be able to ignore.'

'You don't know him like I do,' she said.

He could feel a quiver run through her body. Whether her fear had any basis in reality or not, it was real enough now.

'If he bothers you again, I'll call in the police,' he said. 'We'll put a stop to it. Now, come on, let me pour you a drink.'

He felt her slowly relax in his arms and kissed her then.

'I'm sorry,' she said. 'It's just that I've never been so happy before. I don't want anything to spoil it.'

'Nothing will,' he said . . .

Famous last words, Nemo thought bitterly. He knew what happened then. It was sitting right there in his mind . . .

. . . been a wonderful day. In fact, as he walked up the hill from the beach, water still dripping from his hair, he thought it had been an altogether splendid week. First, Phillip finally landed Louis B. Mayer as a client, a *coup* that would bring at least $100,000 a year to his company. Like all the studio heads, Mayer had been a tough nut to crack. If Phillip's company didn't perform for him as promised, he'd drop them like a hot potato. But they would perform, and Phillip foresaw a long and profitable relationship.

Then came the wedding. Beside it, everything else paled. Originally, they wanted a small wedding, far from

198

the glare of publicity. But once Lela began to prepare the guest list, it became obvious that they had a major social event on their hands. Close to two hundred luminaries from the entertainment and business worlds, representatives of both families, and a circle of close friends attended. It was a joyous event.

They planned to spend their honeymoon on Santa Catalina Island, one of the more popular resorts of the time. Soon after the reception began, they were driven to the harbour, and sailed across to the island in a private yacht provided by Mayer himself.

The house, provided by another friend, was delightful. A small but elegantly furnished Victorian above the town with a view of the ocean. In fact, it had all been delightful. Dinner at the Casino, the wedding night, and the morning after.

Finally, however, Lela pleaded exhaustion. While she slept, he went down to the ocean for a swim. He gave her plenty of time to nap, stopping off for a drink at a small corner bar before returning.

He opened the front door and called her name. Poked his head into the living room. She must be upstairs, he thought.

Halfway up the staircase, he noticed the first ominous signs. Blood streaked the walls. He stopped and looked, seeing but not understanding. Giant smears, handprints – as if someone had tried to hold onto the flat surface and been dragged along.

What the . . .

'Lela!' he screamed, and began to run up the stairs, taking them three and four at a time, the blood pounding so hard in his head it almost blinded him.

The bedroom door was open, as if to let in the trail of blood he was following.

'No!' he screamed, skidding to a stop, just inside the doorway.

199

She lay on the bed in a pool of crimson, still and white and dead.

Slowly he moved closer.

Wounds blotted her arms and chest. Gashes, punctures, deranged cuts and stabs.

'Oh, my God!' he said, falling to his knees beside the bed, unable to stand, barely able to see through the mist that covered his vision. 'Oh, no! Oh, no! Oh, my God!'

He touched her still warm cheek and willed her eyes to open. 'Lela,' he said. 'Lela, I'm home.'

He was sobbing then. Oceans of grief choked him and pained his throat.

'Oh, no!' he said again.

Who could have done this? What madman would have done this to beautiful Lela? Terrified her, deformed her, murdered her.

And then he felt the sharp prick of steel against his neck.

'Don't move,' said the voice. 'All right. Slowly now. Turn your head.'

He turned to see Terry Jones, blood on his face and hands and clothes, his eyes filled with a manic brightness, his mouth twitching, just a foot or two away.

Jones held the knife against his throat, his arm outstretched.

'You made me do it,' Jones said. 'It's all your fault. You took her from me, turned her against me. We loved each other and you ruined it. You destroyed our lives.'

'You killed her,' Phillip said, his voice a whisper, a hate filling his being.

'You made me. I couldn't let you have her,' Jones said. 'Nobody will have her now.'

And then the rage overpowered Phillip and he howled his agony at the brutality and unfairness of the world and reached out with his hands for the neck of the animal

200

who had taken the woman he loved. And he felt the knife enter his neck.

Still, he reached Jones and put his hands around his neck and began to throttle him with all the strength at his disposal, seeing the man's face grow purple and his eyes bulge, and feeling the knife pull free of his neck and enter his chest again and again.

He ignored the burning pain and the bubbling blood in his throat, intent only on his task of murder.

But then he saw the redness fade from his victim's face and saw the eyes grow normal and realised that his hands had lost their strength and were limp around Jones' neck now, and that everything was beginning to fade like a receding picture and that in a few minutes he too would be dead, as dead as his sweetheart, dead on the bed behind him.

The picture grew red and then grey and finally a blinding white covered everything and he sighed and gave it up, falling back to lie across the woman he loved . . .

Nemo felt an emptiness so vast he could not move in it. He sat frozen in a core of nothing while twilight faded into darkness. And then came a grief that was past the point of tears, and still he sat. Finally, he reached a bitter anger.

'Come on, Lela, I won't let anything happen to you.'

Wonderful.

He had spoken those words more than sixty years before.

Just a few days ago he had sat on the bed behind Sam. He had finally found her again after half a century. What had he said? 'I love you, Sam. I'm not going to let anything happen to you.'

Patterns.

Were they doomed to repeat themselves through

eternity? Had this happened to them before even, before the Twenties? Had it happened again and again through the centuries?

'No!' he cried, finally breaking free of the spell of emotion that held him. 'No!'

They weren't helpless puppets, doomed to travel in circles, ignorant of where they had been or where they were going. He knew now. He remembered. He wasn't a prisoner of the past. Somehow he would learn from it and free himself and create the future they wanted. He would find a way.

It had been a warm day, but now a surprising chill filled the air. At the far end of the garden, a bird cried once and then fell silent. Nemo left his half-finished drink on the ground beside the chair and went into the house.

Chapter Fourteen

For a wild moment that morning Sam couldn't remember how many days she had been held in this house. It scared her because she knew that loss of time sense would be the first loss of reality and, above all, she had to maintain reality. The confusion lasted only a few moments though, and then she realised with some relief that this was the fourth morning.

The woman, unsmiling and silent, brought her breakfast. After eating, Sam did her exercises. Then, hot and sweating, she put the chair back against the door and took a shower.

There was a tendency not to do her hair, not to put on make-up, for there seemed no point, but she forced herself. It was the pointless everyday things that anchored her in the reality she needed.

She sat in front of the dresser and carefully applied make-up. The paleness of her skin and the shadowed marks around her eyes gave her face a haunted appearance. She had not slept well and suspected that if the ordeal continued for much longer, she would look like a concentration camp survivor. If, of course, she survived.

Jones came for her at lunchtime. He greeted her cheerfully and took her arm as they walked downstairs.

His loafers, brown slacks and grey Kashmir sweater, were dapper enough for a garden party. But she noticed signs of tiredness around his eyes as well.

He went through his ritual of polite patter while they ate at the long table. She ached to ask him about Nemo, remembering the violent madness in his eyes when he spoke of him the day before. She was afraid that Jones had done something since then to Nemo, but she knew it was better not to mention Nemo, not ever again. Perhaps Jones would simply forget that he even existed.

'Do you remember the time we went to San Diego?' he said conversationally. 'We went there for the weekend and stayed at that wonderful old hotel, although for the life of me I can't remember the name now. We had champagne for breakfast and by mid-morning we were both so tight you pushed me into the pool with my clothes on. What a wag! Do you remember?'

'You know I remember nothing,' she said, sullen at his insistence.

He looked at her intently and said, 'Yes, I'm afraid that's true. Would you let me hypnotise you to help you remember?'

Sam almost laughed. Let him have power over her will? 'You've got to be kidding,' she said, and added, 'Anyway, I'm not a good hypnotic subject. Someone tried when I was younger and couldn't put me under.'

'Yes,' he said thoughtfully. 'Some people resist, just as you resist remembering. Well, we'll have to do something else, I suppose.'

'What do you mean?' she asked.

Jones shrugged cryptically. 'I don't know yet. But I'll think of something.' He put sugar in his coffee and said, 'You must remember soon, you know.'

'Operating on a strict timetable are you?' she asked

204

flippantly. 'Well, I'm sorry to screw it up for you.'

'My patience has its limits,' he said quietly, the menace evident beneath the casual tone.

She ignored it and said boldly. 'So has mine. When are you going to let me go?'

He smiled. 'Let you go? Our fate is tied together tighter than any rope could bind you. Don't you see that yet? We will always be together, Lela. It was meant to be, my dear.'

She had no defence against this talk. In her mind it was so insane, nothing rational could puncture the pose. She changed the subject instead.

'Do you think I could have some paper and a pen?' she asked. 'I have nothing to do. Perhaps I could draw or write.'

Jones hesitated, then nodded. 'Yes. That may not be a bad idea. Have you ever heard of unconscious writing? If you just let yourself go and write what comes into your mind, you might find yourself writing the truth.'

God spare me, she thought, and said, 'I just thought I'd do some drawings or keep a diary or something.'

'All right,' he said. 'I'll give you some utensils after lunch. Delicious salad, isn't it?'

When they finished eating, he took her into his study and gave her a pad of unlined paper, a ballpoint pen and a pencil. She waited for him to lead the way out of the room, but instead he sat at his desk and gestured at the armchair. 'Please sit,' he said, 'I must explain something to you.'

She sat almost primly on the edge of the chair, her back straight, the pad on her knees, and waited.

He stared out of the window for a moment and then swung his head back to face her. 'I told you at lunch that our fates are entwined,' he said. 'I want to show you how unavoidable this is. The decisions we make in past lives

205

are the backbone of the script we write today.

'After our life together, I was reborn in Germany,' he began, his tone matter-of-fact. 'I lived there, fought there, and was killed there in 1945, by Russians. It was an uneventful life, an hiatus after the loss of you.

'In this life, I was born in Poland. In Gdansk, a seaside city with a large harbour – its only redeeming feature. I was born in 1945, of course. My father was a worker in a factory, my mother was a schoolteacher. It was not an easy life, however. The Poles have never had an easy life.

'All the time I was growing up, I was driven by one desire: I wanted to come to America. I knew my destiny was there. My mother told me I had cousins who lived there. How I envied them! I would dream, day and night, of how to get there. To begin with, I begged my mother to teach me English and, secretly, she did.

'In 1957, when I was twelve years old, I stowed away on a British freighter going to Liverpool. I made the journey undiscovered and hungry. In Liverpool, I lived on the strccts for three weeks until an American ship docked and, once again, I stowed away.

'I was close to starvation by then and after two days at sea I could stand it no longer. Late that night I left my hiding place in the lifeboat and tried to reach the galley. I was caught by the third mate and taken to the captain.

'There is such a thing as luck. The captain was a Polish-American. Oh, he made me work while we were at sea, but he also arranged to get me through immigration and to my relatives in Boston. And so, in 1958, I arrived.

'Later, I became an American citizen. My name was Jozef Platek. Later, when I began to write, I used the pen-name Terence Jones. Why did I choose that? Because subconciously that is who I wanted to be again.

206

Interesting, isn't it? Before I even knew of my past life, I took my name back from that past life.'

Jones cocked his head to one side and pointed his finger at her. 'You see, all I wanted to do was find you again. All those years, over thousands of miles, you led me here.

'I knew my destiny was here in Los Angeles. I came to live here seven years ago. And all the time, I looked, although I didn't know what I was looking for.

'And then I found out about my past lives. And then came that remarkable day when I saw you and knew that I had found my destiny and reached the end of my journey.'

When he finished, Jones leaned forward on his elbows and waited, expecting her to say something. She said nothing, but just stared defiantly back at him.

'Don't you see the miracle of it?' he asked. 'How every step of that tortuous journey was meant to be and led to this very moment as we sit here in this room?'

'I see that you've had an interesting life,' she said finally. 'Things have happened, as they tend to do for everyone. The reasons that they happened though, lie only in your imagination.'

Jones shook his head sadly. 'Lela, you have become very prosaic in your incarnations, my dear. Things do not just happen on this earth. The seeds of all that happens lie in the past, and just as trees have no choice but to grow upwards from their seeds, so we have no choice but to take the steps that lead us to the present.'

'I don't believe that,' she said flatly. 'We all have choices. It's what makes us human.'

Jones waved his hand. 'You still refuse to understand. That's one element of your character that hasn't changed – your stubbornness. You always were pig-headed. You're the type of person who would watch two stars travel through space for a million light years. You'd

207

see them dodge every obstacle thrown at them, and then when they finally met and collided, you'd call it an accident. There are no accidents in this universe. It's all planned.'

'I don't believe that,' she said. 'I believe in free will.'

'Then you are a fool,' he said.

Alone in her room Sam began to write.

He believes that everything is predetermined, that free will is an illusion, and this gives me a clue to his behaviour.

She put the pen down and walked to the window. Clouds scudded across the sky, bumping into each other like hurried commuters. The housekeeper appeared on the driveway, carrying an armful of flowers from the garden. Beyond her were the lawns and then the walls. Beyond that was freedom.

Might as well be a hundred miles, Sam thought.

She went back to the dresser, tore a sheet of paper from the pad and wrote: *My name is Sam Barry and I am being held against my will by the writer Terence Jones. I am in his house, but I do not know where it is. Please tell the police.*

Carefully, she folded the paper into quarters, wrote *Police* on the outside, and slipped it in her pocket. And then she waited.

Later in the afternoon, the housekeeper brought tea. Sam took the tray from her and smiled. The woman merely looked back on her, her old eyes without interest.

Sam pulled the paper from her pocket and pointed at it.

'Police,' she said. 'Give police.'

The old woman regarded her and the paper blankly.

What was his real name? 'Jozef, no, non,' she said, pointing at the paper and shaking her head. 'Police, yes.'

208

No response from the woman.

'Polizei,' Sam said. 'Polizei.'

The housekeeper reached out, her face expressionless, took the paper and put it in the pocket of her apron. She turned and left the room, locking the door behind her.

It was an outright gamble. Much depended upon who the woman really was and what her relationship was to Jones. If merely a servant who had been given some wild tale about Sam's presence, there was a chance the note would get somewhere. The problem was, she had no idea. For all she knew, the woman could be his mother.

In the evening, when Jones came to collect her for dinner, his face told her nothing. He greeted her pleasantly and took her arm as they walked downstairs.

Maybe, just maybe the housekeeper had kept the note, Sam thought hopefully.

But when she sat and looked down at her plate and saw the note sitting on her napkin, her heart fell.

'That was very foolish, Lela,' Jones said. 'She has been with me for many years, ever since she came from the old country, and would never do anything to harm me.'

She felt like weeping, but only a slight tremor in her chin showed it. She clenched her jaw and looked directly at him. 'I don't want to harm you either,' she said. 'I just want my freedom. I want to get out of this place and away from you.'

Jones poured red wine from a carafe and handed a glass to her. 'I'm very disappointed in you, Lela. Your lack of gratitude for my hospitality hurts me deeply.'

'Hospitality!' she snorted. 'I'm your prisoner and you know it.'

Jones shrugged. 'I thought that by now you would have come to terms with your situation, and recognised the realities.'

209

Sam felt an almost overpowering urge to scream, to throw plates at him, to attack him with her fork – anything to shatter this insidious façade of calm, rational, patient interest that cloaked his madness.

She clenched the edge of the table until her knuckles whitened and said, 'Never! That will never happen.'

Jones smiled and said, 'Drink your wine, Lela.'

She picked up the glass and threw the wine at him. It hit him in the face and dripped down, staining his white dinner shirt with red blotches.

He kept the smile fastened to his face. 'If it weren't so foolish, your spirit would be admirable,' he said. He picked up his napkin and dabbed at his face and shirt.

'This is not a book!' Sam shouted, not bothering to contain her anger. 'This is my life you're playing with. You talk like some character out of a goddamn book. When are you going to realise what you're doing?'

'I am perfectly conscious of it,' he said. 'You are the one who has to reach a realisation.'

'Oh, Jesus!' she said in frustration.

'Lela, I love you,' he said, his voice gentle. 'Your resistance is based upon fear, unfortunately a fear with some validity, but I would never hurt you again. You must believe that.'

'You've said that before,' she said. 'When did you hurt me? What do you mean?'

'I'll explain after dinner,' he said.

'I don't want to eat. I'm not hungry,' she said.

As she spoke, the housekeeper entered with the food. She looked at Sam with the same bland disinterest as before, as if nothing had happened between them.

'All right,' Jones said. He spoke to the woman in what Lela knew of as Polish, and she left, carrying the food.

'Bring your wine,' Jones said. 'I have something for you to hear.'

He gestured for her to sit on the couch in the study. She chose the armchair.

He reached into a drawer of his desk and said, 'This is a recording of one of my hypnotic regression sessions. I think you should hear it.' He opened a cabinet and revealed a tape deck. After loading the cassette, he pressed the rewind button.

There was a perfunctory knock at the door and the housekeeper entered, carrying a tray.

'If you won't eat, at least have some coffee,' Jones said. He poured them each a cup and handed one to her. The woman left with the tray.

'Now listen,' he said, going back to the tape deck. There was a woman's voice: 'You are back with Lela now. You have gone to her house to talk with her. Now, what is happening?'

Although slightly slurred and soft, the next voice was unmistakably Jones': 'She is angry with me. She opens the door and stands there, just looking at me. And then she says, "What do you want?"

'"To talk with you. I just want to talk to you," I say.

'"I have nothing to say to you. But if you don't stop following me, we are going to inform the police," she says.

'I tell her I love her, that the man she is with is nothing and that he will betray her. She laughs at me and tells me she loves him and then I grow angry and grasp her by the shoulders and push her inside. I close the door behind me and see that she is afraid and tell her not to be afraid and that I will not harm her but that I am there to protect her.

'And then . . . and then . . .'

The sound of sobs interrupted the voice then. It was Jones. 'No,' he said. 'No, I can't.'

Sam looked at him. He sat behind the desk, his eyes

211

closed, the muscles in his jaw jumping with tension.

The woman's voice: 'Tell me what happens then.'

'No, no, no! I can't do it, I can't . . .' And then the agonising sobs again.

The woman's voice: 'All right. Take a deep breath . . . Good. Now relax . . . relax. Good. Now, when I click my fingers you will awaken feeling refreshed and relaxed. One, two, three!' And then there was the click of her fingers.

There was a pause, followed by an indecipherable noise on the tape.

Jones' voice: 'Oh, God!'

The woman: 'What?'

Jones: 'I remember it all, what happened.'

The woman: 'What happened?'

'We talked. I grew angry then and hit her, slapped her face with my open palm. My God, I hurt the woman I loved! And yet, somehow it seemed to make her see. I promised her I would never hurt her again and I told her how much I loved her and, finally, she came to see it. We made up. We kissed and then went upstairs and began to make love.

'Her boyfriend came into the room then. He was insane with jealousy.

'He was carrying a knife.

'He came at me first, stabbing me in the chest. I lay on the floor, too weak to move, and watched him murder her, stabbing her until she no longer breathed.

'It was a terrible experience. I tried to rise, to help, but I couldn't and, finally, I died.

'He cheated us. He killed us and killed our love. He murdered it all.'

And then the sobs began again.

Jones opened his eyes then, pushed his chair back and went to the cassette deck. He switched it off and turned

212

to face Sam. There were tears in his eyes.

'This is what happened,' he said. 'I tried to protect you and failed. I hit you and hurt you and then I failed you.'

Sam tried not to react, but couldn't suppress her feelings. The emotion, particularly in the first part of the tape, was undoubtedly genuine. She had lied when she said she never cried at movies. She always cried at movies and, in a way, listening to the tape was something like watching a movie.

She chose her words carefully. 'I can sympathise with your experience,' she said. 'I can understand your emotions. I won't even argue the validity of your beliefs with you. But there is something you must understand. I am not Lela. Never have been. I don't know who Lela is, or anything about her, or where she could be, if that's possible. But I'm not her and you must believe that.'

Jones rose and came around the desk. He kneeled on the floor beside her and said, 'I love you. You must believe that.'

His eyes were still misted, his voice choked with emotion.

'You may believe that,' she conceded, 'but I don't love you.'

'Drink your coffee,' he said.

She reached for her cup, thankful for something to do. She was confused, and couldn't understand why. She felt pulled from four directions.

She had already finished most of her cup and drained it now.

A bitterness that didn't fit. She knew then that she had been drugged.

She lay on the bed, her head resting on a pillow, her eyes heavy, her breathing slow.

213

By the soft light of an oil lamp, she saw Jones on the bed beside her. He sat upright, holding her hand, stroking her arm in soft, rhythmic motions from the elbow down.

'You are feeling tired,' he said. 'You are feeling sleepy. Your eyes are growing heavy. You are lying on a soft white cloud and feel relaxed and safe and peaceful. Your eyes are heavy and you cannot keep them open.'

It was so hard, she thought. So hard to resist. Waves lapped at her, one after the other, seducing her, calling her like sirens from the sea. It would be so easy to simply follow, to stop resisting and let the flow carry her along as nature intended.

No! She fought to open her eyes.

'Now, enjoy this relaxed feeling,' he said soothingly. 'Let the clouds carry you along. Let your eyes close. Let the weight press down on you and surrender.'

'You —' she said, her throat thick. 'You drugged me,' she forced out.

'You are floating now,' he said. 'There is a gentle, relaxing light all around you. There is nothing to fear. Your eyes are heavy.'

It would be so easy, she thought again. She could just flow down the river and see where it led. She could stop fighting and let it all happen.

He didn't want to hurt her. He loved her. He had always loved her, he claimed. Why doubt it? Why fight it? Sleep would come. Fear would leave. The terrible ordeal would end.

'Good,' he said. 'Now your eyes are closed. You feel at peace with the world. You feel relaxed and alert. You feel as if soft rain is falling on your face. As if you are surrounded by delicate clouds.'

Yes, she thought. It could feel so good. *What did he give me?* Why do I feel so passive? Listen to nothing.

214

Believe nothing – not from him, not from you. It's the voice of the drug you hear now. Close your ears. You're being tortured. You're being raped. Don't listen. Fight!

'And now you are completely relaxed, completely at ease. You feel at home. You trust me. You will now do as I say. You will –'

'NO!!!' It was a scream from her soul, from reserves she didn't know she had.

It reverberated around the room like a bouncing ball. It even scared her, but more importantly, it scared him and he bolted back as if struck.

She forced herself to sit, and made her eyes open, driven by the anger, the sense of violation. She lifted her arms and beat them against his chest.

'No! No! No! she said. 'Damn you! Fuck you! Animal! Rapist! Murderer!'

He bounded back then, leaving the bed and standing beside it, his fists clenched.

'What are you saying?' he asked.

She mustered her energy, made herself move and sit on the edge of the bed.

'Get out!' she said. 'Get out and leave me. Go! Go!'

She lifted her arm and pointed at the door. It felt as if a weight was tied to it, but she held it there through sheer will.

'Go!' she said again.

And, as if by miracle, he backed away towards the door.

She stood unsteadily beside the bed and shouted again, 'Go!'

And he left.

Staggering, weak, drained of resources, she stumbled to the chair and somehow dragged it to the door. She pushed it against the handle, locking him out, safe for the moment.

And fell.

Chapter Fifteen

Lieutenant Marshall was in no mood for small talk. He stood on Nemo's doorstep, a morning newspaper in one hand. In response to Nemo's greeting, he said, 'You sonofabitch! Do you have any idea what you've done?'

'Would you like to come in?' Nemo asked, standing aside.

Marshall barrelled past him and headed for the living room. 'I could have you for obstructing justice,' he shouted. 'And I could probably dream up a few more charges.'

'You're forgetting that I'm a lawyer,' Nemo said, coming into the room, 'I've done absolutely nothing illegal and you know it.'

Marshall glared at him. 'Do you know how many phone calls we've had this morning so far on this? About forty. Ranging from a lady who also remembers Sam Barry in her last life, to a man who says he's been in touch with the aliens that abducted her.'

'I've had a couple of calls myself,' Nemo said mildly.

'And this part about the police dropping leads for political reasons, according to a source you have in the LAPD. If I get out of this with my rank intact, not to mention my job, it'll be a miracle.'

Nemo frowned. 'I'm sorry if I've placed you in a bad position. I tried not to – to be as discreet as possible. But you really left me no choice. As far as I'm concerned this is the only valid lead we have and you were about to drop it.'

'You promised to make no more statements to the Press,' Marshall complained.

Nemo sat on the couch. 'No, I didn't. You told me not to and I said nothing. I wasn't about to close my options.'

'All right, all right,' Marshall said, pacing across the living room carpet. 'Water under the bridge. What's done is done. The question is, what have you got in your mind to do next?'

'Nothing,' Nemo said innocently. 'I'm going to wait and see what response there is, that's all.'

Marshall stopped and scowled at Nemo. 'What's in your mind? You didn't just do this to get the weirdos to call.'

'Not exactly, although something might turn up,' Nemo said. 'I've had four calls so far this morning. No, take a look at the story. Stinger's done rather a tongue-in-cheek job. It makes our T. sound like a raving lunatic. I don't think he's going to like that. I'm betting we get some reaction from him.'

'You could be putting the girl in danger.'

'Yes, I thought of that, of course, but I don't think it will. It's a calculated gamble.'

Marshall resumed his pacing. 'You say you got some calls?'

'Nothing useful,' Nemo said. 'But I asked my office to refer all calls here.'

Marshall wagged his finger at Nemo. 'If you turn something up . . .'

'You'll be one of the first to know.'

'Jesus! What I have to put up with,' Marshall said in

217

disgust, walking towards the door.

'Oh, Lieutenant,' Nemo called. 'Any luck on the composite drawing?'

Marshall glowered at him. 'That's the other forty phone calls. All just as looney,' he said, letting himself out.

Nemo couldn't help smiling at the policeman's problems. He understood them all too well. One of the calls this morning was from a self-professed psychic who offered his services for a small fee of $5,000 – with only half to be paid in advance. When Nemo asked the man if he had ever found missing people through the use of psychic powers before, the man had said, 'No. But I have real strong feelings about this one.' For a moment, Nemo was tempted, but judgement claimed him and he declined the offer. When you were desperate you took desperate measures, and the circling vultures knew that well.

The waiting was the hard part. He had almost religious faith that *something* would happen soon, but it was a blind faith demanding saint-like patience, a quality he had never practiced. When waiting, you could still everything but your mind. He knew of no tricks to stop the mind creating mental image pictures – pictures of Sam in terror or in danger, pictures of the discovery of her body, or of her eternal absence. Those last were the worst. The fear that he would simply never hear from her again, that she would just disappear off the face of the earth and become one of those unsolved mysteries you read about in true crime magazines.

When he wasn't worrying, he spent his time going over and over the events so far, seeking a fresh angle, a new alternative. There had to be some way to find T. Unless the man was perfect, a genius or the luckiest man in the world, he had to have left some trail to be fol-

218

lowed. But no matter how many times he looked at it in his mind, nothing came. He couldn't help but feel he had exhausted every available alternative.

His first lucky break of the day came at about eleven that morning with the ringing of the telephone.

'Nemo Riley,' he answered.

It was a woman, her voice husky with a slight Southern accent. 'My name is June Devereaux. I think I have some information that might help you.'

'Yes?' he said.

'I think the man who kidnapped Sam Barry may have been a client of mine,' she said.

Later, Nemo would reflect on how strangely emotions react to events. When he heard her words, his first response was elation, but it was immediately followed by suspicion.

'A client?' He asked, his tone conservative. 'What service do you offer, Ms Devereaux?'

'I'm a hypnotist,' she said. 'I do hypnotic therapy. You know, help people stop smoking, get over phobias, stuff like that. But I also do past life regression on a smaller scale.'

'And what makes you think that one of your clients is involved in Miss Barry's disappearance?'

'The newspaper mentioned a name, Lela Edwards, and a time, the Twenties. That coincides with what I know. This client described such a person.'

'How long –' Nemo began, and stopped, excitement building in spite of his protective scepticism. 'No. Listen, could I come and see you, now?'

'Yes, this would be a good time,' she said, and gave him an address in Glendale.

'I'll be there in fifteen minutes,' he said.

❉   ✳   ✦

June Devereaux lived in a small stucco duplex bounded by three freeways on the northern edge of Glendale. Nemo knocked at the door and looked down to find a large black cat rubbing itself against his leg. He reached down to stroke its head and the door opened.

Nemo discovered a long time ago that you could never anticipate appearances from telephone voices, and this proved no exception. The voice on the telephone belonged to a young, sultry Southern belle; the woman standing in the doorway was about fifty and overweight with a blowsy face and blonde hair that had come directly from a bottle.

'Are you Mr Riley?' she asked.

He said he was and she invited him in, pushing the cat back with her foot. 'No. You stay outside Portia,' she said, and closed the door. 'Cats love a sucker,' she said with a smile. 'I get them from all over the neighbourhood.'

When she smiled, you could see that she had once been beautiful. Remnants still lurked beneath the lined and folded skin. Perhaps she had once been a sultry Southern belle, Nemo thought.

The apartment was well-furnished and comfortable, with the usual accoutrements such as a stereo system, television set, bookshelf and framed prints on the walls of the living room. 'Please sit down,' she said, gesturing at the couch. 'I've just made a fresh pot of coffee. Would you like some?'

'No thanks,' he said, anxious to hear what she had to say.

'All right,' she said and sat opposite him in an armchair. 'I suppose you'd like me to get right to the point.'

Nemo nodded. 'I'd appreciate it.'

'I'm a State licensed therapist,' she began. 'Perhaps I

220

shouldn't be telling you this. Information I get from clients is confidential, you know. But this seems to be a matter of urgency with the possibility of danger to life, so I decided to call you.

'Just go ahead,' he said impatiently.

'Well, this man came to see me about nine months ago and he was interested in finding out about his past lives through hypnosis.'

'What was his name?'

The woman pursed her lips. 'He called himself Henry James, obviously a pseudonym. But he said his privacy was important and his name wasn't. I didn't insist.'

Nemo masked his disappointment and said, 'Okay, carry on.'

'Well, we did a few sessions and he contacted a few past lives. But there was one in particular that fascinated him and he kept on asking to go back to it. It was in the Twenties when he was an actor here in Hollywood and in love with a woman named Lela Edwards, a famous model according to his story.'

'Anything unusual about this?' Nemo asked.

She rose and went to her stereo system. 'I always tape these sessions,' she said. 'I keep one for my records and make a copy for the client. Maybe you should hear this one.'

Nemo settled back on the couch while she fiddled with the recorder, 'Here,' she said and pushed a button. 'I'll start it here.'

There was a woman's voice, obviously June Devereaux's: 'You are back with Lela now. You have gone to her house to talk with her. Now, what is happening?'

Although slightly slurred and soft, the next voice was unmistakably T.'s. Nemo had heard it enough to recognise. 'She is angry with me. She opens the door and stands

221

there, just looking at me. And then she says, "What do you want?"

'"To talk to you. I just want to talk to you," I say.

'"I have nothing to say to you. But if you don't stop following me, we are going to inform the police," she says.

'I tell her I love her, that the man she is with is nothing and that he will betray her. She laughs at me and tells me she loves him and then I grow angry and grasp her by the shoulders and push her inside. I close the door behind me and see that she is afraid and tell her not to be afraid and that I will not harm her but that I am there to protect her.

'And then . . . and then . . .'

The sound of a man's sobs. He said, 'No,' he said. 'No, I can't.'

The woman's voice: 'Tell me what happens then.'

'No, no, no! I can't do it, I can't . . .' and then more sobbing.

The woman's voice: 'All right. Take a deep breath . . . Good. Now relax . . . relax. Good. All right now let's try this again. I want you to tell me what happened with this woman. Tell me what you are afraid to tell me. Go back to that time and nod your head when you are there. Good. Now what happens after you go into the house?'

'We argue. Terribly. She – she says things that hurt me, that hurt me and I get so angry and I tell her that if I can't have her nobody can have her, and I take out the knife in my pocket and I begin to stab her with it and stab her and stab her and she runs from me and there is blood every-where. And she screams and I grab her hair and drag her up the stairs to the bedroom and throw her on the bed and stab her again and again until she stops screaming and stops moving. And –'

Nemo sat petrified at the horrible scene. This was the murder of Lela he was hearing.

The rasping sobs continued until the voice of the woman said gently. 'And then what happened?'

'I hear a noise then and hide in the closet and a man comes into the room. It is her lover. He falls to his knees beside the bed and I slip from the closet and come behind him. We fight and he tries to choke me, but I still have my knife and I stab him until he falls. He cannot have her.

'I – I run from the house then and throw the knife in the bushes and –'

The man began to cry again.

Miss Devereaux rose from her chair and turned the tape off.

Nemo froze in his seat, his mind a turmoil of thoughts and emotions. Yes, he had already remembered his murder, exactly as T. described it, but to hear about Lela's death was different . . . It shook him.

'It's a terrible thing,' Miss Devereaux was saying. 'I've heard some strange things in hypnosis, but never anything as brutal as that. It upset me terribly. But now, when I see what's happened . . .'

'What do you mean?' Nemo said weakly, trying to get himself back into the present.

'The client came back once. He picked up the tape and thanked me and said he wouldn't need my services anymore. It was what he said then though that makes sense now. He said he had to find Lela again, that he couldn't leave things unfinished. And then I read the article in the paper this morning and I knew it was him.'

'And you think this man's dangerous?' Nemo asked.

'He was a strange man. Withdrawn, you know. Secretive. Yes, I think he still could be dangerous. He took this reincarnation stuff very seriously.'

223

Nemo asked her to describe her client. It matched what he'd heard of T. from the other sources.

'Did you find out anything about him, about who he was?' Nemo asked.

'No. He always paid in cash. Never showed any ID. I have no idea what he does or where he lives. I think he's wealthy. He wore good clothes and drove an expensive car. He's either independently wealthy or self-employed, I'd guess. He came here during regular working hours.'

'You said an expensive car. What kind?'

'It was one of those old cars, maybe from the Twenties or Thirties, you know. But done up real good, shiny chrome, spotless paint job. It was red.'

'You don't know what kind it was? Or the licence number, by any chance?'

'No,' she said. 'I'm not real good on cars. And I didn't see the plates.'

'If you saw pictures of old cars, could you recognise it?'

'I doubt it,' she said apologetically. 'I told you I didn't think I could be a lot of help.'

'Anything else about him at all?' Nemo asked. 'Any mannerisms anything he said?'

She thought for a moment and then shook her head. 'No. Not that I can remember.'

Nemo scuffed the carpet with his toe until another idea came. 'Do you have tapes of your other sessions with him?'

'Yes,' she said, brightening up. 'Yes, I do.'

'Could I borrow them?'

She hesitated for a second and then said, 'Yes. Of course. Anything that could help that poor girl.'

'I might, well, I probably *will* have to give them to the police,' Nemo said. 'They'll probably also want to talk to you.'

'Yes, I understand,' she said.

'I'd like to try something else as well,' Nemo said. 'I'd like to send one of my staff over with some pictures of old cars and see if you can identify the one he had. Would that be all right?'

'Yes,' she said. She knitted her fingers nervously. 'In a way I feel responsible for this. God knows what I helped stir up in that poor man. I mean, if he hadn't have come to see me and if I hadn't –'

'You can't blame yourself,' Nemo said, interrupting. 'People do what they do.'

'Well, I won't be doing any more past life regression after this,' she said. 'I'm going to stick to helping people give up smoking and stuff like that.'

'Probably not a bad idea,' Nemo said. 'But don't blame yourself for this. He is responsible for what he does. We all are.'

His words didn't do much to console her. When he left with the package of tapes, her last words were, 'I'm sorry.'

'For what?' he asked.

'The girl. She's close to you?'

'Yes.'

'I'm sorry if what I did has helped anything bad happen to her,' she said, close to tears.

Nemo patted her on the shoulder and left.

He made two calls when he got home. First, he called his office and asked Marion to get someone to June Devereaux's house immediately with a book of antique cars. 'As soon as she identifies a car, I want him to call me. From there,' he ordered. Next he called Marshall and left a message for the lieutenant to call him.

There were eight or nine sixty-minute cassettes in the

225

package, although he had no idea how much of each tape was filled. He took coffee into the living room, and sat beside his cassette deck with a notepad on his lap. He was ready for a marathon.

The tapes were dated, thank goodness. He began with the earliest.

T. was both nervous and suspicious at first, but the hypnotist had little difficulty getting him under and once there, he was as receptive as a child. In fact, during the first session she didn't even attempt to reach a past life, but sent him back into his childhood.

Nemo scribbled the following information in his pad: that the man had grown up in a foreign country and run away, that he had lived in Boston with relatives, that he spoke a foreign language. Nemo wrote down the words phonetically. They sounded East European, but he wasn't sure. It would be easy enough to check, he thought.

The second tape involved their first venture into a past life. T. was a German this time, a young soldier, killed by the Russians in '45.

The third tape took T. back to the Twenties in the United States. It was the story of a struggling young actor with a monumental ego, embittered by the fact that nobody appreciated his talent as much as he did.

Some hours and tapes later, on his fifth cup of coffee, Nemo looked down at what he had. Not much really. After the third tape, T. wanted only to return to the life in the Twenties, apparently trying to discover all he could about it. However, the first tape had given Nemo the most information about the man's present life. At least he had some background. A few of the tapes contained some preamble before the hypnotic trance was induced, but there were no clues there. T. was remarkably close-mouthed about himself.

He was interrupted by a phone call from the law clerk at Miss Devereaux's house. 'Sorry,' the young man said. 'It took me a while to find a book with pictures of all the old cars.'

'Did she identify it?' Nemo asked.

'No, sorry. The closest we got was that it was probably from the Twenties. The lady doesn't know much about cars, old or new.'

Disappointed, Nemo thanked him and, after hanging up, added that piece of useless information to his pad. How many cars from the Twenties still around? Hundreds, if not thousands. And how would you find them? T. didn't seem to be the type of person to join clubs. Another problem to solve.

Nemo decided to take a break. The man's voice, his posturings, his delusions were beginning to tire him. Each time he heard the voice he couldn't help thinking of Sam. And that didn't help either. Time was passing, and as it did, he knew Sam's position grew more precarious.

His own memories intruded as well. The man, Terry Jones his name then, had loved the same woman he did. Before Nemo had even met her, Jones had dated her, slept with her and, apparently adored her. He spoke of those times often during his hypnotic trances and on many occasions Nemo found they acted as a catalyst on his own mind.

There was one point in particular where Jones spoke of taking her to San Diego. He too had taken Lela to San Diego. They had gone there for two days to get away from the pressures of business, and Lela had even mentioned going there with Jones before, although to a different hotel. He hadn't minded. She loved him now.

During those idyllic two days they had talked of marriage for the first time. Before, it had been one of those assumed and unspoken things. Sooner or later they would marry. It was something they had both known. On this particular day, however, they walked on the beach and one of them, he wasn't sure which, had brought the subject up.

'Do you think we should marry soon?' he remembered asking.

'Whenever you wish,' she replied.

She was beautiful then. Long brown legs, bared by a skirt that flowed behind her, hair blowing in the breeze, her hand in his.

'Let's do it soon,' he said.

She laughed and said, 'The sooner the better. I wanted to hear you say it.'

'What about children?' he asked.

'Oh, I want children,' she said. 'I love children and I want dozens of them. But not yet. I have to follow my career for a couple of years and see where it leads.'

'There's no rush,' he said. 'We have plenty of time.'

The ring of the telephone brought him back to the present. It was Lieutenant Marshall returning his call.

'I got nothin' for you,' Marshall said, launching immediately into a tirade. 'All we've been getting all day are calls from whackos. Nothin' from the drawing and nothin' from the line of crap you fed the *Times*.'

'I got something for you, Lieutenant,' Nemo said smugly.

'You what?'

'I found the hypnotist who handled our man and I have tapes of all his sessions and I know a bit more about him than I did when I saw you this morning.'

'You got tapes?' Marshall asked.

'Yep.'

'Anything that can lead us to him?'

'Not on the face of it. I'm listening to the last couple of

228

them now. But you guys are the pro's, you can go through them and see what you find.'

'I'll – what time is it? – I'll be over in about an hour to pick them up. Okay?'

'That's fine,' Nemo said. He'd be finished with them by then.

'Give me the name, address and phone of the hypnotist. We'll have to talk to him too.'

'It's a her,' Nemo said, and gave him the information.

'All right. See you soon,' Marshall said and hung up.

Nemo returned to the tapes. He didn't have much time left. He'd just have to ignore his dislike of the process.

He listened for another hour, but it was merely more of the same. The man was cagy. He gave nothing away. The past may have been an open door, but the present was closed.

In fact, Nemo thought he gained more from listening to the man's conversations after he was woken from the hypnotic trance, than what went on during the session. It wasn't what T. said that interested him, but the tone in which he spoke. He began to get an idea of the man's character: impatient, arrogant, secretive, and a man with an inflated opinion of himself.

As for the facts, well, T. was of European extraction, once lived in Boston, spoke a foreign language and drove an old car. The language would be easy to discover, and that would add another piece to the puzzle. Piece by laborious piece, a picture would form to finally reveal the identity of T.

Time was the only arbitrary now. Sooner or later he would see the entire picture; Nemo had faith in that. What he didn't know was how much time Sam had.

Chapter Sixteen

The sound of the turning door handle woke Sam. She lay on top of the bed, still dressed. Sometime during the night she must have made it to the bed and collapsed again.

The door handle turned a couple more times and someone pushed against the chair, but it held. The shuffling steps of the housekeeper retreated down the hall.

Her head felt like a block of wood on her shoulders. Whatever he gave her last night was still there in residual form. She went to the bathroom and splashed water on her face. She looked in the mirror, her face still wet and cringed at what she saw.

An old hag stared back at her; puffs of darkness surrounded her eyes and stress pulled her mouth and cheeks into a tight mask. Sam Barry, fashion designer, she thought derisively. She looked about as fashionable as a MacArthur Park bag lady.

She went back to the door and made sure the chair was tight. She didn't intend to let them in. Not after what happened last night. If they wanted to keep her as a prisoner, a prisoner she would be – by her choice.

The thought of mind-altering drugs filled her with revulsion and she wondered what he had given her last night. Some kind of major tranquilliser probably – the type of thing used in mental institutions to pacify patients. It had sapped her will and weakened her judgement and she could still feel a fuzziness to her thoughts. Damn him! What he had done angered her even more than the abduction, for some reason. It was a more gross personal violation than anything he had done before. Thank God she had found the strength to muster up enough resistance.

Would the chair hold against a forceful attempt to enter? She looked around the room for additional support. The dresser was too heavy to move. Likewise the canopied bed. Perhaps the mattresses would help. She pulled them from the bed and dragged them, one at a time, to the door, propping them against the chair. It wasn't much, but it would stop the chair from skidding back.

Heavier footsteps in the hallway. The doorknob turned. There was the sound of a shoulder being pushed against the door. It opened perhaps a quarter of an inch, but the chair held.

'Lela?' It was Jones. 'Lela, don't be silly. Open up. We have your breakfast here.'

'I don't want any,' she said.

'Are you upset about last night?' he asked. 'It was only Thorazine I gave you—a sedative to relax you. You were under a lot of stress.'

'Screw you,' Sam said. What kind of fool did he take her for? Thorazine wasn't a sedative like Valium, it was what doctors called a major tranquilliser, just as she had suspected. He must have given her a massive dose.

'Open up,' he said, his voice harder now.

She ignored him, went to the dresser, and applied make-up to her face. After this she'd do her exercises, she thought. She had to hold it together and not let him sap her spirit.

231

'Open up or you'll be sorry,' he said, his voice growing louder.

The handle turned again and he banged his shoulder against the door. 'Open the door, damn you!'

The chair held.

'Don't you want some food? Some coffee?' he asked. He sounded to her like a pervert trying to entice a child into his chair.

'Leave me alone,' she said, and applied a light red lipstick to her mouth.

'Aren't you getting hungry?'

She didn't bother answering. For the first time since being held there, she felt a sense of security. She was in here and he was out there, and never the twain shall meet.

'Open the door,' he said, shouting now.

'All right,' he yelled. 'All right, I'll be back.'

She heard his angry footsteps pound on the hardwood floor of the hall.

What would he do? She looked around. The windows were barred, the door blocked. There was no other way in. She wondered how long she would be able to keep it up. And the answer came: until Nemo finds me. Nemo, she thought again.

She tried to picture his face in her mind. And failed. Nothing materialised. She closed her eyes and saw only bland pink fuzz. No, she thought desperately, I can't have forgotten what he looks like!

And then she saw an image of him standing at her door, beer and wine in his hands, and she almost cried with relief.

She had to hold on to Nemo. He was all that gave her hope. Without him, she might remain in this house for years. Her file would gather dust in some police department drawer. Her friends would say, 'Poor old Sam.

232

Wonder what ever happened to her?' The public would say, 'Sam Barry, fashion designer? Don't remember that one. Funny name for a woman, isn't it?' And Jones would be there saying, 'Lela. Do you remember, Lela, when . . .'

It was a nightmare.

Such strange thoughts. She wondered if it was the drug, still in her system. She felt so tired. No, exhausted was a more correct description. Perhaps she should lie down, just for a little. No. The bed. The mattresses were at the door.

She leaned back in the chair and closed her eyes. Yes, she would just close her eyes a little. Maybe it would clear her mind.

The day was not working out as well as Jones had planned. He went back to the dining room, wondering how to handle Lela. Stubborn woman. You would think she would have discovered by now that pig-headedness brought only grief. He would have to teach her a severe lesson.

The housekeeper came in with the morning newspaper and laid it on the table. By now the story of Sam Barry would be buried somewhere in the Metro section, he thought complacently. The media would soon grow bored with the lack of police progress and drop it entirely.

He scanned the headlines on page one and turned to page three. He drew his breath in sharply, his eyes riveted to the headline: *Reincarnation Motive in Barry Abduction Lawyer Claims*.

Jones grew angrier and angrier as he read. The reporter had really done a number on the story. A UCLA psychiatrist was quoted as saying that '*the man is obviously compensating for a failure to attain early goals.*' A

233

psychologist claimed that '*the delusory belief in reincarnation is usually based on an inability to accept the realities of life and is the sign of an immature personality*.' And the lawyer, Nemo Riley, was blunter, saying, '*The man is apparently a raving lunatic*.' The only saving grace was the inclusion of a wildly inaccurate police composite drawing of him.

'That bastard,' Jones said aloud. He had no doubt that Riley was behind the story. The man wouldn't leave him alone. He would always try to spoil it for him.

He closed the newspaper with a violent gesture. He had taken care of his rival once before and would do so again. He had hoped it wouldn't be necessary, preferring to concentrate his attentions upon the awakening of Lela, but the man was becoming too much of a thorn in his side.

Damn! he thought. He lifted his hand and rubbed his temple. The headache was back, worse than ever. It had plagued him for months now, slicing into his head like a cleaver, riding with his emotions. He would have to take something for it again.

Then he would handle Lela. She would learn not to take him lightly. After that he would fix Mr Riley, once and for all.

There was a shattering, crashing noise that seemed to be right in her head.

Sam's eyes shot open. The gleaming head of an axe pushed through the splintered door panelling.

There was a grunting sound and it pulled back. Another mighty thud, and the axe appeared again, shattering more of the panel.

'Just wait,' Jones said. 'I'll teach you a lesson. Just wait.'

234

Again and again the axe thundered against the door.

Soon, she saw his movements through the hole. She sat motionless on the chair and waited. There was nothing she could do to stop him.

The banging stopped after a while. His hand came through the door, moving like a blind man's until it found the top of the chair. All it took was a little push and the chair fell to the side.

The door opened and he came in, sweat pouring down his face, his eyes fiery with anger. The axe hung from his left hand like a weapon, making him look like some wild Viking invader.

'How dare you lock me out,' he said, walking to her.

She sat on the chair and stared up at him, strangely unaffected by what was happening. Let it happen, she thought.

He stopped in front of her and glowered down. 'That will never happen again!' he screamed.

And his right hand darted out like a snake and struck her on the side of the head, sending her spinning to the floor. He dropped the axe, grabbed her arm and bent down, hitting her with his open palm again. And again. One of the blows hit her mouth and she tasted blood.

This is real, she thought, not bothering to defend herself. She felt outside of herself, like an observer watching it all happen. Curiously, there was no fear.

Finally, after what seemed a void of timelessness, he stopped.

She clambered to her feet then and touched her face with her hand. When she drew it away she saw blood.

He stood with his fists clenched, his chest rising and falling and his breath rasping. 'You shouldn't have done that,' he growled.

She just looked at him, a perfectly objective glance, devoid of judgement or criticism.

'You shouldn't have done that!' he screamed, his face reddening and the veins of his neck jumping out like roads on a relief map.

He took her arm and pushed her ahead of him into the hall. They went downstairs, down another hall towards the back of the house and came to a door. He opened it, put his arm in and searched the wall until he found the light switch.

'Go on. Go in,' he ordered.

Stairs led down to a basement, an unfinished dusty room that reeked of age and neglect.

Sam hesitated at the top and felt his hand shove her back. She stumbled to the bottom, looked up, and saw him standing at the door.

'You can think about your situation here,' he said. He stepped back and closed the door.

She stood in the middle of the room and looked around. The walls were made of brick, the floor of concrete. The only contents were a couple of broken pieces of furniture and a pile of boxes against one wall.

Sam's legs trembled then and she sat down where she had been standing, crossing her legs. She pulled up the end of her blouse and dabbed at the blood on her face.

Chapter Seventeen

Jones felt ill. His head still hurt and he wanted to vomit. He walked back and forth from one side of his study to the other, his hands clasped behind his back, his thoughts bouncing around.

Lela was like a child; she had to be taught how to behave, to respect her elders. She needed a firm hand, discipline. And yet . . . God! He hadn't meant to hit her. It was just that she provoked him. She made him so angry.

When he was angry, he wasn't responsible for what he did. Was anyone? When angry, he was lost in a red fog. It swirled through his mind, obliterating thought. It made him want to grasp the object of his anger and shake it and shake it until it stopped what it was doing.

Should he apologise to her? No! She appreciated his strength, demanded it. He should show no signs of weakness or regret to lessen her respect for him. Women were like that. They wanted their men to be strong, even if they were beasts. She was no different. Yes, she would be outwardly upset, but deep down she admired his masterful ways. One day she would admit it.

One day . . .

It shouldn't be taking this long. She should have

remembered by now. In fact, according to his original projections, by now they should have been on their second honeymoon, so to speak. Was he doing something wrong? Or was she simply stupid? No, he couldn't believe that. She was an intelligent woman. It was one of the reasons he loved her. But how could she continue to deny the realities? He had given her every opportunity to remember. Gone out of his way to create an environment to stimulate her memories. But she spurned his help, threw up these ridiculous barriers. Mocked him!

The anger thundered up again.

How many men would go to these lengths for the sake of love? Surely she couldn't doubt his love of her. The evidence was too powerful. He was risking everything for their love. Surely she could see that.

Agreed, women were fickle creatures, given to infatuations and fleeting emotions. But Lela was different. Of course, she had spurned him before. Thrown him away like an old rag. He remembered the day she told him they could no longer be lovers. It was the saddest day of his life – that life . . .

They went out to dinner. She was unusually subdued throughout the meal. He drove her home and stopped the car outside her apartment building. He was about to get out to open the door for her when she put her hand on his arm.

'Wait. I must talk to you,' she said.

She was blunt and did little to soften the blow.

'We can't go out together anymore, I'm sorry,' she said.

He couldn't believe it, thought it was some joke. 'What are you talking about?' he asked.

'I'm sorry, Terry, but it's over,' she said gently.

'What do you mean?' he asked. 'How can it be over? We love each other. I want to marry you. I love you, Lela. You know that.'

'I don't love you, Terry,' she said, and he flinched. He never thought he'd hear those words from her lips. Never!

'Are you serious?' he asked.

'Yes,' she said.

He didn't know what to say then, just let it sink in. She was calling it off, rejecting him! It wasn't possible. He had given her everything, taught her everything.

'Why?' he asked. 'Why the sudden change of heart? What's happened? What did I do?'

'Dear Terry, you haven't done anything. You're the best friend a girl could have. It's just something that's been growing for a while. Everything changes in time and it's time to end it now.'

The suspicion grew and then burst out. 'Is there some-one else?'

'Yes,' she said.

She said it so simply. There were no excuses, no apologies, she just said it and looked at him, waiting for his reaction.

'Who?' he finally managed to say.

'It doesn't matter,' she said. 'There's another man and I love him, I truly do. I've never felt anything like this before. I hope you'll be happy for me.'

He wanted to scream then. She claimed she'd never felt anything like it before! What was he? Chopped liver? What about what they had together?

'Who is it?' he asked again, anger threatening to burst out.

'It doesn't matter. It's immaterial. It has nothing to do with us,' she said.

'Who is it?' he demanded again, gripping her arm and squeezing. 'Tell me. I'll take care of him, you'll see.'

'Let go of my arm,' she said.

'Not until you tell me. You can't just say it's over and

239

expect to walk out of my life with no consequences. What do you take me for?'

'Let go,' she said, fear in her voice. 'You're hurting me.'

'You can't do this to me,' he said, shaking her.

'Let go or I'll scream,' she said.

There were people walking on the sidewalk. A kid sat on the steps of the apartment building and watched them. He released her arm.

'I was hoping you'd accept it better than this,' she said, rubbing her arm with her other hand.

'I love you, Lela,' he said in a choked voice.

'I'm sorry,' she said, and opened the door. 'I hope you'll still be my friend,' she said, and stepped out.

He just sat there as she walked away, his head bowed. After a while he began to sob.

By the next day he came to his senses. He needed to find out who his rival was. He began to follow her.

He saw him for the first time that night. The man came to pick Lela up. He drove an expensive car and dressed well. Tall, sandy-haired, relatively good-looking in a conservative way.

They went to dinner. And then they went to the man's home in the Hills. A big place too. The man was apparently well-off. He sat in the car and waited, but she didn't come out.

Finally, at about ten the next morning, the man drove her back to her apartment.

He continued to follow the man. He went into an office building in downtown Los Angeles and entered an office on the third floor. The sign said, *Phillip Bates, Attorney*.

He stuck his head into the reception room and said to the secretary, 'Was that Mr Bates who just walked in? I have an office here and I've wanted to meet him for some time.'

'Yes, it was,' she said. 'I'll tell him you're here.'

He looked at his watch and said, 'Gee, I forgot. I have an appointment. I'll come back later.'

Phillip Bates was his rival, he thought as he went downstairs. He was the man who stole Lela away from him. A thief and a scoundrel.

It was then that he decided to kill Bates . . .

Jones looked around his study, trying to remember where he was. It's the 1980's, he reminded himself. I'm here now and *I* have Lela.

He had killed Bates.

But Bates was still here too.

His name was Nemo Riley now. He was a lawyer again, and he was still hanging around Lela. Some people never learned.

He should have shot to kill when he had Riley in his sights a few days ago. But he hadn't known who he was then, only that he was some fellow hanging around Lela, an amorous neighbour, someone she was just having a casual affair with to pass the time. If only he had known.

Riley knew what was going on. Somehow, he had remembered. He was positive Riley knew. That story in the newspaper. In spite of Riley's comment that the 'abductor' was 'a raving lunatic,' you could read between the lines and see that Riley knew.

It came to him then. This was why things weren't working out as planned. Riley was the wild card. Riley was responsible for Lela's stubbornness. The man had seduced her again, captivated her mind and warped her values.

Riley. This time he would take care of him properly. Without Riley to fixate her attention on, Lela would turn to him again.

His error last time was to try and persuade Lela of her mistake. She had been too blinded to see. This time, he

241

wouldn't make the same mistake. This time, he would simply get rid of Riley first.

The telephone jangled. He let it ring a few times and regained his composure. It was his literary agent in New York.

'How's the new book coming?' his agent asked.

'Fine but slowly,' he replied.

The agent hesitated and then said, 'Your publisher's getting impatient. It's four months overdue already, you know?'

'Yes, of course, I know,' he said irritably. 'They're going to have to get patient. It takes as long as it takes.'

'What shall I tell them?'

'Tell them anything,' Jones said. 'But don't promise a time. I don't know when I'll finish.'

They exchanged information about royalty statements and then Jones hung up. The truth was, he hadn't worked on the book for months. Compared to what was happening in his life, the story was as flat and dull as a board. He had lost interest in it long ago. Besides, there were more important things to be done.

He turned his mind back to the immediate problems facing him – Lela and Riley.

She obviously needed more stimulation to get her memory flowing. With Riley out of the way, it would be easier, of course, but even then he would have to encourage and guide her. For starters, he would leave her in the basement room and show he meant business and wasn't to be trifled with. She would understand in time and see that he was doing it all for her own good. She would learn to appreciate strength and resolve.

As for Mr Riley . . . his time was limited and his prospects bleak.

Jones rubbed his hands together. He felt better now. He knew what he had to do.

242

Chapter Eighteen

The trial of Terry Jones for the honeymoon murders of Lela Edwards and Phillip Bates made good copy at the time. The reporters milked it for all it was worth. Nemo reread the newspaper stories. He couldn't afford to miss a single element that could add to the growing picture of T.

He found nothing he hadn't seen before. He tried some of the magazine articles written after it was all over. One particularly sensational approach caught his eye. It spoke of '. . . *the flamboyant young actor . . . struggling for recognition in a competitive field . . . wealthy in his own right . . . a disappointment to his prestigious family.*'

Nemo rose to his feet and stretched. Something the writer Bill Hazel had told him came back. It seemed to make sense. 'People get stuck in roles. A psychotic, for instance, is someone who cannot escape the role he is playing.' This seemed to describe T. What else had Hazel said? Something about it being a compulsive form of behaviour.

Nemo knew the answer lay within these parameters. The more he learned about the Jones of the past, the more easily he would be able to predict the behaviour of

243

the man now. The theory was good; the difficulty was translating it into practical terms. But somewhere in the past was a clue which would lead him to the man. He was sure of it.

The doorbell rang. It would be Maddy. She had called earlier, saying she had to go to Sam's house to look for some papers and would stop in to see him.

She came in, a ball of nervous energy. 'I'm getting totally paranoid,' she said, following him into the kitchen. 'Today I was driving along and thought somebody was following me. Totally nuts.'

'You're sure somebody wasn't?' Nemo asked.

'Of course I am,' she said, perching on a barstool. 'Are you getting paranoid too?'

'It's safer to be paranoid apparently,' he said. 'Coffee?'

'Sure. I might as well. It'll stop me from eating. God, the last few days I've been putting it away. I'm getting bloated. Starting to look like one of those fish that blow themselves up, you know?' She blew air into her cheeks and bulged her eyes.

Nemo laughed. 'You look fine to me.'

'Ugh,' she said. 'I look like a pig. But thanks anyway. Anything new, any news?'

'Nothing that I didn't tell you on the phone,' Nemo said, pushing a cup of coffee over to her.

'Something has to happen soon. This is dragging out too long,' she said, echoing his own sentiments.

'You keeping the business going?' he asked, changing the subject.

'The vultures are coming out, wondering how Sam's disappearance is going to affect them, wondering when they're going to get paid. But, yes, I'm managing things okay.'

'Well, hang in there,' he said. 'Something will happen soon.'

244

'I've been having nightmares,' she said. 'I keep seeing Sam in a whirlpool, her hand outstretched. I reach for it, but I'm a foot too short and she gets sucked under.'

'She's not going to go under,' Nemo said firmly.

'I know. It's only a dream, but . . .'

There were tears in Maddy's eyes. She wiped them with the back of her hand. 'I'm not much help like this, a big crybaby,' she said.

Nemo took her hand in his. 'Don't worry about it. I feel like that myself sometimes. But I know this is going to turn out okay, Maddy. We're getting closer all the time.'

She nodded and sniffed. 'I try so hard to believe that, but this whole thing is a nightmare. It's –' She began to cry again and pushed herself back from the bar. 'Listen, I've got to go,' she said.

'Are you all right?' he asked.

'No, of course I'm not,' she said, 'but I will be. Don't worry about me. Keep worrying about Sam.'

After she left, he continued to do just that. Finally, for lack of any better course of action, he called Marshall.

'Did I miss anything on the tapes or with the hypnotist?' he asked.

'If you mean do we know any more than what you told me yesterday, the answer is no,' Marshall said. 'We have one of our psychs doing a psychological profile based on what we know and the voice on the tapes, but that's about as useful as having your own witchdoctor – maybe less.'

'What about the language?'

'Polish.'

'Doesn't that give you a lead? A Pole who once lived in Boston, and moved out here?'

'Do you know how many Poles there are in this country? I had one of my men do a quick research job on that. Turned up nothing. Unfortunately, this isn't Poland – we don't keep dossiers on everyone.'

'So it was no help,' Nemo said.

'No immediate help,' Marshall contradicted. 'We still may come up with something.'

'I've been hearing that for a long time,' Nemo said disappointedly.

'We're doing our best,' Marshall said curtly. 'You call me if you come up with anything else.'

'Right,' Nemo said.

They were doing their best, a thought terrifying in its finality. What chance did Sam have if the best continued to turn up absolutely nothing? Once again, the weight was squarely on his shoulders. He was the one who would have to make things happen. He alone could find Sam. Somehow he could and would.

Nemo sat in his study. The pad before him bore the doodlings of a deranged mind, he thought. Guesses, suppositions, diagrams, and a few facts – his attempts to make sense of what was happening and glean new data.

He pushed his chair back and put his feet on top of his desk. The key was in the past. But where to look?

He scanned back, allowing the images to flash through his mind like photographic slides. A dance, a smell, the touch of Lela, the sounds of traffic, music, casual snatches of conversation . . .

And then, like a bird surveying the ground below, he landed on something. A memory blossomed . . .

'I wish he'd leave me alone,' Lela said. 'He called me again today, begging to see me.'

'He'll give up once he knows you mean it,' Phillip replied.

'You don't know him.'

'Who is he? Tell me something about him.'

Lela finished pouring the drink and brought it to him.

246

She sat gracefully on the couch beside him.

'He's a spoiled brat who's used to getting what he wants. That about sums it up,' she said.

Phillip smiled. 'Come on, there must be more to him than that. After all, you were friends once.'

'Yes, I know,' she said regretfully. 'I shouldn't talk about him like that, but he is irritating me so. He's never able to take no for an answer.'

'So tell me more about him.'

'He comes from a wealthy family. His father is in textiles and oil and something else. He has money of his own now. Plenty of it, I think. Although he once told me it's nothing to what he'll get when he turns thirty. He disappointed his family terribly when he came out here, but he had this dream of being an actor. A consuming passion, if you know what I mean.'

Phillip nodded. 'You see it all the time out here. They flock here from everywhere, longing in their eyes.'

'He had the bug bad. He's not a bad actor, you know, but he hasn't been terribly lucky. It's been a struggle for him to get accepted, even though he has money and lives in a mansion and drives an expensive car. To most people, he's just another struggling actor. But he's stubborn. He'll never give up.'

'Apparently he's exhibiting that stubbornness as far as you're concerned.'

'Yes. First he tries pouting until he gets his way, then he gets nasty.'

'In what way?' Phillip asked.

'He has a foul temper. I've seen him shout at a waiter in a restaurant and scare the poor man out of his wits. He tried it with me once, but it didn't work. I refused to let him dominate me. He didn't try again. If he thinks he can dominate people he will.'

'Sounds like a bully,' Phillip said.

Lela looked at him, a realisation dawning in her eyes. 'Yes, I think you're right. I never thought of him in those terms, but that does describe him. He'll be terribly nice to people stronger than himself, people that he needs or can't push around. But he's nasty to his inferiors and takes advantage of them.'

'Well, I don't think he'll be bothering you for much longer.'

'I hope not,' she said with a sigh. 'It's such a waste of time.'

. . . and a few days later, Lela told him about meeting Jones on the sidewalk . . . his comment about putting the flowers on her grave . . . Phillip decided to pay him a visit . . .

Jones lived in a large brick house on the back side of the Hollywood Hills. It was surrounded by a high stone wall and overlooked rows of orange trees and vegetables. Phillip drove through the gates and parked beside a red Cadillac.

Jones answered the door himself. 'What can I do for you, Mr Bates?' he asked, his tone unfriendly. He was a tall young man, thin and wiry. He was almost handsome, but his mouth was too thin and the trace of a permanent sneer on his lips subtracted from his charm.

Phillip had called and asked to see him 'on a matter of some urgency.' Jones must have guessed the nature of the matter. It was obvious.

'May I come in?' Phillip asked politely.

'I think you can say what you have to say here.'

'Very well. I want you to leave Lela alone. She was willing to retain a friendship with you, not a romance. She and I have plans.'

'Just like that? Jones said tautly.

'You are bothering her and upsetting her with your persistence,' Phillip said firmly.

248

'I knew her before you did, long before. We loved each other. How dare you come here and give me orders,' Jones said, his voice rising.

'Don't shout at me,' Phillip said.

'You leave!' Jones said, pointing his finger to the gate and truly shouting now, his face an apoplectic red. 'Get away from here. How dare you presume to speak for Lela, you, you, nothing!'

Phillip stepped forward then and pushed his face close to Jones'. 'You stop bothering her. If you don't, I'll report it to the authorities, or give you a good thrashing myself. Is that understood?'

Jones pushed at his chest then, but Phillip had expected it and his stance was firm. He put one large hand on Jones' neck and began to squeeze.

'Leave her alone,' he said. And then he pushed Jones back and turned to walk away.

'I'll get you,' Jones shouted. 'You can't do this to me. You can't have Lela. You can't steal her from me and expect to get away with it. You'll see, buddy, you'll see.'

Phillip ignored him and entered his car. Empty threats he thought. The fellow would probably just let it drop now. He'd done a good job of scaring him off . . .

Nemo focused slowly on his desk, drifting back to the present. He hadn't done a particularly good job, had he? Jones had come back and murdered them both.

Was the man's character the same now, he wondered? Hot-tempered, irrational and basically still a coward? What portions of a life did a person carry forward into the next? There were obvious changes in attitude and approach, but inside, as far as the basics of his character, little had changed. There was no guarantee, however, that T. would follow the same pattern.

Where was the pattern? The memory he had just relived had been enlightening in some ways, but gave

249

him nothing to act on now. And now was when he needed it.

Damn! he thought in frustration. Somewhere there had to be something that could help.

The telephone rang, as if in answer to his need. It was the hypnotist, June Devereaux.

'Have you come up with something else?' he asked eagerly.

'No. No, the police came by to see me and I told them everything I told you. I hope it was a help.'

'I see,' Nemo said, masking his disappointment. 'Well, what can I do for you?'

'I just wanted to see if *you* have any news,' she said. And then she broke into sobs. 'I feel so terrible about this, so responsible.'

'It's not your fault,' he said. 'You couldn't have fore-seen what would happen. Don't blame yourself.'

'It's just that I – I don't know. That poor girl. I wish there was something I could do.'

'All you can do is let us know if you think of anything else, anything that could lead us to him. It doesn't matter now insignificant it seems. Perhaps just something he said in passing. But it may be something that could help us find him or who he is.'

'I will, I will,' she said. 'I'll think about it some more.'

'All right,' Nemo said. 'You just take it easy on yourself, okay?'

'Yes,' she said. 'Thank you.'

He said goodbye to her and stared bemusedly at the phone. Here he was comforting everyone, it seemed. Who would comfort him? No one except Sam, and she wasn't available.

An ugly, persistent mood of self-pity began to rise and he quickly quashed it, angry at himself. He needed to get out.

250

He took his car and drove aimlessly. Almost without knowing it, he found himself on the Hollywood Freeway. He took the Franklin Boulevard exit and then drove down Franklin.

It was foolish, he knew, but he was hoping to see something.

Every woman pedestrian looked like Sam, if only for a split-second, and every man could have been T. He scoured their faces, slowing down every time he saw someone. At one point he even followed a car up Beachwood Canyon because the man in it had dark hair and seemed tall.

When all else fails, we pray to the goddess of luck. Just a little luck, he thought, that's all I need. One break. One glimpse of Sam being taken somewhere in a car, or walking on a street. It was impossible, but he had nothing else.

Finally, he took the road up to the Griffith Park Observatory, stopped the car and got out. He walked around the building, ignoring the tourists, and stood on a balcony overlooking the city. She was somewhere down there.

His eyes fixed on the Cinerama Dome, as familiar a landmark as Graumann's Chinese Theater. With its stark white roof, it looked like a half-buried egg. It was funny, he thought. It all began in Hollywood more than sixty years earlier, and here he was in Hollywood again. Life flowed in infinite and mainly incomprehensible circles. Of all the people in that teeming city below, only a relative handful had any concept of their true nature as beings who lived and died and lived again – and again, and again.

He had not given himself much time in recent days to dwell on the ramifications of his newly won knowledge. Now, however, viewing the city from his vantage point

251

on the hill, it began to sink in. The sceptics claimed that those who believed in reincarnation feared death. It was an attempt, they said, to deny the extinction we all face. The truth of the matter was that the sceptics feared life. Poor lost souls, they dreamed only of the comfort of nothingness. They said also that a belief in reincarnation encouraged a fatalistic acceptance of the ills dished out by life and led to an apathetic existence. Again, the truth as he knew it now was different. If you accepted that your present was created by the seeds of your past actions, it could lead only to total self-responsibility. There was nobody to blame for your failures; they were a result only of your actions.

He wondered then how he had brought the present conditions with Sam? What were his responsibilities in the matter? What were Sam's? They had started something back then and were now attempting to complete it – again. T., or Terry Jones, as he was then known, had his responsibilities too. Each one was trying to fulfil the pattern of their lives, and one of them at least, had long-held and opposing purposes. One appeared destructive, the others creative; one evil, the others good, but it was probably not that simple. T. was held in the tracks of a circle and could not escape. His free will had deserted him and he was acting like a puppet manipulated by strings of emotions he did not understand. Perhaps that was the difference between sanity and insanity.

There was a tap on his shoulder. He turned to face a Japanese man who gestured at him with a camera.

'Picture, please,' the man said with a grin. He pointed back at two women and another man.

'Of course,' Nemo said.

He took the camera and stepped back until the four of them were framed against the western horizon.

'Smile,' he said.

They grinned obediently.

Click!

He drove around a little more and then stopped for a bite at an Italian restaurant on Hillhurst Avenue. The sight of people talking, eating, laughing, all the normal, everyday things that people did, comforted him in a curious way. No matter what happened elsewhere, for most people life continued. And in spite of their fear and ignorance and uncertainty, they continued with an astonishing degree of dignity and courage. It was altogether admirable, he thought.

It was dark by the time he arrived home. He parked in front of the house and walked to the front door. A pale moon hung low in the sky and, looking over at Sam's house, he saw a lone light in the maid's quarters over the garage.

Perhaps there would be a message from Marshall, he thought hopefully, as he unlocked the door. Maybe the police had come up with fresh leads since they had last spoken.

He stepped inside and flicked the light switch in the hall. It didn't come on, so he flipped it a couple more times.

Damn, he thought, moving cautiously down and trying the living room light. Nothing. Blackout, or fuse perhaps?

No blackout, he realised, remembering the light next door. It had to be his fuses.

He fumbled his way back to the hall, his eyes slowly growing accustomed to the darkness. He had a flashlight in the kitchen. The fusebox was somewhere on the back patio, he wasn't sure exactly where.

And then he heard the shuffling sound behind him.

His hands automatically rose to protect himself and he

253

began to turn. There was a sudden burning sensation on his left hand as it reached the level of his neck and he realised he was holding a razor-thin length of wire. At the same time, he felt the man's body press against his back.

'The gunshots were just a warning,' the man's voice said. 'You went too far. Now I'm going to finish you.'

The piano wire cut into his hand. And Nemo struggled for his life.

He'd heard of piano wire being used by professional assassins. It was thin and sharp and slided through a throat as if it was butter. Thank God he had caught it with his hand. But the pain was excruciating.

His senses were as alive as they had ever been. He smelled the aftershave of the man behind him, heard the jagged breathing, felt the weight of his body.

They struggled silently – one for death and the other for life.

Nemo tried to move his hand so the wire would press against the sleeve of his sweater rather than his flesh. But it tore into him as he pushed.

No. The wire was embedded in his flesh now. There was nothing to be done with it except to hold it, keep it away from his throat.

He looked down and saw the man's black leather shoe. A target.

He lifted his own foot and brought it down as hard as he could on the man's instep. At the same moment he bent his arm and hit back with his right elbow. Both connected simultaneously bringing a yelp and a gasp.

The pressure loosened on the wire.

Nemo pushed his bloodied hand forward and ducked under the wire, turning at the same time to face his attacker. The man had doubled over with the blow to his midriff, but now he straightened and came towards

Nemo, the wire held out high in front of him. He would try to loop it over Nemo's head and slice through the back of his neck.

It was Jones. Even in the dark, Nemo knew the face, knew the man. Pale skin, a narrow face, thin lips, burning eyes. This was Lela's murderer, Sam's abductor. It was a different face, another body now, but the person behind the mask was the same. He knew it as well as he knew himself.

Jones rushed him and Nemo kicked, aiming for the man's knee. He missed and hit his lower thigh instead, but it slowed him down. Jones, realised he had lost the advantage of his weapon, dropped one end of the wire and began to whip it through the air like a sword.

Nemo raised his left arm to protect himself and swung with his right. Missed again. Went off balance. Felt a fist pound against his ribs. Started to fall. Lashed out with his right again and felt it hit the man's skull.

When he hit the floor, he rolled. He had to gain time. But Jones was there and his swinging foot caught Nemo in the solar plexus, causing him to gasp for air. Still, Nemo managed to grab the foot as it departed and pull Jones off balance as well.

Nemo rolled again, still gasping like a grounded fish, still needing time. He would get his breath and get this guy. The urge to survive was stronger than the urge to murder.

He came to one knee, one arm raised as a shield to protect himself from the attack that would come. But nothing came.

Instead there was the thump of footsteps leaving, the opening of a door.

He staggered to his feet and made it to the back door. He leaned against the jamb. Jones was running, a blur near the fence. And then he was over it and out of sight.

255

Jones had fled rather than confront him in a face to face fight. The man had known he would lose.

Nemo began to chase him but hadn't gone ten paces before he stopped, gulping in air. The man would have a car on the road on the other side of the block and he'd be there by now. He could try driving around, but it was a long block and Jones would be long gone by the time he made it there.

He looked at his hand. There was one deep cut and a host of smaller ones. Blood dripped to the ground.

An opportunity lost, he thought bitterly. But then he realised that his life had been at stake and that was what he had won. He'd live to face Jones another day.

He went back into the kitchen and unravelled a roll of paper towels. After washing his hand, he clamped them in a bunch over his wound.

His hand was shaking. No, his entire body shook. With trembling fingers, he dialled Lieutenant Marshall's number.

Chapter Nineteen

The fear came later for Sam. In fact, hours passed in the dusty basement room before she fully realised the enormity of what had happened. The blood on her face oozed out slowly, then hardened into the beginnings of a scab. Every now and then she reached a hand up and touched it and during one of those moments she saw with a strange, detached clarity that the rules of the game had changed.

She had been hurt – physically beaten, and it was a significant step in the wrong direction. The pressures of the situation, pressures she was only too well aware of, were apparently affecting Jones as well. Desperation had pushed him from the pose of charming suitor, to a covert attempt to drug her, to an overt and open physical attack. It was a downward spiral with the ultimate goal of . . . what?

It was then the fear came. The conclusion was too obvious to ignore.

She knew that fear fed on itself, but there was nothing else to do in her prison but think. And thought brought little solace. Try as she might to do otherwise, her thoughts focused on her predicament.

She spent half an hour poking around the basement,

inspecting the walls and dark corners, hoping to find a laundry chute or air vent, something through which she could crawl to freedom. But there was nothing. It was a sparse room with no apparent function.

The boxes piled against one wall intrigued her, but when she opened them she found only tattered old magazines with crumbling, yellowing pages.

She forced herself to exercise, but after forty-five minutes of that, she realised it was only weakening her. She had not eaten since the previous night, and hunger was becoming a factor. It was also a problem. If Jones offered food, should she eat it? Would he attempt again to drug her? She feared the drugs more than anything, more than physical abuse and perhaps even more than death. A beating hurt only her body. She would suffer from it, but she would be able to withstand it, she knew. But drugs were another matter. They weakened her will, and only her will supported her resistance.

She wondered again what Nemo was doing. Whenever she found herself sinking into despair, she thought of him and sifted through the memories of their short relationship. She had recalled the first time they made love a hundred times now. She remembered their dinners, the other times they made love, their walk through Studio City, their visit to the museum, and, above all, his promise that he would not let anything happen to her. Because of that, she knew he would be doing everything he could to find her.

The thought comforted her, but the mind is a curious thing. No sooner did she allow hope to rise, than despair of equal or greater weight crashed down on it like a hammer. Yes, he would be trying to find her, but, no, he would not succeed. It was an impossible task. Jones had appeared from nowhere, entered her life like an invisible wraith. There were no connections to be seen.

How could he be found? Anyone who attempted to track her with a logical approach would be facing almost certain failure. There was nothing logical about what had happened. How could one predict or perceive a mind as unbalanced as Jones'?

She dozed on the floor, her thoughts jumbled between sleep and wakefulness. She dreamed of being with Nemo. They were on a mountain above the city. It was night and the flickering lights below seemed to be dancing only for them. 'Think of them as stars and make a wish,' Nemo said.

'I wish we were together,' she said.

She spread her arms and flew from the mountain, swooping above the city, clothed in exultation, a joyful song bursting from her lips.

And then Nemo was beside her, holding her hand, and they went out above the ocean and travelled for a while with the grey whales who were going south to mate.

And then the power of flight seemed to desert her and she felt herself fall.

Down she went, faster and faster. Until . . .

She was lying on a bed and Nemo was crying beside her and she wondered why.

She wanted to ask him what was happening, but she couldn't because she was dead.

There was a noise and she opened her eyes and sat up. The door began to open and a figure stood silhouetted against the bright light in the passage. After a moment she saw it was Jones.

She rose to her feet as he came down the stairs. He stopped a yard away from her and looked searchingly at her face. 'You made me do that,' he said.

259

Sam didn't answer, but lifted her chin defiantly. Damned if she'd cower before him.

'I hope you learned a lesson,' he said.

Still she said nothing.

A momentary indecisiveness crossed his face and then he said, 'Come on. Your room is ready.'

When they reached her room she saw the door had been replaced. He gestured for her to go in and said, 'Dinner will be in half an hour. I'm sure you wish to wash.'

She heard the key turn in the lock.

She went to the mirror and inspected the damage. She hardly recognised her own face. The left side of her lip was all that had been cut, although the blood caked in a dribble on her chin. There was also a bruise on her left cheek where he had struck her. And dust covered it all – face, ears, arms, hands and clothes.

She stood under the shower for twenty minutes, turning the water as hot as she could bear. She wished it could wash everything away, but of course it didn't. The fear was still there and another feeling as well – the sense of degradation that accompanied being a victim. She recognised it for what it was, but it was a hard one to shake.

The feeling of degradation came from a strange self-blame associated with her predicament. Somehow, she was angry at herself for getting into this situation. Of course, she knew it was illogical and irrational, but she couldn't help feeling that in some way it was her fault she was a prisoner in this house. She must have done something to bring about this retribution. These things didn't just happen. Some fault in her character must have attracted the man. Stupid thoughts, she knew, but that knowledge did nothing to eradicate them.

She towelled herself hard, rubbing her skin until it

burned, trying not to think, but only to act. As soon as she finished dressing, the door opened and the house-keeper stood there, her face as sullen and vacant as always.

Jones waited for her at the head of the table. ·

'Ah,' he said when she entered, and stood while she sat.

'You must be hungry,' he said.

The choice faced her now. Would there be drugs in the food or drink? Should she eat or not?

'Are you going to try to drug me again?' she asked, antagonism coating her voice.

'I told you, those were only relaxants,' he said, 'No, I shall not give them to you again.'

'I don't trust you,' she said. 'Why should I?'

'We shall drink from the same bottle and eat from the same dishes,' he said.

'No drink,' she said. 'I'll eat some food.'

'This is a very good year,' he said, showing her the wine bottle.

'No drink,' she repeated.

Jones shrugged and poured himself wine. He sipped it appreciatively and looked at her over the glass. 'I met your boyfriend today,' he said casually.

Sam had to stop herself from gasping. Nemo? He'd seen Nemo? 'Oh,' she said, in an uninterested voice. 'What boyfriend?'

'Yes,' he said, forcing a smile and ignoring her ques-tion. 'We bumped into each other, but unfortunately I had to leave rather quickly.'

'Are you referring to Nemo Riley?' she asked.

'Nemo Riley/Phillip Bates – the man who took you away from me back then. I planned to prevent that from happening again, but it didn't quite work out as I had planned.'

261

'What did you do to him?' she asked, unable to hide the concern any longer.

Jones held his wine up to the light and admired the colour. 'Not enough, unfortunately. But don't worry, I will.'

'What in God's name has he ever done to you?' she said angrily. 'Leave him alone.'

'He killed you,' Jones said. 'In your life as Lela, Phillip Bates was the lover who killed you. Nemo Riley was Bates.'

'Oh, God,' she said, pressing her hands against her cheeks. 'Is there anyone who isn't a part of your perverted fantasy?'

'It's no fantasy. He took you away from me,' Jones said.

She looked at him uncomprehendingly. How could this man think thoughts like these and still function. He slept, he rose, he dressed himself, he worked, he conversed, he did all the things that people normally did and yet he was completely insane.

He sipped his wine and said, 'I shall have to kill your Mr Riley.'

'You can't mean that!' she said in horror. 'How can he hurt you now?'

'Oh, I do mean it. In fact, I have already tried. I don't mean the time I shot at him. That was just a warning. No, I visited him this evening. However, plans do not always work out. Next time, I will be more efficient.'

'Leave him alone,' she screamed, banging her fists on the table.

Jones pretended to be surprised. 'Oh,' he said, raising an eyebrow. 'Is there something more than platonic love here?'

'He's done nothing to you. He's a good, decent man whose only fault is to be a friend of mine. Leave him

262

alone,' she said more quietly.

'He will try to ruin me again,' Jones said. 'He remembers, even if you don't. He is an evil man and must be prevented from ruining us again.'

'Oh, God,' she said in frustration.

He looked slyly at her. 'Perhaps we could come to an agreement? You remember and I will leave your friend alone to his devices.'

'Remember! Remember! I can't remember. Can't you get that through your head. I don't believe in this insanity of yours. You have to believe in order to create the memories you want.'

'Yes, I thought that would be your response. You are nothing if not consistent, Lela. Always have been,' he said.

She nibbled at her food, hunger deserting her in the onrush of fear for Nemo's safety. What could she do? Could she pretend to remember? Make the deal with him and fake it? She doubted she would be able to pull it off. The man was crazy, but as cunning as a fox. The only consolation lay between the lines. He had apparently tried to do something to Nemo and failed. Nemo had proved too much for him to handle. Either that, or simple fate had intervened. If anyone could look after himself, it would be Nemo. Perhaps it would serve them both better if she didn't worry about him and concerned herself instead with the problem of how to get out of here.

'You are very quiet tonight,' Jones said.

'I have nothing to say to you,' she said.

Anger infected Jones' face. 'I should think you know by now that my patience has its limits. I told you that before,' he said sharply.

Sam rested her elbows on the table and stared hard back at him. 'Are you going to hit me again?'

Jones looked sullenly back at her.

'If you are,' she continued coolly, 'do it now. I don't care. Do what you like.'

'You made me do that,' he said.

'I made you do nothing,' she said. 'You chose to do it. You chose to keep me here. You chose to react. You chose violence.'

'You made me. You made me,' he said.

Suddenly he looked like a child protesting its innocence after being accused of some transgression. His face, normally so controlled and studied, now seemed immature and weak and petulant.

'Nobody else is responsible for your actions,' she said softly, pushing it.

'You don't understand,' he said, a glassiness in his eyes. 'I never wanted to hurt you. He made me do it. You made me do it. I never wanted to.'

'He made you hit me?' she asked.

'He made me do it. I had no choice. If I hadn't done it he would have taken you. And then you said those things to me. Such cruel things. I had to do it, Lela. The knife was there, it came into my hand and I had to do it.'

'Had to do what?' she asked, puzzled now.

'To kill you!' he screamed, his face livid. 'I had to kill you!'

'What are you saying?' she asked, not understanding.

His face changed instantaneously, the anger replaced by a childish cunning. He smiled thinly at her and said, 'I know what you're doing. I'm not saying anything. You just got me upset that's all. I didn't know what I was saying.'

'I made you say it,' she said ironically.

An expressionless mask dropped over his face then and he stared back at her in stubborn silence.

Sam sighed and pushed her plate away. 'I need some

264

sleep,' she said, and added with a touch of sarcasm, 'May I please be excused?'

Jones nodded. There was still no expression on his face, but there was a new look in his eyes, a wariness, the watchful look of a man who suspects he is about to be attacked.

Sam felt a surge of triumph. The man wasn't holding it together. If she could maintain herself, he could crack before she did. The problem was, she had no idea what he would do when he finally snapped altogether. She fervently hoped she wasn't around to see it.

'Excuse me,' she said calmly, and stood. She turned and walked from the room. She could feel his eyes pushing into her back like fingers.

There was something different about the room, apart from the new door. After looking around and failing to spot what it was that had changed, she placed the chair against the door. If he wanted to creep in there during the night, he'd have to batter it down with an axe again. She wasn't leaving it unguarded.

She stretched out on the bed without bothering to change her clothes. Exhaustion soaked her body. The last two days had multiplied the stress cumulatively.

She switched off the bedside lamp and lay still in the dark. The bruised spot on her cheek pounded in rhythm with her pulse. What had Jones been talking about? Apparently he thought he had killed this Lela woman in his other life. What then of the tape recording he had played of his hypnotic session? Had he edited it, changed the end of the story, so to speak, merely to impress her? It was an ominous development. If he thought he was capable of murder back then, what of now?

Drifting on the edge of sleep, she suddenly sat up, lifting an arm automatically to protect herself.

'Lela? It was Jones' voice, but she saw no one.

She turned the light on.

'Lela, I have something to tell you. You must listen now.'

Where was the voice coming from?

And then she saw what she had sensed or perhaps seen earlier out of the corner of her eye – the addition to the room, a speaker high on the wall above the dresser.

'Lela, I want you to listen to the sound of my voice. Relax to the sound of my voice and remember who you were. I want you to try and remember, to allow the pictures to come into your mind as I speak.'

There was an almost sing-song quality to his voice. It sounded as if he might be reading from a script.

'You were Lela Edwards,' the voice continued. 'You lived in New York and you were a successful model. But your success meant nothing. You were unhappy until you met me at that party.

'Remember the party? High above the city . . . a large mansion . . . the finest society of Hollywood . . . the stars, the men handsome in dinner jackets, the women in gowns, the orchestra playing at one end of the huge room. Remember?'

Sam got off the bed and walked to the speaker. She stood below it and looked up while the voice droned on. He was speaking from another room, or perhaps he was playing a tape recording of something he had prepared earlier. There was a certain tone to the voice, as if it was spoken into a machine.

'Now, let the picture of the party come into your mind,' he continued. 'See the colours of the dresses, the huge chandeliers on the ceiling, the liveried waiters. Hear the music . . .'

266

A scratchy old dance tune came on then. Harry James? She wasn't sure.

How long did he plan to keep it up? If it was a recording, it could go on all night and she desperately needed to sleep.

The speaker was set into the wall, probably fastened from the hallway. There were no screws or wires visible. What if she bashed against the outer shell? With what? The chair was too heavy to lift that high. There was no broom or similar length of wood in the room.

The music ended, there was a momentary pause, and then the voice returned. 'Do you remember when we first made love? Do you know that it was in this very house? Yes, I owned this house then. At least, my family did. I found it again six months ago and luckily it was on the market. I bought it and intended to bring you back here.

'We made love, not in this room, but in one down the hall, the large master bedroom. Remember it? The big bed had a canopy like this one. Your passion was boundless. You cried my name at the end. Remember?'

God, Sam thought wildly, how can I stop this drivel? She picked up a shoe and threw it up at the speaker. On the third try she hit it, but the shoe just bounced off and the voice went on.

'I thought when I brought you here that you would recognise the house. We had many happy hours here, my dear. Think on it now. Remember . . .'

The voice went on and on with its reminiscences and instructions. 'Remember . . . remember . . .'

Sam threw herself on the bed and pulled the pillow up around her ears, but still the voice penetrated.

'We drove down the coast. There were few houses then. We stopped and watched dolphins cavort near the rocks. You wanted to make love on the beach, but I suggested we wait until we reached San Diego . . .'

Jesus! She had to stop it, had to find a way to rest. The bathroom! She took her blankets and pillows into the small bathroom. The tub was dry now. She threw them into it, closed the door behind her and climbed into the tub.

She lay down and pulled the pillow up around her head again. The voice was only a soft murmur now, soft enough to ignore. It was uncomfortable, but bearable.

Within minutes she sank gratefully into sleep. She dreamed of driving beside the ocean in an old car, her hair flying back in the wind, a joyous smile on her lips. But the man beside her wasn't Jones. It was Nemo.

She called his name in her sleep.

In the other room, the voice rolled on.

'We had dinner at the Brown Derby. Ben Turpin was there. He came over to our table and talked to us. He complimented me on my taste in women. Remember . . . ?'

Chapter Twenty

'You're sure he was wearing gloves?' Lieutenant Marshall asked.

'Yes, I'm sure,' Nemo replied wearily.

'Shit,' Marshall said disgustedly. 'Well, as usual, he left nothing and nobody saw him. Didn't even leave his goddamn piano wire.'

The paramedic finished bandaging Nemo's hand and said, 'You be certain to go and see your doctor tomorrow. We don't want this getting infected.'

'A strange weapon to use,' Marshall said. 'Type of thing you read about in books – "Strangled by piano wire" – but I've never seen it employed before.'

'Well, I guess the guy has a wild imagination,' Nemo said.

He shook the medic's hand and showed him out. 'You want a drink?' he asked Marshall, back in the living room.

The policeman looked at his watch. 'Don't mind. I'm off duty now.'

'I could use one myself,' Nemo said. 'Scotch okay?'

He poured them each two fingers of Scotch and sat heavily on the couch. The fight had taken more out of him than he realised. His body felt suddenly old and heavy.

Marshall sipped his drink appreciatively and said, 'He didn't say anything except those few words at first?'

'We were both too busy to talk,' Nemo said grimly. 'But I got a good look at him. I'd know him anywhere.'

'I'll get the artist around tomorrow. Maybe we can get a better composite and get the television stations to run it.'

Nemo shrugged. 'If you think it'll do any good.'

It was Marshall's turn to shrug. 'Who the hell knows,' he said.

Nemo noticed the disappointed lines around Marshall's mouth and felt relieved he wasn't a policeman. It had to be one of the most frustrating jobs on earth. Nor did it give you a generous view of human nature. You dealt constantly with people who were emotionally disturbed, who were conscienceless, or depraved, or without the normal attributes of humanity. Sometimes you were able to help people, but rarely. Usually you arrived on the scene when it was too late to help.

They drank in glum silence for a moment and then Marshall said he was leaving. Nemo walked him to the door, not bothering to ask what he was going to do next. It would only embarrass him. They both knew Marshall still had nothing tangible to pursue.

Marshall turned at the bottom of the front steps. 'You got a gun?'

'Yes, I do,' Nemo said. 'A couple of revolvers. Why?'

'Keep one handy.'

'You think he'll try again?'

'I don't know,' Marshall said. 'But he wants to kill you, doesn't he?'

Yes, he did, Nemo thought when he was back in the house. Jones wanted to kill him because he knew who he was, or who he had been. When Marshall asked what motives Jones had for attempting murder, Nemo quite truthfully said, 'Jealousy, probably.' Marshall didn't have any problem accepting that. What he didn't know was that the jealousy went back sixty years and other lifetimes.

And he probably would try again, Nemo thought. This hadn't been an attempt to warn him off. The man wanted him dead and he was prepared to do something about it. It was a chilling thought. He'd never been a target before.

He couldn't dispel the thought that he'd blown it. T. had been in his house. Right here. They'd struggled, hand to hand and man to man, and T. had got away. The man came to kill him, of course, and he *had* been able to foil him, but he should have been able to turn the tables. If he had, Sam might be sitting in the living room at this moment.

He berated himself for about fifteen minutes and then decided it was a useless exercise in masochism. He needed to do something. He needed to talk to someone.

He called Maddy.

'Would you like to go out for a drink?' he asked.

'No,' she said. 'Why don't you come over to my place?'

She lived in West Hollywood in an apartment building with potted palm trees and a false façade that proclaimed, 'East of Eden Apartments.'

'It's a dump, but it's home,' she said when she opened the door. She wore faded blue jeans and a large sloppy sweatshirt.

She looked as if she hadn't slept for days. But in spite of her tangled hair and drawn features, she still had a welcoming smile and the usual humorous glint in her eyes. 'It's a singles building,' she said. 'I thought I could meet guys here, but it's actually single homosexuals. Ah, well, the story of my life.'

271

The apartment was by no means a dump, as she claimed. It was expensively and comfortably furnished with attractive prints on the walls and a jungle of indoor plants on shelves and on the floor. A top-of-the-line stereo system was occupied with a Miles Davis record.

'*Sketches of Spain*' Nemo said with a smile of recognition.

'You know it?' she asked, surprised.

'I think it was the first album to introduce me to modern jazz,' he said. 'I loved it.'

'What happened to your hand?' she asked, noticing the bandage for the first time.

'I had a little visit from our friend, T.,' he said, and gave her a shortened version of what happened.

'My God,' she said.

'I'm just pissed with myself for not getting the guy,' he said. 'I had him there and let him go.'

'I imagine you were kinda busy saving your life,' she said drily.

He shook his head and said, 'Still . . .'

'What?' she said. 'Are you being hard on yourself, or sorry for yourself, or a combination of both?'

Nemo couldn't help smiling at her tone. 'Both, I guess.'

'Well, you have no right to feel sorry for yourself,' she said firmly. 'Sam's the one in trouble and that's not going to help her.'

'Yeah,' he said.

'Come on, snap out of it,' she urged. 'I know it's tough, but you have to keep going for Sam's sake.'

'I'm not getting anywhere,' he said. 'I just keep going in circles and not getting any closer to her.'

'Something will happen,' she said optimistically. 'If you keep on trying, something will happen.'

'I've been telling myself the same thing,' he said, not at all encouraged.

272

'God, you're a mess,' she said unsympathetically. 'What do you want to drink?'

He asked for wine and she went to the kitchen. A moment later she returned and handed him a glass.

'What have you been doing anyway?' she asked, sitting beside him on the couch.

'I've been remembering the same past life that T. claims to remember,' he said.

He hadn't intended to say anything like that, but he just blurted it out, without thought of consequences. It had been balancing on the edge of his mouth and simply tumbled away from him.

Maddy put her glass carefully on the end table. For the first time concern filled her face. 'Give me that again?' she said.

'It started with dreams and then the memories came,' he said. He backtracked and explained the sequence of events – the dreams of Lela, the coincidences, the discovery of facts he thought to be the imaginings of sleep, and then the open and accessible memories. Maddy listened to it all, not saying a word.

'We all knew each other, here in Los Angeles in the Twenties – Terry Jones, Lela Edwards and myself, Phillip Bates,' he said, summing it up. 'We formed what was called a fateful love triangle. Lela and I died together, murdered by Jones, who was later hung for the crime.'

'And Jones remembered all this through hypnotism?' she asked finally.

'Yes. But the man's psychotic. He can't let go of it. He's like one of those horses going round and round, tied to a post.'

'And you just remembered?'

'Through necessity, through being exposed to all of this again, through being in the right place at the right

273

time. All of those things, I suppose.'

Her silence told him as much as the stiffness of her face.

'You think I'm crazy too?' he asked with a weak smile.

'Yes, I think you're nuts,' she said. But then she shook her head in contradiction. 'It's only my first reaction,' she added honestly. 'Then come the second thoughts. I remember you telling me earlier about the dreams. The thing with the dress – the fact that Sam designed a dress exactly like that. I never could explain that. I don't know what to think.' She spread her hands out helplessly. 'I really don't. I'm a practical person. I believe in what I can see and touch and all of this is too much for me to handle. I can't help but think that the pressure has become too much for you to handle, Nemo.'

'I don't have any doubts, you know,' he said. 'I know now that it's true. But the thing is, it isn't important. Here and now is important, and getting Sam away from that crazy is important.'

'Why did you tell me this?' she asked.

'I don't know. I had to tell someone, I guess. Maybe a new perspective is what's needed now. I don't seem to be getting anywhere. I keep thinking the clue that'll lead me to her is in the past, but I can't see it. I just can't see it.'

'Perhaps you're looking too hard.'

'What do you mean?'

'Sometimes when I have a problem, if I stop thinking about it the solution pops into my mind after a while. If I try and force it, nothing comes.'

'That may be right,' he said, 'but I don't have the time to wait around for inspiration to strike.'

'You really believe that you're remembering your own past life?' she asked.

'Yes.'

274

She shook her head and said, 'I just can't accept that.'

'It's all right,' he said. 'I'm sorry I placed you in this position. I had to tell someone.'

'Yes,' she said, a determined expression replacing the confusion. 'Let's put aside my scepticism for the moment. Let's suppose that this is true – that both you and this guy are remembering this past life. Let's pretend that it's true. Tell me what you've remembered in more detail. Let's go over it in detail.'

'Really?' Nemo asked, interest lightening his features. 'You'd be willing to listen to it all again?'

'If it helps Sam, I'll listen to anything,' she said.

'You'd better put on some coffee. This may take a while,' Nemo warned her.

They talked until after two in the morning. Nemo dredged up every recollection he'd had. Then they started comparing it to what they knew of the man now. It led to the same dead end, the same tired old conclusions.

'Look, it boils down to this,' Nemo finally said. 'He murdered her in a jealous rage last time. I keep thinking that it's going to happen again.'

'Not necessarily,' Maddy said. 'He's trying to get her back this time. It's you he wants out of the way.'

'He wants her to remember. The dress, the telephone call, the use of the name, Lela. What if she doesn't remember?'

'If he has her, why would it bother him?' Maddy asked.

'Because the man is crazy. If he was sane and happened to remember this past life, he would have simply met her and wooed her and maybe explained things to her in a rational manner. Assuming even that he'd want to continue with this long-dead relationship. But, no, he abducted her and he tried to kill me. He's caught up in

275

this thing in some insane manner.'

'Well, how would he try to get her to remember?' Maddy asked thoughtfully.

'He'd talk to her, I guess. Try to force her.'

'Maybe he'd take her to places they were at together in the other life,' she suggested.

Nemo grimaced negatively. 'Too risky. Someone might see her.'

'Maybe he'd show her things she owned in that life.'

'That was the dress,' Nemo said. 'Somehow he found it. Perhaps in some thrift shop or some private collection. But that must have been lucky. A coincidence, or whatever. I doubt he'd find much else. Things simply don't last that long.'

'Yes, I guess you're right.'

'Back with nothing,' Nemo said gloomily.

After talking more without obvious progress, they both began to yawn.

'I'd better go,' Nemo said. 'I've imposed on you long enough.'

'I only wish I could have helped,' Maddy said.

'You have. You let me share this with you. I didn't know how much I needed to do that.'

'If I think of anything else I'll call you,' she promised.

Nemo drove home with a sense of failure sitting like a passenger in the seat beside him. It had been a relief to blurt it all out, even to a disbelieving audience. But it brought him no closer to Sam. Maddy was right. His own feelings were not what mattered now. Only Sam mattered.

Stopped at a traffic light, a red glow flushing his face, he said aloud, 'Where are you, Sam?'

Nobody answered.

*   *   *

276

The same plump, blotchy-faced artist he had met at the florist's shop arrived at Nemo's house in the morning. Although it was not yet eleven, there was an unmistakable bouquet of alcohol on his breath.

The artist, Gabby Hauser pulled out the earlier drawings and layered features over them, according to Nemo's directions. After about an hour, a fairly good likeness emerged of the man Nemo struggled with.

'Good enough,' Hauser said, gathering his materials. 'An improvement on what I had to go on before. Marshall is waiting for this. I'd better get it back.'

'When will it get on the air?' Nemo asked.

'How would I know?' Hauser replied. 'I suppose Marshall's going to try for the evening news. There's still a lot of pressure on this one from above.'

'Good,' Nemo said.

'Easy for you to say,' Hauser grumbled.

Nemo felt more optimistic after he left. It really wasn't a bad likeness. Perhaps this time someone would know the man. It was the best he could hope for.

Maddy called to see if he'd come up with anything new since they talked. He mentioned the drawing and then said, 'I was so busy talking about myself last night, I forgot to ask how the business was doing with all this happening?'

Maddy groaned. 'Terribly,' she said. 'I'm beginning to get the feeling from the people we deal with that they think Sam's dead. Most of them are not answering my phone calls. They're just waiting for the body to be found and then they're going to tear up those nice little contracts.'

'It won't happen that way,' he said.

'I know. But I can't expect them to have the same faith we have.'

'Well, hang in there,' he said. 'Maybe something will

277

come of the police drawing.'

His laundry was piling up – sweat-stained shirts, rumpled sheets and underclothes all accused him of neglect. He attacked them energetically, thankful to be engaged in a task requiring no thought. Was it faith they had, he wondered as he worked? He thought not. The man would not have bothered to come after him if Sam were already dead. He was a rival in T.'s eyes, and to be a rival, there had to be an object of mutual attention. She *had* to be alive still.

I'll grab any straw, he thought. He held hope, no matter how futile, like a banner – a blind soldier riding into battle. But will I ever find Sam, he wondered?

He banged his hand against the thin metal of the washing machine, causing a dent. It was too much for a man to bear. He couldn't go on like this, hoping and despairing. Time was on the side of despair. It had to end soon. It had to.

He slid down the wall and sat on the floor of the laundry room and cried while the blades of the machine beside him swirled the clothes around and around.

Chapter Twenty-one

Amanda Baker and Janet Desmond smiled warily at each other over the restaurant table. Although socially friendly for years now, they still tended to circle each other like hungry predators waiting for an opening.

'I will have the Caesar's, please,' Amanda told the waiter.

'Coquille St Jacques,' Janet said. 'And another glass of white wine.'

Their relationship was based on mutual admiration. Janet respected Amanda's social skills and ability to manipulate people, while Amanda admired the younger woman's sexual boldness and equally awesome ability to manipulate in a different context.

'I hear you went home with one of my writers the other night,' Amanda said when the waiter left.

The use of the possessive didn't escape Janet. 'Terence Jones?' she asked. 'I didn't know he was yours.'

'Only in a social context, dear.' She sighed deeply. 'My appetites are, unfortunately, different from yours these days.'

'He's an interesting man, but quite bizarre,' Janet said with a self-satisfied smile.

'Then you must have enjoyed him?' Amanda asked ambiguously.

'On a certain level,' Janet said. 'He may be a little too weird, even for me.'

'How so? There's a certain intensity, a stiffness about him, but I wouldn't have thought of him as that unusual. Are you referring to his performance in the bedroom?'

'I think he hates women, for one thing. Then there's this strange reincarnation trip that he's on,' Janet said. Her eyes fell on the man at the next table. He had a nice body, but she could tell by the way he crammed food into his mouth that he'd be a hasty lover.

Amanda's ears perked up. 'Reincarnation trip?' she asked. Terence told her at the party he wasn't interested.

'He was talking about faithfulness. He said some people were faithful to those they loved for lifetimes. Something about real true love transcending death. Selflessness, and all that. Demonstrating his fidelity as opposed to mine.' Her eyes came back to Amanda. 'He thinks I'm a slut. Do you agree with him?'

'Of course not,' Amanda said. 'Promiscuous, certainly, but a free spirit, not a –' She refrained from uttering the word. Really, Janet's compulsive frankness was tiresome at times. 'Are you going to see him again?'

'Perhaps. Perhaps not. He offered a certain kind of excitement lacking in most men. But he might be a little too strange for my taste.'

'When he was talking about reincarnation, was it from a personal point of view?' Amanda asked, getting back to her interest. 'Something he experienced, or . . .'

Janet shrugged. 'Who knows? Maybe he'd been reading about that woman who was kidnapped. What's her name?'

'The designer?' Amanda had read the newspaper stories as well. The kidnapper claimed to know her in a past life. Of course, the papers tended to sensationalise these things, but she had found it fascinating. Unfortunately, people like that gave reincarnation a bad name.

280

'Yes, Barry. Sam Barry,' Janet said. 'In fact, he's weird enough to be the one who kidnapped her.'

'Terence? Oh no, he's much too proper,' Amanda said.

'Proper?' Janet said with a knowing smile. 'You don't know him in the same way I know him.'

Amanda smiled sweetly. 'The conversation always returns to the bedroom with you, doesn't it, dear?'

'It's what I do best,' Janet said, unabashed.

They talked of other things during the lunch and then went their separate ways: Janet to her hairdresser and Amanda to Bullocks to buy a birthday gift for a young niece.

Later, when she arrived home, Amanda's thoughts returned idly to the conversation. Why, she wondered, had Terence denied an interest in reincarnation? She sighed. The answer was obvious, of course. He was a strange and insular man, obsessed by privacy. Intellectually brilliant and charming but he never revealed much of himself. It was one of his most fascinating traits, in fact. The air of mystery that surrounded him.

It would be just like him to take her advice and see a hypnotist and then tell her he hadn't. She smiled at the thought. Perhaps she had got through to him after all. An unacknowledged convert was better than no convert at all. She took the blouse she had bought for her niece from its box and held it up. It was beautiful, she thought, but then fell victim of doubt. You never knew with young people these days. Tastes and fashions changed so quickly, you couldn't be certain what they would like. She should have stayed away from clothes and bought her a piece of jewellery. Oh, well, she thought fatalistically, the girl could always take it back and exchange it.

She went into her library and began to make her daily round of afternoon telephone calls to her circle of acquaintances. One had to keep in touch.

281

At six o'clock, after preparing a small snack of crackers and camembert cheese, Amanda sat in the television room and turned on the set. She was going to the theatre with a group of people in a couple of hours and planned to have supper afterwards at a newly discovered French bistro. The snack would keep her going.

Like much of her social life, the evening was obligatory rather than freely chosen on the basis of personal pleasure. At least one of the women accompanying them was a deathly bore. Still, she took her responsibilities seriously. One of the couples, Daphne and Carson Agutter, were socially prominent and well worth developing.

Her mind occupied with the evening ahead, she inattentively watched the evening news. The Agutter's were *nouveau riche*, as so many people were these days, desperate for acceptance in the more important monied circles. Perhaps they could be convinced to become patrons of the young artist she had recently discovered. He needed the help and they the status. It would be mutually beneficial and everyone would be happy, which was always the best end result.

And then her attention riveted on the television screen, all thoughts of social manipulation vanished.

It was a picture, one of those awful cartoon-like police composite drawings. She listened to the announcer say that police had, '. . . reissued an updated composite of the suspect in the Sam Barry abduction . . . and if anyone knows who this man is, please call the police.'

No, she thought, it's impossible.

The picture bore a remarkable likeness to Terence Jones.

It was difficult to tell, of course. Those drawings were seldom more than caricatures. And yet, it had the same narrow face, the same deepset eyes. But it couldn't be.

She used the remote control to find another newscast.

282

About two minutes later, the same story came on. This time she studied the picture carefully.

If someone showed her the picture and asked who it was, she would find herself saying, 'Well, it looks like a bad drawing of the brother of writer Terence Jones. There's such an obvious family resemblance.' Taking into account the limitations of police artists and witnesses, however, it could well be Terence.

Her mind went back to the luncheon conversation with Janet Desmond. He'd talked familiarly of reincarnation, of love in a past life – all after denying an interest in the subject to her at the recent party. Janet's words came back to her: 'He's weird enough to be the one who kidnapped her.' It struck her at the time as just another of Janet's idle and outrageous remarks and she had quite rightly scoffed at it. But how well did she really know Terence? They were friends, weren't they? But how well did she *know* him? Only what he chose to let her know. He had a barrier that social acquaintances never saw through.

Could he have kidnapped that young designer? For the first time, she asked the question outright. Goodness, she thought, what am I going to do?

It wasn't her job to decide. She should call the police and tell them her suspicions. They would investigate and ascertain the truth. If she were wrong, and the picture wasn't of Terence at all, but simply happened to bear a strong resemblance to him, he would at most be inconvenienced. If it was him, the police would handle it.

Her mind made up, she reached for the telephone on the shelf behind where she sat. She lifted the receiver and dialled information to get the number of the police.

'What city, please?' the operator asked.

But what if it was Terence? She had been the one to introduce him to the subject of reincarnation, hadn't she? In the resulting fuss, it would all come out. Would

283

she be held responsible? Of course not. But the media would grab onto that juicy little titbit and create a scandal. There would be talk. Her name would be linked to that of a criminal's forever.

'What city, please?' the operator repeated.

Amanda replaced the receiver.

She needed to think of the consequences before she did anything rash.

She had a reputation to consider, a position to uphold. She had no desire to become involved in anything remotely seedy. Of course, people knew she associated constantly with artists of one kind or another, and they could be considered seedy, she supposed. On the fringe, anyway. But their scandals had never touched her. In this case, however, she had actually suggested he go to her hypnotist and find out about past life regression. In a way, she was responsible for his actions. At least, it could be argued that way.

She picked up her phone again and called her hypnotist.

'Alan? How are you dear? I just have a quick question. I suggested to a writer friend of mine, Terence Jones, that he come and see you. Did he?'

He hadn't, Alan said. Perhaps he had used another name? She described him. No, he hadn't come. Positively not.

She hung up again. Well, thank God for that. But he might have gone to someone else. And it had still been at her suggestion.

There was really only one thing to be done, she thought, coming to a conclusion. She should go and see Terry and confront him with her suspicions. If he had done this foolish thing, she should talk some sense into him before things went too far. It was her responsiblity.

Her mind made up, she reached for the telephone

284

again and excused herself from the theatre party. She apologised profusely, saying she was suffering from a migraine headache. She promised to arrange an alternate outing soon.

It was probably a mistake, she told herself as she dressed. More than likely it was a coincidence. The real kidnapper bore some slight resemblance to Terence. The rest could be due to her active imagination.

Before she left, she told her housekeeper she was going to see Mr Jones. 'I'll be back in a couple of hours,' she said.

Sam sat at the dinner table and watched Jones dab a napkin at the corners of his mouth. It was the first time she had seen him since the previous night. The recording of his voice had never stopped. She had managed to sleep, but then she woke in the morning the patter was still going on. And it continued through the afternoon as well. He must have set some kind of loop on his tape recorder, she decided finally. She figured that the entire monologue lasted about two hours before it began to repeat. She had spent much of the day in the bathroom. However, by late afternoon, her nerves were on edge.

He came to get her for dinner a short time ago, putting on his usual act of complete normality. When she complained about the recording he simply smiled and said it was for her own good. 'A part of your ongoing education, Lela.'

She ate dinner in sullen silence.

It had come down to a battle of wills now, she decided. His against hers. She was afraid she was losing it, however. Every now and then her eyes would go out of focus and the world would look as it did to someone who stood up too quickly. Her thoughts were wandering too. She found herself thinking the oddest and most insignificant things. It was hard for her to concentrate. And growing harder to see things as they were. Imagination kept intruding. At times, the barrier between reality and unreality seemed little more than a thin, transparent veil.

'How is your memory coming along?' he asked, his words piercing through her fog.

The sound of his voice made her shiver. She'd been hearing it on the tape forever it seemed. Now it was like a rusty nail scraped on metal.

She could not let him know how weak she felt.

'My memory is perfect, as it has always been,' she said defiantly.

'Hmm,' he said.

A short time later, he poured wine in her glass and cleared his throat. 'You know, Lela,' he said, 'you must understand that everything I'm doing is purely out of love for you. It's all for your own good, for your happiness. You'll see the truth of that one day.'

She said nothing. It was an old speech, one she'd heard many times before.

He leaned back in his chair and looked directly at her. 'It won't be too much longer now,' he said. 'Soon you'll remember everything.'

And yet even as he spoke, she heard the quiver of uncertainty in his voice. He was trying to hide it, but it was there, she thought triumphantly. *He was no longer certain.*

'You're beginning to realise that I'm not going to remember, aren't you?' she asked daringly. 'You're beginning to see that you've made a mistake.'

Quickly he sat upright. 'I have not made a mistake. You will remember,' he said forcefully.

Sam smiled. 'No, I won't. Because there's nothing to remember. And you know I'm not going to.'

286

He put his glass down on the table with a crash. 'Stop it!' he ordered. 'You have to remember. If you don't . . .' He looked away, leaving it unsaid.

'What?' she asked. 'You'll murder me, as you think you murdered Lela, the woman in your imagination? Go ahead. It would be better than living as a prisoner here, subject to your sick fantasies.'

He glowered at her, seemingly not knowing how to respond.

'I'd rather die than keep this up forever,' she continued. 'And I'd definitely rather die than play the part of your lover. I can't stand you. Can't you see that?'

He was about to speak, when a flash of headlights brightened the window. He got up quickly and took her arm.

'Come on. Up to your room,' he said, pushing her hastily. 'If you make a sound, you may get your wish.'

They almost ran up the stairs. He shoved her into the room, saying, 'Who the hell could that be?' He locked the door. 'Now, you be quiet,' he said, and she heard his footsteps thunder away.

She couldn't suppress the rising hope. Maybe it was the police. Maybe it was Nemo. Help of some kind. She sat on the bed and waited. Thank God, at least, the tape was not running.

The doorbell rang. Jones straightened his tie and took a deep breath. He walked slowly to the door and opened it.

'Amanda!' he cried, wondering what in the hell she was doing here. 'What a lovely surprise!'

'Hello, Terence. May I come in?'

'Of course,' he said, stepping aside. 'I'm afraid I'm leaving in a few minutes though.'

He led her into the living room and asked if she wanted a drink.

'Thank you, no,' she said. 'I must ask you something very important.'

'Oh?'

She did not sit, but stood facing him. She held her handbag before her like a shield, hands fiddling with the gold clasp.

'Were you involved with the abduction of that fashion designer, Miss Barry?' she asked.

The blood left Jones' face and his mouth opened involuntarily. It took a moment, but then he recovered his composure and said, 'What are you talking about?'

His reaction was enough to increase her certainty. 'There was a police composite drawing on the television this evening,' she said. 'It was a picture of you, Terence.'

'Of me?' he asked, forcing a choked laugh. 'That's ridiculous. It must have been some kind of mistake.' But he'd been the one to make a mistake, he thought, his mind flashing through the possibilities. Damn! It was that Riley again. He should have worn something over his face when he went to his house. But he hadn't expected the man to live to give any descriptions.

'I don't think so,' she said firmly. 'I talked to Janet Desmond. She told me of your interest in reincarnation.'

He spread his hands out in a gesture of amazement. 'So I'm slightly interested in the subject. You know that. How can that lead to a suspicion that I'd have anything to do with this – this crime?'

She ignored his outraged show of innocence and said calmly, 'I was going to call the police and let them sort this out, but we are friends, Terence. I thought we could discuss the matter intelligently and find some way to rectify the situation. You could get into a great deal of trouble, you know that, don't you?'

'Amanda, I really don't know what you're talking about,' he said sincerely. 'Perhaps there was some superficial resemblance in the drawing you saw, but many people look like me. If you are my friend, how can you judge me so easily?'

'Then you won't mind if I call the police and let them investigate this?' she asked.

'I –' he hesitated. 'I, of course not.'

'Very well. If you direct me to your telephone, I'll do it now,' she said.

'Yes. No!' he said. 'Amanda, can we talk about this? You know how I avoid publicity. I really don't want, can't afford to get involved in something like this.'

'I want to see the girl,' she said.

'Amanda there is no girl. You've made a mistake. I just don't want to become a media clown. You, of all people, should understand that.'

'I want to see the girl, she repeated stubbornly.

He glowered at her, trying to decide how to handle the situation. She had him, and he knew it.

She knew it as well, but as she looked at his angry face she felt the first stirrings of fear. How foolish she had been to come here alone like this!

'You haven't talked to the police about this yet?' he asked.

It only increased her misgivings, but she determined not to show it. 'I want to see the girl and then we can discuss what to do,' she said.

He sat down. 'Let me explain,' he said. 'Please sit down.'

She sat opposite him, knees primly drawn together, her bag on her lap.

'I did see a hypnotist,' he admitted. 'And I did remember my past lives, many of them. I did as you suggested.' He looked at her before continuing, as if to confirm her complicity in his actions. 'One of the lives I remembered concerned my soul-mate, the woman I have loved, probably for many centuries. Well, I found her, and she is

289

staying with me here. She hasn't been harmed. I am simply helping her remember. That's all there is to it. The media has made the usual song and dance out of it. You know how they do that.'

'She is free to leave when she wishes?' Amanda asked.

'Of course. She's the woman I love,' he said.

'Then let me see her and ask her for myself,' Amanda suggested.

Surely you of all people can understand the idea of a pure love, a love that transcends time, that lasts forever, that is unforgettable and irreversible,' he pleaded. 'I ask only that you trust me on this.'

'Let me speak to her,' she persisted, unmoved by his emotional remarks. Something wasn't right here, she knew. She had come this far and now she was determined to continue.

He hesitated and then said, 'All right. You can talk to her. Wait here, please and I'll bring her down.'

Jones walked stiffly from the room. Now what, he thought? Now fucking what? He'd have to play it through, brazen it out. There weren't many alternatives. He was running out of time. How long would it be before someone else recognised the drawing?

He'd get Lela. Put the fear of God into her first so she shut up. Maybe he'd have to put the woman in the basement. No, he'd have to find out who she told of her visit. Keep her here and leave the country with Lela? Now? Tonight? It wasn't in the plan. His plan was to get her to remember first and he still had one more card to play. He had to make some time.

He unlocked Lela's door. She sat on the bed and stared back at him. He saw hope flee from her face.

'There's a woman here,' he said, talking urgently. 'She's a friend of mine and figured out that I was the one who – who, abducted you. She wants to see if you're all right.

290

'I'm going to take you downstairs, Lela. I want you to tell her you're fine. That you're here willingly. Do you understand? If you don't do as I say, I will punish you severely. I promise you that.'

'I don't care,' she said. 'I won't go down there and lie for you.'

He strode quickly across the room and grabbed her arm and began to shake her. 'You will,' he said. 'You will do as I say or I'll . . .'

'Kill me?' she asked, a smile coming to her face. She began to laugh then, feeling the hysteria climbing but not bothering to suppress it. 'I don't care,' she added. 'I really don't. It's all unravelling for you.' And then she raised her voice to a shout. 'I'm a prisoner!'

Jones drew his hand back and slapped her across the face, sending her falling back on the bed. 'Quiet!' he said. 'Quiet!'

Amanda's voice came from the doorway. 'This is your idea of good treatment, Terence?' she asked.

She stepped into the room and hurried over to the bed. She pulled Sam up and put her arm around her. 'You poor child,' she said. She turned to Jones. 'How could you do this? An intelligent, cultured man? How could you?'

'You don't understand,' he shouted, his face red. 'You meddling old fool, you don't understand.'

'I understand enough,' she said. 'Come, my dear. I'm taking you away from here.'

'No!' Jones screamed. He leaped across the room and gripped her arm. 'Leave us alone!'

Amanda stood and faced him. 'You either let me take her with me or I call the police,' she said. 'You have no choice. You need help, Terence. I promise you that I'll help you get it.'

'I need help? You think that I'm unbalanced, that I'm crazy or something? You narrow-minded old fool,' he snarled. 'You have it wrong, Amanda. You need help.'

His hands went to her neck then and fastened around them like a tight collar. 'You can't just walk in here and ruin my life with your middle-class views. I won't allow it. I won't have it.'

She began to make choking sounds as he increased the pressure. She tried to kick him with her foot, but it was a futile gesture.

'No!' Sam screamed. She got off the bed and began to flail at Jones with her fists.

He continued to hold Amanda with one hand and lashed out at Sam with the other, catching her on the side of the head. She fell back, almost blacking out.

He gripped Amanda again and shook her back and forth like a rag doll. 'No,' he said. 'You can't do this. You can't. Not now. Not so close to the end. So close to victory after so long a time. No. No.'

Horrible gurgling noises came from her throat. Her eyes bulged, her face darkened to an almost purple colour. His hands gripped tighter and tighter, like a man wringing water from a cloth.

Sam staggered up from the bed again. She tried to hit Jones, but it was difficult for her to see – for some reason her vision was blurred – and her blows were weak. He struck her again and sent her reeling back.

There was no sound from the old lady now. Her body was limp in Jones' hands. But still he shook her, uttering his litany of frustration and hope and hate. 'Not so close to the end. Not after all this time. No. No.'

He released his hands finally and she fell to the floor like a sack.

Sam covered her mouth with her hands, her eyes filled with horror and loathing. She could see the woman was dead. There was no further point in trying to help her. There was nothing to be done for her now.

292

Jones looked down at the body on the floor and then at Sam, disbelief on his face.

'You murdered her,' Sam said finally, fighting down the nausea in her throat. She wanted to vomit, to scream, to cry, to waken from this terrible nightmare.

She wasn't ready to die, she realised then. Not like this. All her talk of dying hadn't prepared her for a reality like this. She had thought only of death as an escape, an end to this living nightmare. But this was different. She had no wish to become a lifeless, empty body on the floor.

'You made me do it,' Jones said dully. Slowly he looked up from the floor and when his eyes reached her he said, 'You made me do it! If you had cooperated, if you had done what I said, if you had remembered like you were supposed to, none of this would have happened. *You made me do this*!'

He roared the last words and sounded more like an animal than human. A wounded animal. A dangerous one.

He moved around the body on the floor and gripped Sam's arm. 'We don't have much time,' he said, his voice feverish. 'We have to hurry now. Move everything up. I don't know who she told. But I have a plan for you. It's my ace in the hole. Oh, yes. This time you'll remember. Oh, yes. Come on, come on.'

He dragged her forcibly from the room. She took a last frightened backward glance at the dead woman who had tried to help her.

'Where are you taking me?' she asked, struggling against his pull.

He jerked her forward. 'This time you will be silent. One word and you will be as dead as she is.'

'Where are you taking me?' she said again.

'Back to the beginning,' he said. And then he added with a skeletal smile on his lips, 'Or the end.'

293

Chapter Twenty-two

The despair didn't pass. It sucked Nemo down to a depth where he could barely function. In the past days he had grown used to the feeling; something always happened to lift him, some vision of hope or act of will. This time, however, the feeling pressed on him like an unliftable weight.

He saw the picture of T. on the evening news, but he had no hope anything would come of it. In fact, as he watched he was almost certain he had given the artist the wrong information. Now it didn't look anything like the man he remembered.

The best he could muster up for dinner was a bowl of corn flakes. He forced himself to eat. He drank half a bottle of beer and poured the rest in the sink.

Peter called and told him they landed a new corporate client that day – a lead they had been developing for more than six months.

'Great. That's fine,' he said unenthusiastically.

'Are you all right?' Peter asked.

He had to suddenly swallow to keep from crying again. 'Yes, I'm okay. A little down, that's all,' he said.

'Do you want to go out tonight? By some miracle of timing I happen to be alone.'

'No. Thanks, but I'm really okay,' he said.

The call left him feeling worse than before. What right had he to have business successes at a time like this, he thought unfairly? His only right was to feel miserable.

The patent inanity of the thought helped. It even brought a small smile to his lips. Man, you're wallowing in it, aren't you, he said to himself?

He decided to go for a jog. Any action was better than no action and a physical activity would take his mind off his mind, so to speak. After changing, he walked out to the road and set off at a slow pace, trying to think only of his movements and the sound of his breathing.

It was a dark night. No moon, just a thin haze covering the sky. He could still smell traces of the daytime smog lurking about and every now and then a car passed, leaving a fresh trail of noxious fumes.

His attempt to think of nothing was disturbed by an intrusive thought, not really a thought but more an unverbalised persistent feeling that he was missing something. It had to do with Maddy.

He gave up his try at meditation and put his attention on the problem. Something Maddy said held an answer for him, but he couldn't remember what it was.

His leg muscles began to ache and his breathing quickened. He was out of shape. Normally he tried to jog at least once every two days or, if that wasn't possible, to get a game of racquetball in with Peter.

'Maybe he'd show her things she owned in that life.'

That was it! Maddy had made the comment when she was trying to figure out how T. would try to get Sam to remember. They'd looked at the example of the dress and then decided that it would be too hard for the man to find anything else.

'Things simply don't last that long,' he had said in refutation of the theory.

But some things did.

Houses did.

He swung around and ran back to the house, his pace twice as fast.

What if T. had managed to get back the house he had owned in that past life as Terry Jones? Lela had spent a lot of time there before she met Phillip. Wouldn't he try to take her back there in the hope it would jog her memory? At the least, she'd probably get a feeling of déjà vu. At most, it would bring back a flood of memories. Or so T. would assume. Wouldn't he? It was a long shot, Nemo thought, but it was the only one he had.

When he got home, his sides ached and sweat poured down his face. He grabbed a towel and wiped himself off, not bothering to shower.

How could he find the house again?

He'd been there once – sixty years ago in another life. A large brick house in the back of the Hollywood Hills. My God, it was like looking for a needle in a haystack. Worse even. In those pastoral bygone days there had been a relative handful of houses up there. Now there were thousands.

He found a city map and spread it out on the dining room table. Where would that house have been? He looked at the string of cities running along the Santa Monica Mountains: Studio City, Sherman Oaks, Encino, Woodland Hills and further out. No, that didn't seem right. It was closer to Hollywood. Along Mulholland Drive? No. There had been a canyon . . .

Laurel Canyon! It had been somewhere around there. Up Laurel Canyon Boulevard and down a winding road into the hill. Confusing pictures entered his mind. Curves, trees, houses with large grounds. God, it was hopeless.

No it wasn't. He contradicted himself firmly. This was

296

no time for defeatism. Not now. It was a chance, the only one he had, and he'd grab it.

Could Jones have actually bought the house he owned in a previous lifetime? Possible, but not probable. That the particular house would be on the market when Jones was looking for a house, that he remembered it, that he bought it – they all seemed remote possibilities. And yet, stranger things had happened, Nemo thought hopefully. I remember my past life. How strange and remote a possibility is that?

He dressed quickly and left the house, driving towards Laurel Canyon. It was foolish to expect to find anything in the dark, and yet his little voice told him to follow his instincts. It was about time he got a break.

But his little voice had lied to him. He drove for four hours along narrow winding streets and saw nothing like the house in his ancient memories. He saw big houses and small houses, old ones and new. He drove down dead-end streets and along some that never seemed to end. He even drove up someone's driveway, propelled by the vague notion that he would see the house at its end. It wasn't there. It never was. One house began to look like another. Finally, close to exhaustion, he turned the car home.

He resolved to get some sleep and rise with the sun. He was on the right track. He knew it. All he had to do was persist.

He found the house the next morning – not through following his nose, as he thought he would, but through a far easier method. He remembered that Jones' address was mentioned in the old newspaper.

It came to him in the shower. Not bothering to dry himself, he ran to his study, dripping water through the

297

house. Excitedly, he rummaged through his pile of research. It was in one of the newspaper stories on the murder of Lela Edwards.

'The police today arrested a man in connection with the murder of Lela Edwards. He was Mr Terry Jones of 1178 Domper Drive . . .'

'Right,' he said aloud.

Clutching the clipping, he went back to the dining room where he had left the city map.

Domper Drive was off Laurel Canyon. A winding little road ending in a cul-de-sac. He had probably driven down it during his search last night.

So easy. Why didn't he think of it before? There was no ready answer to his question. Maybe the gods want me to suffer, he thought grimly. And then added a plea to the gods, whoever they were, saying, I've suffered enough.

He was naked, he realised. And cold. He ran back upstairs, towelled himself off and dressed in jeans and a loose-fitting shirt that hung out over his trousers. Finally, he took a .38 revolver from his closet and, after loading it, tucked it through the belt of his jeans so the shirt covered it.

Downstairs, he called Marshall's office. The lieutenant wasn't in, a man said. He was probably on his way to work.

'This is Nemo Riley,' he said. 'It's urgent that he gets this message the moment he walks in the door. Tell him to meet me at 1178 Domper Drive off Laurel Canyon.'

'May I say what it's about?' the man asked.

'He'll know,' Nemo said, and hung up.

The gun was uncomfortable. He took it out of the belt and carried it by hand to the car. He put it on the seat beside him.

The drive seemed endless, even though it was only a

matter of about two miles. He ran one red light and left the others with squeals and the smell of burning rubber. When he reached the winding canyon road, he took the corners like a pro, only once narrowly missing a slower car ahead of him.

The Domper Drive sign was right where the map said it would be and he skidded eagerly around that corner. It was a narrow serpentine street, lined with trees and high shrubbery and houses sitting well off the road.

Even numbers on the right, he noted, and flew by them until he reached the 1100 block. He slowed down and looked more carefully.

1100, 1120, 24, 30, 50, 60, 70. He slowed the car to a crawl. There it was – 1178.

He was operating on pure adrenalin by then, but his view of the house through the iron gates sent a fresh burst through his system.

A large brick house. Red brick. Yes, and a high stone wall. Rolling green lawns. Roses. A long driveway that circled in front of the house. That's it, I swear, he said to himself.

He'd been to this place before. A long time ago. He'd stood on the front step and argued with Terry Jones. It was the same house, he was sure of it.

Now what? He couldn't just drive in and announce himself.

He parked the car dangerously on the side of the narrow road a few yards down from the house, took the gun from the seat and stuck it back in his belt. He walked back to the double gate.

It was open, he noted with relief. That made it easier. A Mercedes was parked in the driveway right in front of the house. No sign of movement inside the house or out in the grounds.

There was no cover between the gate and the house,

299

just an open space. He'd have to take a chance.

He pushed the gate open with his foot and stepped through. He stood there for a moment and then sprinted for the house. Speed and luck were his only allies, he reasoned.

Panting, he reached the front door. He stopped there and leaned against the wall, listening. There was only the sound of his breathing. The house was silent.

He wondered how many laws he was breaking as he reached for the handle of the front door and turned it. What if it was the wrong house? What if it was the right house and his hunch that T. lived here was wrong? There was no time for misgivings now.

He pushed the door and it opened.

Quickly, he stepped in and closed the door behind him. Squinting to adjust to the gloomy interior, he looked around and took in the furniture, the old pictures on the wall, the expensive but old carpet.

He felt as if he had stepped into a time warp. This had to be it, he thought, excitement rising.

He listened again. Still no sound. Slowly, he walked forward, wondering where to start. He took the gun from his belt as he moved and held it loosely in his right hand.

He stopped in front of a door that led to what appeared to be a dining room and listened again.

Music. It came from the other side of the dining room. The kitchen perhaps?

Quietly, he moved through the dining room and stopped at the door. Yes, a radio played at low volume. There was also the sound of someone moving about in the room, the noise of dishes.

He took a deep breath, put his hand on the door handle, opened it and stepped in. He fell into a crouch and held the gun out before him.

The elderly woman at the sink dropped the dish she was holding back into the water. Her eyes grew wide with fright and she opened her mouth, exclaiming in a foreign language.

A foreign language! He was right, he thought exultantly. It was probably Polish, which was what T. had used on the tape.

'Quiet!' he said.

But she began to chatter to him. He couldn't understand the words, but he could see the fear on her face.

He let his gun hand drop and held up the other. 'No. No,' he said. 'I won't harm you. Where is the girl? Where is the man?'

She eyed him warily, mollified somewhat by his gesture. Then she shook her head and said, 'No Ingliz.'

'Man,' he said. 'Woman.'

She shook her head again.

He pointed at himself and then at the house in a searching motion. 'Man? Where man?'

'No,' she said.

He put the gun down on the table beside him and, using both hands, made the universal curvaceous gesture for woman. 'Woman?' he asked. 'Where woman?'

Was that understanding in her eyes? She shook her head again and said, 'No,' this time pointing out of the house towards the driveway.

Gone? Had they gone?

He made the motion of holding a steering wheel and the sound of a small kid would make to describe a car, feeling stupid as he did so. 'Man? Woman? Gone?'

She nodded eagerly and pointed out again.

'Shit,' he said.

He picked up the gun and gestured at the woman with it. 'Come on,' he said, 'let's go and look around.'

She was an old woman with a lined face and a bent

back, but she moved remarkably quickly for her age, leading the way back through the dining room to the hall. She stopped and looked at him and then at the gun, the fear still obvious on her face.

He moved through the hall, opening doors and looking in each room. A living room, a study, another large sitting room. The 1920's motif was everywhere – in the furniture, the art, even the glassware and other utensils.

No sign of people.

'What's upstairs?' he asked, turning to her, forgetting for a moment that she wouldn't understand.

She shook her head.

'Come on,' he said, pointing the gun at the stairs.

She trudged ahead of him, looking as if she had carried loads of wood on her back all her life.

He opened the first door. A bedroom. It could only be described as lush. An enormous brass bed, red cover, dark wood furniture. The drawers of the dresser were open and so was the closet door. Men's clothes were scattered carelessly on the bed. It looked as if someone had hurried through, looking for something. Or as if someone had been packing.

Back into the hall. He tried the next door. It was locked. He pushed at it but it wouldn't budge.

'Key?' he said, pointing at the lock.

The woman shrugged and pointed again out of the house as if to indicate that the key had gone.

He banged on the door and said, 'Anyone there?'

There was no answer, of course. It was a slim hope at best.

He stood back from the door and lifted his foot. He kicked at the lock with the flat of his shoe, again and again. Finally there was a crunching sound and the wood gave. One more kick and the door flew open.

It was another bedroom. The crumpled body of a

302

woman lay on the floor. He went in and kneeled beside her. She was quite dead. Bruise marks on her throat showed that she had been strangled.

Nemo heard a gasp behind him. He turned and saw the elderly woman, her eyes wide. She began to wail, a high keening sound. And then she fainted.

Lieutenant Marshall arrived ten minutes later. Nemo took him upstairs and showed him the body.

'Did you touch anything?' Marshall asked.

'Only the door.'

'I'd better call it in,' Marshall said.

They went downstairs and used a telephone in the hall. Marshall spoke to someone and told him what had happened. 'And for Christ's sakes get someone out here who speaks Polish,' he said.

'Let's have a look around,' he said when he put the phone down. 'Do you know who this house belongs to?'

'No. There's a study. There'll be papers,' Nemo suggested.

He led the way into the office and Marshall began to rummage around on the desk. Nemo glanced at the bookshelf.

'My God!' he exclaimed, and hit his forehead with the palm of his hand. He pointed at one of the shelves. 'Terence W. Jones. The historical novelist. The same name. Terry Jones. He used the same name. I never thought for a second that he'd use the same goddamn name!'

'Right,' Marshall said, holding up some envelopes. 'Addressed to Terence W. Jones.'

'All these books are written by him,' Nemo said. 'It's probably a pen name. But it's probably the one he goes by.'

'Most of the time,' Marshall said. 'Some of this correspondence is addressed to a Polish name. Platek. Probably his real name.'

There was a telephone on the desk. Marshall picked it up, called his office again and asked that an All Points Bulletin be put out on Terence W. Jones alias Jozef Platek. When he finished he turned to Nemo.

'Do you have a licence for that gun in your belt?' he asked Nemo.

'Not to carry it.'

'Better let me keep it for now,' he said, holding out his hand.

Nemo took the cartridges out of the revolver and handed it over. Marshall slipped it into his jacket pocket.

'Have you searched the house thoroughly?' he asked.

'No,' Nemo said. 'Not all of it. Where do you think they've gone?'

'Let's make sure there's nobody else in the house,' Marshall said 'or no more bodies.'

The possibility that Sam's body might be somewhere in the house hadn't even occurred to Nemo. He'd assumed that wherever Jones was, Sam had been taken with him. The thought made him blanch.

'You don't think that Sam's here, do you?' he asked.

'I don't think anything,' Marshall said. 'Let's look around.'

They looked through the remaining rooms upstairs, the downstairs area and went into the basement.

'Looks like somebody was here,' Marshall said. 'Footprints in the dust.'

They went back to the hall. 'I assume that's your car out on the road,' Marshall said. 'The Mercedes in the driveway may be the woman's. Let's look at the registration.'

304

He opened the glove compartment and found the papers in a small plastic bag. 'Amanda Baker. Date of birth, August 2, 1926. Address in Pasadena. Sounds like our lady.'

'Did you notice the speaker in the bedroom?' Nemo said, as they walked back into the house.

'No, where?'

'Up near the ceiling. Wonder where it leads?'

'There it was a stereo setup in the office,' Marshall said. 'Let's go and have another look.'

It didn't take them long to find the collection of tapes. There were the copies made by the hypnotist, which they had already heard, and then there was the tape he played to Sam to 'jog her memory.'

They were ten minutes into it when the first police cars arrived. Marshall excused himself and left Nemo with the tape.

He listened to the wheedling voice of Jones and first felt only rage. Then, at the thought of Sam's ordeal, it changed to nausea. Obviously the man had used the tape to try and brainwash her. It made him wonder what else the man had done?

An army of police descended on the house then. They went through the house like rats looking for food, inch by inch, Marshall took the officer who spoke Polish with him into the kitchen and suggested Nemo listened in.

'We'll find out what she knows,' he said.

He began to question the woman through the interpreter. She was obviously afraid, but she seemed eager to speak to someone who could understand her and answered willingly. She looked only at the interpreter when she talked. Even when Marshall interrupted with questions, she avoided his eyes.

An hour later, Marshall sat in the study with Nemo and began to reconstruct. 'All right,' he said, 'we know

305

that Sam Barry was here at least since the morning after she disappeared. Most of the time she was locked in the bedroom, although she spent some time in the basement. The woman is a distant relative of Jones'. He told her that he and Sam were having a lover's quarrel. The woman didn't particularly believe him, but decided it wasn't her business to interfere. She swears she didn't know anything illegal like abduction was happening.'

Nemo put in his data. 'We know that he spent most of his time trying to get her to remember that she was Lela Edwards in another life. The décor of the house, the films he showed, the music, the tapes. All of that was designed to awaken those memories in her.'

'Yeah, that was probably his opinion. The guy was trying to brainwash her into sharing his delusions,' Marshall said, disgust in his voice. 'If she stood up to all of that, she's a tough lady.'

'Tougher than she looks,' Nemo said.

'We know they left sometime last night,' Marshall continued. 'Also that the housekeeper assumed the woman in the Mercedes had left with them. He took the key to the upstairs room with him apparently, because she says she didn't have one.'

'So we know that as of last night Sam was alive,' Nemo interrupted.

'Yeah. But we have no idea where he took her. Jones left with a suitcase and told the Polish woman only that he had to leave for a while. He was quite willing to leave her holding the bag. God knows how long before she'd discover the body in the upstairs room. Time for him to put some distance on, I guess.'

'Do you think he's left the country?' Nemo felt his stomach sink. He had come so close, but now she was even further away. 'I mean, where could he go?'

'The woman said he was very upset when he left.

Talking strangely. Which considering how weird he is anyway, must have been very strange. Said something about one last chance. Does that mean anything to you?'

Nemo shook his head. 'Not really.'

'If he left the country, we'll know,' Marshall said. 'Airports, borders – they've all been alerted. Someone will have noticed something.'

'A man and a woman travelling together?' Nemo said dubiously. 'Not particularly unusual.'

'We'll find out,' Marshall said.

'One last chance,' Nemo said thoughtfully. 'He's been trying to get her to remember and obviously she's been resisting. Maybe that's what he's talking about.'

'By the way,' Marshall said. 'I've been meaning to ask you . . . how did you find this place?'

'It's where Terry Jones lived in 1924,' Nemo said.

'Jesus,' Marshall said, bemusement in his voice. 'This is the weirdest one I've ever worked on.'

'CATALINA!' Nemo shouted, the sound echoing in the room. He slapped the desk with his hand. 'That's where they are!'

'What?' Marshall asked.

'He's taken her to Catalina Island. It's his last shot.'

'Why? How do you know that?'

'Because that's where Terry Jones murdered Lela Edwards and her new husband Phillip Bates in 1924,' Nemo said triumphantly. 'It's where the whole thing started, or ended, or whatever.'

'He's taking her back to where he thinks he murdered her in another life?' Marshall said. 'Why?'

'Call it shock treatment. He thinks that maybe she'll remember everything if confronted with where she actually died in another life.'

Marshall watched him silently.

Nemo looked back at him and his heart fell. It must

307

have showed on his face, because Marshall nodded and said, 'Yes. Or he's taking her back there to kill her again.'

Nemo looked at his watch. 'Burbank. We can get a plane to take us over. I know the house where the murders took place. I can find it again.'

'How do you know that?' Marshall asked.

Because I remember it well. It's where we had our honeymoon, and where we were killed, Nemo wanted to say. But instead he said, 'The newspaper articles after the murders.'

'Come on,' Marshall said. 'We'll get an escort to the airport.'

They jogged out of the house. Nemo prayed they were moving quickly enough. Sam was in more danger now than ever before. Jones had his back up against the wall now. He'd make a last effort to win the game and then God knew what he'd do. He didn't want to think about it. He just wanted to get there.

They tried for a police helicopter, but there wasn't one immediately available. Finally, after what seemed like interminable negotiations, they found a small Cessna to fly them to Catalina.

If Nemo had wings, he would have flapped them to help the small aircraft fly faster. As it was, he leaned forward in the seat, drummed his fingers against his knees and urged the pilot to hurry.

'Don't worry,' Marshall said, allowing a kindly expression to soften his scowl for the first time, 'we'll be there soon.'

'Yes,' Nemo said. 'But will we get there in time?'

Marshall only grunted.

Chapter Twenty-three

They spent the night in a cheap motel in San Pedro. Sam did not sleep at all. She lay like a board, stiff and unmoving and listened to the groans of Jones in the bed beside her. The face of the woman he strangled hovered in the darkness above her like a gargoyle with bulging eyes and swollen tongue. By the time morning came, they both looked like hell.

They ate breakfast silently in the chilly car, after ordering at a drive-up window. He still hadn't told her where they were going. She thought that, if it were possible, he was becoming even more insane. At times he muttered to himself and grinned secretively at his thoughts.

They drove down to the waterfront and when he parked at the pier for the ferry to Catalina, she finally realised that was where they were going.

'All right,' he said before they left the car, 'I want you to wear these.' He handed her a pair of dark glasses and a scarf. 'Tie that over your head and under your chin. I don't want anyone to recognise you. If people speak to you, just ignore them. Act unfriendly. If anyone thinks they recognise you, I want you to laugh and deny it. Say your name is Rita Jones, or something. Say you're my wife. Do you understand that?'

He glared at her, the menace open now. 'You don't want to die. You'll do as I say, won't you?'

It was true. She didn't want to die. She had decided that last night. She wanted to live forever, if possible. If that didn't work out, she wanted to die peacefully in bed of old age – not with the hands of a madman wrapped around her throat. She nodded her agreement.

They boarded the ferry without problem. It wasn't crowded, and they found a seat away from other people. She sat on the hard cushioned board and listened to the throb of the engines. She felt them vibrate through her body.

'Why are we going to Catalina?' she asked.

He just smiled at her and said, 'You'll find out when the time is right.'

He never moved from his position beside her. She asked if she could go to the ladies' room and he said no. 'You can wait until we get there,' he said. She asked if they could stand outside on deck for a while and get some air. He silently inspected the idea for flaws and then nodded.

The ocean was smooth and the ship rode it gently, moving up and down in a soft rhythm. The sun was higher in the sky now and it had grown warm. A thousand glistening particles of light danced on the water. Under any other conditions it would have been beautiful. As it was, however, Sam was only conscious of the man beside her.

Santa Catalina Island is twenty-two miles from the mainland. The trip takes a shade less than two hours. Although one of the major resorts of the Los Angeles area, Sam had never been there. All she knew about it was that in the seventeenth and eighteenth centuries it had been a major hangout for pirates and smugglers off the California coast.

In view of her ignorance, her reaction as they approached the rugged, mountainous island astonished her. Her heart began to thud, her palms grew clammy and her breathing ragged. She had experienced the physical phenomena enough in the past few days to know it was the onset of fear. But why now, she wondered?

They cruised into the bay and the picturesque village of Avalon and tied up at the modern pier. The town was hardly more than five blocks long, dominated still by the Catalina Casino on the other side of the bay. It was a pretty and peaceful picture, yet her agitation inexplicably increased. The prospect of walking from the boat filled her with dread. She had the feeling that if she went onto the island with Jones she would never leave. It was based on nothing she understood, but it was not unlike a feeling of claustrophobia, with the same stifling sensation and urge to run.

'I don't want to go there,' she said to him.

He looked at her strangely and said, 'You have to. You don't have any choice now.'

She thought of screaming or making a fuss, but the picture of the dead woman still hovered in her mind. If she created a scene, people would react in one of two ways: they would either come to help or not want to get involved and leave as fast as they could. It wasn't a gamble she was willing to take. She knew he would react by doing something drastic to her.

They waited until most of the passengers left the boat and then followed. They walked at a fast pace down the pier to the main street.

'I took the precaution of renting the house earlier,' he said to her. 'Lucky thing. I thought we'd have to come here, but not this soon.'

She stood silently in the doorway while he collected the keys from the realtor. He chatted sociably with the

311

man for a moment and made some joke about fishing. Then he said, 'The wife can't stand cooking fish, anyway,' and gave the man a farewell wave.

He took her arm outside and turned down a sidestreet, the suitcase in his other hand.

'Where are we going?' she asked, a dull leaden feeling pressing against her chest.

'Up the hill,' he said with a nod. 'Do you know where we are, Lela?'

'Catalina,' she said irritably, but she knew it wasn't the answer he wanted.

They trudged through the town and up a narrow, winding road. Her feet grew heavier and heavier with every step, and a lassitude crept through her body, pulling her back down to the ocean.

It was an old two-storey Victorian house, painted blue with white trim on the gingerbread windows. Salt and sun had taken its toll and the paint was fading now.

'Here we are,' he said. 'Remember it?'

It was the house she was afraid of, she knew then. It was a trap, a cage, a murderous house.

'I don't want to go in there,' she said.

He gave her that strange look and said, 'It's all right this time. It's different.'

'I don't want to go there.'

He looked quickly up and down the road and then pulled at her arm, dragging her through the gate and down the stone-tiled pathway to the door.

'No,' she cried, trying to dig her heels into the rock. 'No,' she said again.

He dropped the suitcase, slammed her up against the porch wall and fumbled in his pocket for the key, continuing to hold her arm with his other hand. When the door opened, he pushed her ahead of him and closed it behind them.

The house wasn't dirty, perhaps it had been cleaned recently, but a musty unlived-in smell permeated everything. She felt it clog her pores as she stood there.

'It was a splendid place once,' he said.

She narrowed her eyes in the gloom and saw the carpet was frayed at the edges.

'Come on,' he said.

He opened the living room curtains and sunshine streamed in. Large windows looked down on the bay. She saw the pier, the Casino and dozens of pleasure craft dotting the water.

She felt split in two.

One half of her loved the view, the other hated it. Part of her allowed a happiness to rise, but a heavy sadness pushed it down. She wanted to stand entranced by the beauty below and she wanted to run. She felt a rush of life and a threat of death.

She wondered if she was finally going insane. She couldn't understand the turmoil of emotions, and schizophrenic push and pull of her soul tearing her apart. Without uttering a sound, she began to cry, rooted to the floor while tears rolled down her face and down her neck.

Jones watched her silently, but there was a smirk around his mouth. 'Do you remember?'

Jones' voice seemed to travel in slow motion, reaching her without impact.

'Do you remember?' he asked again.

She turned to him and said, 'I remember nothing. Nothing!'

He shook his head at her. 'Do you know where you are?' It was rhetorical, for he answered the question himself. 'This is the house in which Lela Edwards died. The house in which you died, Lela.'

She was melting in tears, drowning in them. He was a

313

madman and a liar. He lived in a tortured world coloured by his insanity. But the cumulative effect of everything that had happened to her was proving too much. She feared that she was going to collapse completely. The battle of wills was almost over and he would win.

She stiffened then. The thought mustered up reserves of resistance she didn't know she had. But he had seen the opening and didn't reliquish his attack. His voice grew harsh and cutting.

'You were here with your lover – your husband, Bates. You were on your honeymoon,' he said. 'I came the day after you were married, to plead with you, to help you see your mistake and take you away from here. Do you remember?'

'I remember nothing,' she said, her voice lifeless.

'I came to save you and you spat in my face!' he screamed.

The volume and anguish of his voice awakened her, as if from a trance. She blinked the tears away and then wiped her face with the back of her hand.

He looked at her through a contorted face, his hands outstretched, pain bending his body so that he almost crouched.

The fear still possessed her, however. It thundered through her body, telling her that this was the crucial moment of the whole ordeal. Now, for the first time, her survival was truly at stake.

He came up to her and put his hands on her shoulders, squeezing them. 'It's coming, isn't it?' he asked.

She shook her head.

'Well, follow me then,' he cried.

He took her back down the passage and up the creaking stairs. Pains stabbed at her chest at each step. She lifted a hand and held her heart as if to prevent it from exploding. They came to a door and he threw it open with a flourish. She took a step backward, feeling suddenly cold, but he pushed her into the room.

'Look!' he ordered her.

She closed her eyes. She could not look.

He put one hand on the back of her neck, the other under her chin, and pulled her head up. 'Look!'

She opened her eyes. It was just a room. There was a large brass bed, a closet, a dresser. It was just a room, she told herself.

The pains in her chest grew more urgent. Sharper. She rubbed it with both hands and strange panting sounds fell from her mouth.

'Yes,' he said. 'Look at it.'

He went to the window with giant manic strides and tore the curtains open. His face was whiter than before and his body trembled. He lifted a shaking hand and pointed at the bed.

'Look!' he said. 'You lay on that bed and bled to death. You made me do it. You made me! I had no choice.'

And then she saw the room as it was sixty years before – new bed, new furniture, a gleaming happy room, the room of her wedding night.

And saw the angry twisted face of Terry Jones.

And heard his scream of rage.

And saw the gleam of the knife in the sunlight as he lifted it up.

And felt it tear into her chest. The burning pain.

Again and again.

And screamed.

It was all true. Every word of it was true.

I am Lela Edwards, she thought. I was Lela Edwards. He was Terry Jones. He murdered me in this room. It happened. It really happened.

It was as if the stormy sky parted and the sun's healing light fell down. The turmoil surrounding her dissipated, the pains in her chest left, the fear melted away.

She looked at him and saw his pain and felt pity for him.

'You remember,' he said, no doubt in his voice.

'Yes,' she said, her voice firm and strong now. 'I remember.'

He held out his arms and took a step towards her.

'No,' she said. 'It's not like you think. I don't love you. I never have. Even when we were having our affair, love was never mentioned by me. You know that. I told you that. I tried to be kind, to continue being your friend, but you were insane with jealousy. Do you remember? You wouldn't let me have my life. Remember, Terry. You couldn't accept it. You said you'd rather see me dead than with another man, and then you killed me. It was wrong.'

'But you made me do it,' he pleaded.

She shook her head. 'Nobody ever made you do anything. You chose to do it. You did it.'

Craftily he said, 'You admitted I was insane with jealousy. I didn't know what I was doing.'

'Yes, you did,' she said. 'You made the decision then and you're making it now. Nobody else does it for you. Not ever.'

'Do you forgive me?' he asked, his voice breaking.

'Yes,' she said.

'And will you stay with me?'

'No,' she said.

They stared at each other, a flow of electrical charge building in the room.

'I loved Phillip,' she said gently. 'I love Nemo. You have to end it now and find your own destiny.'

Slowly he shook his head and then his body stiffened and his neck bulged and he screamed, 'NO!'

316

A knife appeared in his right hand. The push of a button and the white steel blade shot out with a click.

'You're not going to do this to me again,' he hissed. 'I won't have it. If I can't have you, nobody else can either, Lela. You were meant for me, my darling. I can't let you do this to yourself. You're mine, my darling. You belong to me.'

He inched towards her as he spoke, his eyes glazed with an ancient passion.

He was repeating exactly the same words he had used before.

It was all happening again.

'Don't do this to yourself, to me,' she said – just as she had said before. 'If you love me you'll allow me my happiness.'

'You were meant for me. Nobody else is meant to have you,' he said.

She stood rooted to the floor. As she stood sixty years before. She hadn't believed what was happening then. Hadn't believed he could do it. This time she did.

She shuffled back and held out her hand, palm up.

'Don't do this,' she said. 'Don't do this again.'

And then he leaped at her, the knife slashing up above him, poised to fall.

She turned and ran. Out the door, down the hall to the top of the stairs.

She heard him a foot or two behind her and imagined she could feel the heat of his breath. She hit the stairs running and began to fall, clutching the smooth wooden banister for balance.

'I'll kill you!' he shouted, just as he did before.

In the other life, they were the last words she heard.

But that was then and this was now, and she knew that only the insane were doomed to repeat themselves in an endless hellish cycle.

317

The front door opened with a crash and a man stood there and shouted, 'Stop!'

He held a gun in both hands and behind him was Nemo.

Jones didn't stop. Again he shouted, 'I'll kill you!' and the sound of his voice merged into the thunderous roar of the gun.

Close to the bottom of the stairs she truly fell and slid first on her back and then on her stomach and he followed and bounced and rolled and landed on top of her, the knife thudding into the hardwood floor.

She heard the choking rattle of his throat and felt the spasm go through his body like a wave and knew his ordeal was over and that he had been rescued by death.

The weight lifted from her and then she felt Nemo's hands pulling her up and his arms containing her, but she could see nothing through the tears.

They were tears of relief and joy and this time. It was a different story, a different time, a different end.

'Sam,' he said, kissing her face hungrily. 'Oh, Sam.'

She saw through the haze that he was crying too.

'Nemo,' she said. 'Phillip. Nemo, my darling.'

He was Nemo now. She would never call him Phillip again. It was a different story. This one had a happy ending. This one had a future. This was their life.